No Peace for the Wicked

the Wicked

Adrian Magson

Best wishes

Adrian Magson

CREME DE LA CRIME

First published by Crème de la Crime Books in 2004
Crème de la Crime Ltd, PO Box 445, Abingdon,
Oxon OX13 6YQ

Typesetting by Yvette Warren
Cover design by Yvette Warren
Front cover photography by Image Farm Inc. Alamy Images,
www.alamy.com
Printed and bound in England by Biddles Ltd,
www.biddles.co.uk

ISBN 0-9547634-2-4

A CIP catalogue reference for this book is available from the
British Library

www.cremedelacrime.com

About the Author

Adrian Magson became a full-time freelance writer after a variety of jobs, including workshop design, management and teaching *tae kwon-do*.

His work has been published in many mainstream UK magazines, and as far afield as the US, Japan, South Africa, Australia and Scandinavia.

His short stories have been broadcast on BBC radio, and he has written for the comedian Roy Hudd and had a comedy play performed at the Oxford Literary Festival.

His crime writing has appeared in the *Ellery Queen Mystery Magazine*, and shortlisted in the *Crime Writers' Association Debut Dagger Award*. Alongside his next crime thriller, Adrian writes the regular Beginners column in *Writing Magazine*, sister publication to *Writers' News*.

Dedications

To Chris Losh for opening the door; to Cari and Lesley for their honesty; to my parents who knew I would do it; to Lynne and Iain for the opportunity, and Susannah for the gritty bits. Most of all, to Ann, for absolutely everything else and beyond.

1

The first old man died on the beach.

Huddled in a blanket, he watched gulls screaming over a plastic bottle bobbing in the choppy water, while under a heavy sky a tanker plodded up the Channel. The beach was deserted. Too early for day-trippers and too cold for beachcombers with their wretched metal-detectors.

He wasn't interested in seagulls or tankers. The birds were noisy and demanding, like people, and the tankers too remote. He had long ago given up interest in anything much, surrendering instead to deliberate and ill-tempered isolation. Now all he had was the creeping disease of old age, made bearable by the few bits of comfort a well-stocked bank account could buy. As long as the account received regular additions, that was all that concerned him.

A car approached along the promenade and he instinctively sank deeper into his deckchair, pulling the blanket tighter around him. If he'd wanted strangers stopping by for chit-chat he'd have hung out a sign.

Maybe it was Willis. His minder was due about now with a flask of coffee laced with something that would truly piss off his doctor, if only he knew...

A door thumped shut and pebbles crunched as someone dropped down from the promenade. A man. Heavyweight, by the sounds of it. It wasn't Willis then; he'd recognise his footsteps anywhere.

The hairs on his neck stirred as the footsteps approached, bringing faint memories of other times when danger had moved against him. Well, he'd faced that before and usually walked away laughing.

The newcomer stopped just behind him, so close he must have been staring right down at the crown of his head. He fought a strong desire to turn and look. Damn him! He'd sit here and defy the intruder to come round and look him in the eye.

Whoever it was didn't bother. Instead the old man heard a rustle of cloth and a familiar metallic click. It turned his blood to water. Then the seagulls and the wind, the impending rain and the tanker all ceased to matter.

Half a mile away, in a block of exclusive flats overlooking the sea front, another old man stared out to sea, puffing on his first cigar of the day. He knew it would likely kill him, but he didn't give a bugger and puffed all the more enjoyably. Too old to let it worry him now, anyway. He wriggled his toes into the pile of his new Axminster. Nothing like the feel of fresh nap, he thought. About as far from linoleum as it was possible to get…

He brushed a speck of ash from his sweater and debated going for a walk. There were few signs of activity. Over to the east he could see two figures down on the pebbles. One appeared to be huddled in a deckchair, the other standing behind him. Bloody mad, some people, he thought idly. Probably asylum-seekers, looking for something to steal.

The standing figure appeared to be holding a hand out to the other. Offering something maybe, or pointing. There was something familiar in the stance that made the cigar smoker shiver. He decided he was better off staying in. Far too cold to venture out, anyway. Easy way to catch a chill. In any case, the boys would be round later for a game of cards.

He glanced at the coffee table, with its single sheet of paper covered in neatly typed figures. He smiled momentarily. Money was still rolling in, and as long as the managers didn't get greedy and the other two let him run things the way he always had since…well, since the changeover, it should be fine.

The front door clicked. Startled, he swung round. Two figures were standing in the hallway, as if they had materialised out of the walls. Their heavy coats and dark slacks gave them the appearance of men attending a funeral.

"What the fuck do you want?" he demanded. For the first time in years he felt a skewer of fear deep in his stomach. "How d'you get in?"

The leading figure stepped forward and pointed at the smoker. There was a sharp, flat sound and the cigar snapped into the air. It landed on the new Axminster where it sizzled pungently. The old man fell alongside it.

The second newcomer stepped past the man with the gun and carefully retrieved the cigar. He placed it in an ashtray where it could burn safely without threatening the other residents in the tower block.

Both men stepped across to the window and looked out. Over to the east a solitary figure was walking up the beach towards a car parked on the promenade. Another figure was slumped in a deckchair as though sleeping.

The two men turned and left the flat, barely glancing at the man lying on the floor.

2

The young man in the smart suit seemed not to notice the chill in the air as he stood on the patio watching his employer. She was kneeling on a cushion, digging the blade of a knife between the flagstones and levering out stems of couch grass, the crepe-flesh in her upper arms quivering with the effort. The knife strokes were short and vicious, as if the battle with the weeds had become personal.

He looked around, eyes flickering over the tree line a hundred yards away, then turning to take in the house behind him. Set in an acre of prime Buckinghamshire countryside, the house wore sweeping eyelash gables overlooking a magnificent stepped garden, and every brick and tile, each bush and shrub, echoed solid, undeniable wealth. He'd heard it was once the home of a merchant banker. He wasn't surprised.

Inside the house a telephone warbled pleasantly, as if promising only good news. The young man went into the kitchen and through to the hallway, breathing a sigh of relief once he was out of earshot. Guard duties with no danger of action had a definite downside.

He picked up the phone and listened to a brief message, then replaced the handset without comment and returned to the patio. Over the elderly woman's bowed back he checked the garden for signs of movement but saw only borders and flower-beds in perfect splendour: neat, ordered and unblemished. Not that he cared for any of it, save for the fact that intruders had no place to hide. Gardening wasn't really his forte.

The woman glanced up as his footsteps sounded on the stones, her knife hand stilled, the thumb resting on the top of the blade. The way she held it reminded the young man of a combat instructor he'd once trained with. Vicious bastard liked to nick trainees with the point of his combat dagger, to give them a sensation they never wanted to experience again. It worked, though. The memory still made his stomach flinch.

"Yes, Gary?" she murmured.

"It's done," he replied, hands clasped respectfully behind his back.

The woman very nearly smiled. She didn't, much. It was as if she had never learned how. "Good. Thank you, Gary." She gazed down at her handiwork. "Much better without all those horrid weeds, and I must get that back border sorted out – it's looking quite a mess, don't you think?"

Gary made no comment. He had learned not to. When the woman levered herself upright with a grunt, Gary made no move to help, either. Something else he'd learned not to do.

The woman was in her early seventies and dressed smartly as always – even for gardening. There was a hint of the showgirl she used to be, mostly revealed by a taste for gaudy jewellery and too much makeup. Behind Dior glasses and heavily layered mascara were eyes that looked out on the world in a seemingly benevolent manner. Eyes like someone's grandmother, which she was, although not recently. Those eyes made Gary shiver. And he didn't shiver at much.

"Have you called Spain?" she asked, dropping the knife onto the cushion at her feet.

"No, Mrs G. I thought you might want to do that."

Her full name was Letitia Grossman. Lottie for short.

But she liked being called Mrs G; it showed respect. There had been too many times when respect had been denied her.

She reached up and patted Gary's cheek with a wrinkled hand, one of her long fingernails trailing momentarily across his cheek. Then she walked towards the house, leaving behind a sickly trace of sweet perfume overlaid by the tang of damp soil. Like she'd been recently dug up and bought back to life, Gary thought.

For Riley Gavin, the first rays of sun in Sotogrande, on the southern coast of Spain, brought a shiver of a much more welcome kind. The day promised to be hot and still, just the way she liked it. She dropped her towel and bag by the pool and revelled as the heat rolled across her naked shoulders. The long, damp winter had dragged on like a depressing cold, and she had been waiting weeks for this moment when she could forget about the wind and rain, the slogging along grey streets back home looking for stories, and allow herself to relax for a while.

She caught a glimpse of her reflection in the glass door to a changing cubicle. My God, she thought, I'm so white I look like the blood's been drained out of my backside. She flicked back her long, blonde hair, wondering if maybe she hadn't also got a little soft around the chin. Too much junk food while sitting in her car watching and waiting for something to develop. Instinctively she adjusted her stance to pull in her stomach. There was no vanity in the move, simply a self-conscious need to look 'right', as her mother always used to say.

She lowered herself on to a lounger and glanced around. Perfect. No one else about.

The complex was a real find. Small and exclusive, the

only other residents were a few golfers too busy playing the local courses to have any interest in the pool. Casual visitors were politely turned away, and there was little to attract families. The small flat was hers for a week and she didn't intend straying far from where she was right now. Riley reached up behind and pulled at the thin cords of her pink bikini top. The unaccustomed heat, as well as the sudden exposure in the open air, brought an instant tingle to her sensitive skin, and a brief shiver ran the length of her body. Oh, yes, she thought. I'm in Heaven…

She lay back and sighed, wondering why she didn't do this more often. Money is why, you silly bitch, she reminded herself, and stretched her legs out before her. Money and the thrill of it all. The chase.

Well, the chase could go hang itself for a while as she recharged her batteries. She hadn't taken a decent holiday since last August and she deserved one more than usual. God knows, she'd worked her little tush off for it. Her last assignment had been long and wearing, chasing up an investment scam perpetrated on a flock of churchgoers in the Midlands who had put their trust in a self-styled Christian broker. The fact that thirty percent was an unusually high return and the proposed 'opportunity' was a land development fund in Colombia, home of coffee and cocaine but rarely top land deals, had failed to ring alarm bells among the virgin investors. It wasn't long before phone calls by the church's pastor to the broker received nothing but the disconnected tone. It had taken Riley two months to track down the culprit, hiding behind another front company, this time in the Retirement Homes business. By then she had gathered enough information on his activities to put together a fireproof story that made page one of *The National Herald*. Her research, someone else's by-line. But what the hell, the main thing was that the 'broker' would shortly be appearing in front of a jury and would, ripped-off investors and court willing, be in a home of another kind altogether.

Warmed by the sun, she slipped into a shallow sleep. Gone were thoughts of work and earning a living…time enough for that next week.

Half an eternity later there was a click at the side gate and a faint splash as someone entered the pool. She opened her eyes and looked. A dark head of hair and strong brown shoulders slipped smoothly through the blue water. A man, probably young. He turned and swam back to the other end, a smooth, uncluttered crawl with no unnecessary splashing. Mmm…masculine and tidy. Now there's a rarity.

After three lengths the swimmer pulled himself effortlessly from the water and sat on the side of the pool, shaking droplets from his head. He reached for a towel and a packet of cigarettes.

A few years over thirty, Riley guessed, a bit gaunt in a hungry sort of way. Good muscles, but not cover-boy six-pack. She felt a stirring of interest and looked him over some more, enjoying the secretiveness of her survey. Nice, she thought. Can't see his buns, which is a pity.

As the man blew smoke into the air, he seemed to notice her for the first time and nodded. Riley nodded back, inadvertently revealing that she was looking at him. She also remembered she wore no bikini top. Oh, what the hell, she thought. He's seen me now – it would be crass to go all girlish and cover up.

She allowed herself to drift away again. What will happen will happen.

Moments later she sensed him nearby. It might have

been the sudden coolness as his body cut off the sun, or the faint hint of aftershave against the background smell of chlorine.

"Can I get you a drink?" he asked. His voice was pleasant with a faint accent. French? Spanish? Yummy...maybe he's rich and—

Riley snapped her eyes open. It was the waiter, Rafael. He was looking down at her with tactful, unseeing eyes, a drinks menu in one hand, a silver tray in the other. Across the pool, the swimmer was gone, a hint of smoke hanging in the still air to show where he had been.

Riley scooped up her bikini top and shook her head, embarrassed and irritated. "Nothing, thanks," she said, and waited for Rafael to leave before settling back to sleep, her thoughts on the strong shoulders and the sleek, black hair of the man across the pool. She hoped he got sunburn.

The following day the pool was deserted. Riley shrugged off her bikini top, poured liberal amounts of Ambre Solaire into her palm and massaged it gently into her body, concentrating on where her skin was most tender. She was enjoying the sensation of lazily rubbing in the warm lotion when the gate clicked and the waiter entered. He stopped in front of her and lowered his silver tray. It held a cordless telephone.

"Call for you, Miss Gavin. Urgent, the man says."

Riley sighed. "Did he give a name?" Who in *hell* knew she was here?

"Mr Brask, madam."

Oh, damn, she thought, but took the phone anyway.

3

Gibraltar airport was hot and noisy, with a combined smell of baking tarmac and aviation fuel soaking the atmosphere of the terminal building. By the time Riley checked in and went in search of a seat, she was in no mood to humour screaming kids, pushy parents, or the openly lecherous squaddies standing around clutching cans of lager, staring at anything in a skirt.

She dropped her leather holdall on the floor, trying to calm down. Bugger them all, she thought rebelliously. Most of all, bugger Donald bloody Brask.

When a woman in a seat nearby stood up and walked away, Riley nudged her bag over. Before she could sit down, a young squaddie with garish tattoos on his arms and a mass of angry pimples on his chin pushed past, dropped into the seat, smirking proudly at two of his mates on the other side of the room. Then he lifted a can of lager to his mouth and swallowed noisily, a froth of beer escaping down his chin.

"It's your lucky day, love," he said, staring hotly at her. "You wanna seat, be my guest." He patted his bony lap in what he probably thought was an inviting manner, his pimples taking on an inflamed look as his hopes rose.

Riley looked down at him and sighed. Oh, yuck, why do they do it? Everyone's an original half-arsed Romeo.

Before the soldier could react, she took the can of lager from his hand, and with a flick of her wrist, poured a squirt of the foaming liquid directly into his lap.

The man leapt to his feet with a howl of protest, while

his mates and some of the passengers laughed.

"What the bloody hell did you do that for?" he demanded, brushing ineffectually at the spreading stain on his trouser front.

"Because," Riley said icily, "you're an ignorant little shite."

The soldier swore under his breath and made a move towards her. Before he could touch her, a tall figure stepped between them.

"Knock it off," said the newcomer. His voice was soft but carried the unmistakable timbre of authority. The soldier stepped back, the anger subsiding to a sullen glare.

The man watched him walk away, then turned to Riley. "You all right?"

It was the swimmer from the pool. He was dressed in a linen suit and light blue shirt, and his tanned skin proclaimed regular exercise and above average fitness.

"Thank you," said Riley gratefully. She felt a glow coming to her cheeks at the thought of what this man had seen of her by the pool. "You really didn't have to. I was about to drop him."

He nodded. "I'm sure you were. They're young lads, full of vim and too much beer. They get a bit carried away."

"Well," she murmured coolly, "he nearly was, at that."

An announcement called for all passengers to make their way to the departure gate, and the man excused himself and went over to the desk, where a young woman attendant smiled at him, then bent to her computer screen. She looked up at a question from the man and pointed towards a middle-aged woman with a moustache standing in the queue for departures. The man nodded at the attendant and walked across to the woman.

Moments later he was back beside Riley. "Stroke of luck," he announced. "We're travelling together."

Riley looked at him. "Really? And what did you promise that woman with the moustache – a baby?"

He barely batted an eyelid. "I'm sorry?"

"You asked her to change seats."

He had the good grace to look sheepish. "I told her you were my fiancée and we'd been split up by computer error. She was glad to help." He held out his hand. "John Mitcheson."

Riley laughed. "Riley Gavin." As his warm hand engulfed hers, she wondered if he could feel her pulse beating in response.

"Riley? Is that Scottish?"

"Not really. My dad just liked old cars."

As they boarded the plane and settled in their seats, Riley was acutely aware of his body close by and a faint hint of aftershave. She gave a wistful thought to lost opportunities, and hoped Donald Brask hadn't taken up an offer on her behalf which turned out to be a turkey. She'd make his life hell if he had.

Not that Donald usually made mistakes. It was one of the reasons she had decided to use an agent for her work. It saved having to pitch for assignments and she could leave it to him to filter out anything she might not like to tackle. Not that it left much out; she needed the money and so did Donald. They were a good team, although she had only seen him twice. Fat, humourless and gay as a hatbox, he saw Riley purely as a money earner. At least it kept him on his toes.

"Sorry, love," he'd breathed insincerely on the phone that morning. "Big story in the making and I've got an editor who needs some digging done by someone who isn't a known Face." When he mentioned *The Daily Review*, Riley found all thoughts of holidays fading into the background.

Donald was talking high-profile national daily with a reputation for good fees. They specialised in crime stories that usually found their way on to television specials, which was good for the track record of the reporter involved and a near-guarantee of repeat work.

"What's the assignment?"

"A couple of old men have been murdered," Brask explained. "Nasty stuff. The editor smells a story and wants to get the goods before the other rags realise what it's all about, which won't be long. He figures an unknown will have more chance of getting the details before being spotted."

He relayed in succinct terms the execution-style death of two men on the south coast of England. Both jobs were professional and carried out with clinical neatness, and since it seemed the two men had known each other, with no obvious motive available, the police were dropping the word that it was probably an old gangland score being settled. "In other words it'll do as an explanation until something else comes up," he finished dryly. "Or until they find a smoking gun."

"Gangland?" Riley asked. She had met a few crime figures, mostly self-effacing types who dressed well, if a little flashily, and kept themselves to themselves. They were a dying breed, preferring to live in the shadows and let their 'employees' do the legwork, unlike their modern equivalents who saw no reason to hide from anyone, least of all the law, because they used the law as camouflage.

"Used to be. Contemporaries of the Krays, but not in the same league. These two operated a corridor from south London down to Brighton. Gambling, tarts, race-courses, clubs, that sort of thing. But not the heavy stuff. Retired now, according to my sources." He gave a dry chuckle. "Respectable pillars and all that, according to the local rag. Makes your heart bleed, doesn't it?"

She heard Donald rustling paper at the other end, and the beep of a computer. He was first class at building files on assignments. "They were pretty successful in their own way," he continued. "But they'd been out of it for so long everyone thought they were dead. One of them had a plush pad on the sea front; the other owned a Roller and a big house on the Downs. Rumour has it they used to operate with a third partner, but no one knows who. Maybe therein lies the motive."

"Thanks, Donald," said Riley. "Do I get to use the *Review's* resources?"

"Of course. But anything they know won't help, otherwise they'd use their own bodies. He wants you to do some background digging without attracting attention."

"Fine. I'll let you negotiate the fee as usual. Make it a good one and I won't cut off your thumbs for spoiling my holiday."

"Of course, dear heart," he said dryly. "Like you couldn't resist the call." He paused, then added, "You might do well to get some help on this one, Riley."

"Help?" This didn't sound like Donald. Next thing he'd be suggesting she became a housewife with two-point-four and a licence to sell Tupperware. "What kind of help?"

"It's just a precaution. From what I've picked up so far, these people might be a bit too sharp to play with by yourself. I've got a name for you – you can call him when you get back."

"Thanks, Donald, but I don't need help, you know that."

"Listen, dear," he countered bluntly. "This is serious. Get help or I don't represent you again. I'm not talking about taking on a lifelong pal. You simply need someone to watch your back." He hung up before she could argue.

4

Riley was disappointed when the plane finally touched down. The food had been avoidable, but easily traded in for the company of John Mitcheson to while away the journey. At least it had taken her mind off the aborted holiday and Donald Brask's concerns. It turned out Mitcheson was a security consultant working between the UK and Spain, setting up systems for wealthy property owners with villas in the sun. He, too, had been on holiday and was now on his way back. Riley found him interesting, if physically unsettling company, and wondered if his claim to be unmarried was true. He certainly didn't have the aura of a married man.

She had deliberately glossed over what she did for a living, dismissing it vaguely as 'research'. Some men felt threatened when she told them she was an investigative reporter, as if she'd confessed to working for the Inland Revenue or the CID. Maybe it said something about the sort of men she knew.

Mitcheson seemed satisfied by her description, and eventually switched topics, to Riley's relief. The holiday was now in the background, and she was already beginning to focus on the priorities for the job ahead. First thing to do was get the file from Donald and brainstorm the details until they were firmly embedded in her mind. It was the least interesting part of an assignment, but fundamental to success. With much of her time spent on the move, carrying round a research library was a luxury she couldn't afford.

They collected their bags from the carousel and walked through the crowded arrivals area, now simply two strangers who had come together for a short while. Riley wondered if there was a chance they might meet again.

As if sensing her thoughts, Mitcheson turned and placed a hand on her arm. "I'm for the M25," he said. "Can I give you a lift?"

Riley shook her head. "Thanks, but I've got my car here."

"Pity. Could we meet again…say, for dinner?"

She gave him a studied look. It never pays to be too eager with a man, her mother used to say. Take your time. Make him wait. "Sure. Why not?"

"Good. I'll call in a day or two."

It was only after he had gone that Riley realised he hadn't asked for her telephone number. So, that was the end of that. On the other hand, nobody caught a prize by waiting. Perhaps she'd call the manager of the holiday flats in Sotogrande.

Twenty minutes later she was in her car on the way to Donald Brask's Victorian pile in Finchley. Traffic was light and she made good time, calling him on the way to let him know she was coming. He was waiting for her at the front door and, with natural gallantry, lifted her hand briefly to his lips.

"My, you look delicious, sweetie," he breathed, giving her a meaningless once-over. He was wearing a thin, light blue jacket and pale slacks, with a pink cotton shirt that didn't quite match and a pair of trainers. The ensemble, Riley thought, looked as if he had dressed in the dark.

"Donald, you're an old fake," she said. "Why not tell me what's cooking?"

He smiled and released her hand, then led her into his office. In a former life it had been the dining room, but was now lined with books wall-to-wall and contained two state-of-the-art computers linked to printers and scanners. A television sat in one corner, tuned permanently to CNN, with the latest in digital recording equipment wired in and ready to go at the press of a remote.

She counted three phones but there were probably more under the sea of newspapers and documents that seemed to float over every available surface. This was Brask's nerve centre and she knew the disarray was misleading. He had a mind like one of his PCs and by the end of the day would have documented, copied, distributed or dumped every piece of information which had come into this house. Much of it arrived from contacts around the country, and what facts he couldn't locate within this room he could source very quickly by fax, phone or online. As if on cue, one of the phones rang once before a machine took over, and an indistinct voice spoke briefly before hanging up.

"Don't worry," said Donald, waving a hand towards the unseen caller. "They'll ring back." He turned to the desk in the centre of the room and pushed aside that day's newspapers to reveal a buff cardboard file. He flicked it with his fingers and handed it to her. "Everything we know is in there," he added. "I'm sorry it's not more."

"Thanks, Donald," said Riley. The file was light, she noticed – too light to contain much of substance. Considering Donald's considerable resources it wasn't a good sign. She was going to have to do some serious digging. Still, that was her job. "What's the deadline?"

Brask raised an eyebrow. "We're talking *The Review*, here, sweetie, chased by whoever else is feeling wide awake enough to pick this up – which they will. The deadline's yesterday, as always."

"Donald!"

He sighed and sat down heavily at his desk. "You've got a week, max. More than that it'll either go stone cold or totally ballistic. The police are currently trying to play it down as two separate incidents – one as a robbery gone wrong, the other as a revenge killing. That might keep some of the pack off the story for a bit, but it won't stay that way for long; it's very quiet news-wise right now, which means editors and reporters will be getting bored. Once they stop kicking the government or the furniture and begin linking the two murders, this thing will be knee-deep in hacks. You can funnel your reports through me."

He handed her a slip of paper with a name, phone number and address on it. "Remember what I said about help. I strongly suggest you call this man."

Gary opened the front door as a dark BMW crunched into the drive and stopped with its nose pointing towards the gate. He watched with apparent disinterest as the driver climbed out. The same scene was being played on a television screen in the kitchen.

"She in?" John Mitcheson asked. If he thought it odd that Gary kept one hand in his jacket pocket he made no comment.

"No, boss. Went out an hour ago – to the garden centre. She'll be back later." Gary stepped aside, allowing Mitcheson to enter. "You heard the news?"

Mitcheson nodded and shrugged off his jacket. "Where are the others?"

"Keeping their heads down near the airport." Gary followed him across the hallway into the kitchen. "She said to stay away from the house for a bit. The neighbours have been talking."

"Makes sense." Mitcheson helped himself to coffee from

a jug on the side. "How is she?"

Gary hesitated. He had known Mitcheson for some years, and possessed the ingrained caution towards officers to not take anything for granted. But this situation was different. And changing. "She's cool," he said eventually. "Seemed to take it in her stride, in fact." He smiled as if proud of a growing child. "Like weeding the garden."

"Are you okay?" Mitcheson's eyes were on him over the rim of his coffee cup, flickering down to where Gary's hand was still in his pocket.

"Sure. I'm good."

Mitcheson shrugged and poured the rest of the coffee down the sink. "I'm going to the gym, then I'll get some kip. I'll be back later for the briefing."

Gary nodded and let Mitcheson out, and stood watching the driveway as the car purred out on to the road. Only then did he let go of the gun in his jacket pocket.

5

The address Brask had given Riley was somewhere amid a row of glass and steel-fronted refurbishments in Uxbridge. As she climbed out of the Golf, she caught glimpses of high-tech open-plan and discreet lighting, with a hint of tinted glass and tastefully-arranged potted plants. Nice, she thought. Feng Shui lives in the bodyguard industry. Then her glance clicked on the number she was after and she questioned what Donald was getting her into. Between two of the stretches of clean glass modernity was a single brown doorway with an open letterbox, like a shocked mouth in a stretch of dried and peeling paint. A section of plain wood had been clumsily inserted down one side and left unpainted, as if the owners were going for shock value to spite their neighbours.

Riley was glad she had dressed in her customary jeans and a sports jacket. It wasn't the height of fashion but it suited her day-to-day movements. Especially here.

She crossed the pavement, pushing open the weathered door which led into a gloomy hallway. A narrow stairway led upwards to a glass-panelled door at the top, with piles of cardboard boxes vying for space on the treads and spilling on to the tiny landing. She shuddered, stepping past the rubbish, nudging open the door with one foot. There was no name on the frosted-glass panel. Inside, the dull atmosphere of a small, smoke-filled office replaced the gloom of the staircase.

"Always make an entrance, dear," a drama teacher she'd known had often said. The theory was that women could conquer their surroundings by making their presence felt. On the other hand the teacher was unlikely to have seen this dump. The furniture was pre-war MOD surplus, with a touch of rough living thrown in. A sturdy desk, a side table, a couple of chairs and a battered, wooden filing cabinet all came together in an uninspiring collection of grot. And yellowed wallpaper. Decor to jump off a bridge by.

A man was sitting at the desk peering at a computer screen. Riley put his age at about forty, with a good head of dark hair and a face that would have been interesting if it hadn't been screwed up in concentration. He wore a battered jacket of indeterminate colour and a button-down green shirt. Comfort winning out over style. He didn't look up.

"I'm looking for Frank Palmer," said Riley.

He raised a finger for a second, then stabbed it down on the keyboard with conviction. Whatever it did seemed to please him and his face lost the screwed-up look.

"Technology," he announced, "can be a real bitch." He had a pleasantly deep voice, with the huskiness of the long-term smoker. "But I live in hope of mastering it." He smiled vaguely as if the likelihood was imminent but unimportant, and stood up. "I'm Frank Palmer. Who is the client – you or a third party?"

Riley suppressed a tug of irritation. He wasn't exactly the jump-up-and-hit-'em type she had imagined. And his office was the pits. But she had enough faith in Donald Brask's advice to know she needed this man – or one like him.

"I need someone to accompany me for a few days while I do some research," she explained.

"Okay. My rate's a hundred and fifty a day plus expenses." He smiled. "I love saying that."

"Make it a hundred including and I'll think about it."

"'Bye," he said, turning back to his computer. "Close the door on the way out."

Riley felt the slow burn of anger. This wasn't how it was meant to go. She was supposed to tell this Palmer what he was to do, he would then agree the terms and off they would go. Nobody had mentioned morons who could afford to turn away paying customers. Hell, it didn't take much to see that Frank Palmer had a cash-flow problem.

She decided to give it another try. Better that than face Donald Brask's withering sarcasm. "Do you mind if I sit down?"

He nodded towards the other chair. "Help yourself."

Riley flicked at the patina of dust and sat down, while Palmer lit a cigarette.

"I need someone," she started again, "to accompany me on some field research. I was given your name."

"So you said."

"My name's Riley Gavin," she continued, letting a little grit creep into her voice. "Donald Brask recommended you."

"Good man, Donald." He stubbed out his cigarette with a wince of distaste. "I'm trying to give up. It's not easy. Which daily are you with?"

"I'm freelance. My assignment's with *The Daily Review*."

He raised his eyebrows, looking impressed. "How long have you been doing this kind of work?"

"Does that matter?"

"It might. I don't want to end up holding the hand of an amateur and getting dragged into something messy."

Riley counted to five. "What makes you think it could be messy?"

"*The Daily Review* isn't exactly known for tackling soft stories."

"Maybe. But you won't be holding anyone's hand. I've been doing this for four years and if you don't want the job—" She began to rise.

"I didn't say that," he said calmly. "I just need to know who I'm – might be working with, that's all." He smiled faintly and looked across his computer towards one of the grimy windows, as if hoping for divine guidance.

"How about you?" She decided to go on the offensive. "How long have you been doing this work?"

"Same as you," he said readily. "Four years. Well, four years solo, anyway."

"Police?" Donald hadn't given any information about Palmer's background, which could be a good or a bad sign.

"Army – Special Investigations Branch. Redcaps to our clients."

A military cop. Useful.

She told him as much as she knew, beginning with the murders of the two former gangsters and ending with the suspicions that a third person had been involved with them. It was the third person she needed to find.

"Who are the two stiffs?"

"John McKee and Bertrand Cage."

Palmer leaned forward until the front legs of his chair settled with a faint thud on the floor. His face was still. In the silence a fly buzzed about his head before settling on the desk and cleaning its feet.

"I think someone's having you on, Miss Gavin," he said softly. "There's nothing 'former' about McKee and Cage. They may have been a bit long in the tooth, but they never left the business. Even I've heard of them. They and their type are not nice people."

Riley stared him in the eye. "That's where you come in, Frank. I do the digging – you watch my back."

He returned her stare for a few moments, eyes blank. Outside, a van door slammed and a man laughed. It seemed to galvanise Palmer into a reaction. He shook his head. "Sorry. I can't help you."

Riley stared at him. "Why not?"

"I'm busy. Permanently."

6

It took Riley an hour on the phone to discover that London was suffering a shortage of willing, experienced men. She was down to three names and fast losing heart: two like Frank Palmer – one-man shows – the third an agency. So far, none had shown great enthusiasm for the job. Only the agency had admitted any knowledge of the two dead men, and the man she had spoken to had hinted a warning about going ahead with the piece. He promised to get back to her after conferring with his colleagues.

She kicked off her shoes and jacket and padded around her Fulham flat seeking inspiration from the notes she had been given by Brask. The file on McKee and Cage was still depressingly thin and she felt an unusual lack of control; normally she had no problem in planning her strategy. Damn Brask and his warning!

There was a scratching sound at the door and Riley stopped prowling and let in the neighbour's cat. He had decided she was worthy of his company a few days after she had moved in and took to calling whenever he was bored or hungry. Buying a tin of cat food hadn't been the best idea, but it was cheaper than sharing her infrequent television dinners. Anyway, she had always been a sucker for strays.

She spooned out meat into a saucer and, as he ate, she powered up her laptop and opened a new document. She typed everything she knew into the file, adding a few random thoughts for expansion later, before running dry and closing down the machine in frustration. There were times when pushing too hard resulted in brain-fatigue and a blank screen.

"What am I going to do, cat?" she asked. The cat finished eating and climbed on Riley's notes to clean himself. She hadn't the heart to dump him off, so turned out the lights and got an early night.

Next morning she called Brask. He didn't seem surprised at her difficulty in finding help, nor at Palmer's lack of enthusiasm. "He's still the best you'll find," he insisted. "Try him again, sweetie. I think he'll change his mind if you talk nicely to him."

Riley hung up and rang an agency she'd heard of in Luton. They were polite until she mentioned McKee and Cage, then found they had suddenly been awarded a big contract and couldn't spare anyone. And they wouldn't recommend anyone either. Better to forget the whole idea, their tone implied.

She rang two more. The wife of one said he was away on a long contract, while the other man's answer machine seemed to mock her with its request to call back later. The industry workload suddenly appeared to have been given a boost, Riley reflected. Bully for the industry.

She got dressed and went to the local library where she began the task of dredging for gold dust. Her father, a beat copper, always said eighty percent of activity was in research. It was a simple credo but one she found correct. It was a matter of knowing where to look. She concentrated on biographies of criminals from the fifties, trawling the indexes for familiar names that might give her a jumping-off point.

In the afternoon she drove out to the British Library at Colindale and waved her press card for admission to the CD-ROM resources in the reading rooms. She quickly found that in between the strands of often lurid speculation, there was little hard detail about the activities of McKee and Cage, most of it from too many years ago to be of practical help. Whether through lack of criminal convictions or a greater press interest in the Krays and the Richardsons, they appeared to have enjoyed a remarkably low-profile existence. What few references there were seemed to have come from an individual reporter's desire to pad out another story with speculation and name-dropping in place of solid facts. It relegated the two men to being little more than satellites in the outer atmosphere surrounding the bigger names. Maybe, she reflected, that's how they had preferred it to remain.

Riley kept at it, slotting a few names into her memory for later use. Most had been connected with McKee and Cage at one time or another and were either beyond the grave or beyond reach in other ways. But somewhere there would be a person with a story to tell. All she needed was to find them.

From the grainy pictures and the text cataloguing the times, Riley wondered why they had bothered. Most seemed to have been blessed with little skill or luck in their chosen profession, and had disappeared off the radar with no explanation or farewell. The smarter ones, she guessed, must have salted something away for their old age, and were probably now living quiet, respectable lives.

Cage and McKee seemed to be in this group, and the latest information had them living in comfortable seclusion on the south coast near Brighton. John McKee had been a respected member of an exclusive golf club, with his home described by one newspaper as an expensive block of flats near the beachfront, where he entertained friends and lived quietly. There was no mention of a family.

Bertrand Cage had not been so fortunate. Dogged by ill health, he had gradually withdrawn into a hermit-like existence. His sole companion was his chauffeur/handyman, Peter Willis, a stocky, neat man staring solidly into the camera. She checked her notes and found Brask had included a phone number but nothing else. Riley wondered what else Willis was good at apart from driving. From latest reports, the police seemed satisfied that he had taken no part in the murder.

She went back to the reports of the killings. Both men had been shot with .38 calibre handguns. Cage died sitting on the beach, from a single shot to the back of the head; McKee died in his flat – also with a single shot, but to the heart. Time of death for both men had been estimated at between 08.00 and 09.00 hours. There were no recorded witnesses.

Riley closed the files. Both shot about the same time. Close enough proximity for the same killer, or two separate ones? She went back to the old reports and made a note of two names that appeared often enough in the files to be interesting. After cross-checking for addresses, she left the library. On the way back she tried the number for Peter Willis. No reply. It was already getting dark.

The rumble of traffic south of the river built up relentlessly as the last of the afternoon light faded, and cooler air began to float outwards through the streets of Newington as a tall figure arrived beneath a block of flats and waited in a doorway. A door slammed and angry voices bit into the gloom, and a thin drizzle of dirt fell to the ground, kicked out from beneath the railings by a scrape of feet on the balcony overhead. In the distance a dog barked and a dustbin lid clattered to the ground. Above the watcher's head the name of the block had been removed, leaving a grubby outline and a few twisted, rusted screws for those who needed reminding what this place was called.

The watcher had spent most of his life in places like this, and had learned the hard way to blot out whatever did not concern him. Everyone had their own problems, never mind listening to those of the people inhabiting cesspits like this.

A youthful figure appeared out of the darkness, cocky and strutting. As he passed under a lamp near a passage-way, the watcher saw a familiar gaunt face topped by a harsh crew cut, with the dark patch of a tattoo on the side of his neck.

He waited until the figure drew level with the doorway, then reached out a powerful hand and grasped him by the collar, effortlessly cutting off any sound the other might have uttered. The youth struggled instinctively, but was spun round with his face pressed hard against the cold brickwork, a knee in the small of his back pinning him like a butterfly.

"You were told to stay put, Leech," the watcher whispered in his ear. "Where have you been, you little runt?"

Leech wriggled ineffectively, straining against the power-ful grip. "I only went for a bevvy, honest!" he choked. "You never said about not taking any breaks – it's cold out here!"

The watcher released the pressure a little, and leaned in close to breathe against the youth's face. "I never said you could leave your post, neither," he whispered. "Has anyone been near Cook's place?"

"No – honest!"

"You better hope so. The moment anyone does, find out who they are and ring me. Right?" With that he let the youth go and walked away.

Behind him he knew Leech would be congratulating himself that his ugly little face wasn't going to take any more punishment. He might even be feeling a little full of himself. He heard the youth running off into the dark. So far he hadn't allowed Leech to see him face to face, giving him his instructions by mobile phone, which suited them both fine. Undoubtedly Leech would think himself well off: being paid to watch some old git who smelled of piss and booze and never went out would be a doddle. Even with the occasional bruising, it was a break for Leech from pushing pills and any knocked-off goods he could trade in the area.

The big man walked back to his car and drove away.

7

Next morning Riley tried the phone number for Peter Willis again. There was still no reply, so she double-checked with Directory Enquiries and on the Internet. No number was listed. Maybe he'd gone to ground to escape the press. She had a feeling that as a driver/handyman – for which possibly read minder – he might be a more reliable source of information than most. If she could get to him.

She left the flat, pointing her Golf towards the Thames. The first address she had noted was Trinity Court, south of the river near Elephant and Castle. It turned out to be a block of flats set back from the road, and she cruised by to check the layout before slotting into a parking space fifty yards away.

The block was light and airy, with none of the darkened alleys and alcoves typical of council blocks. Trees and flower tubs complemented a bright, hi-tech fascia and buffed-steel handrails along the balconies and walkways. What would probably once have been a breeding ground for scraggy dogs, doubling as a car-breaker's yard into the bargain, was now gone. At least, on the surface.

Riley climbed a spiral stairway, following the numbers to the first floor balcony. Her progress was watched by a group of four children, for the most part hooded and silent, and she wondered if anything had truly changed under the surface. Her suspicions were confirmed when she arrived at the door to number thirty-two. It was a carbon copy of those on either side, all three reinforced with sheets of aluminium or steel, daubed with paint and

31

etched deeply with initials or symbols. Dynamite would not have dented them, and Riley wondered if neighbourhood watch schemes elsewhere couldn't learn a thing or two around here.

She hammered on the door until it flew back without warning, revealing a tall, emaciated man in a string vest. He looked about eighty but could have been twenty years younger. Strands of grey hair hung limply from his forehead and rheumy eyes stared out in a dazed fashion, like an animal emerging into the daylight after a lengthy hibernation. Around his body hung the acid aroma of beer and stale sweat.

Riley swallowed hard. So much for her image of a gang member from the sixties. Reginald Arthur Cook, according to reports of the time, had been an enforcer – a strong-arm man – for Bertrand Cage and John McKee. In December 1968, one of his strong arms had put a bookie into a coma, resulting in a five-year prison sentence. Back then he had been bad news.

"Reggie Cook?" she asked bluntly.

He blinked slowly. "Who wants to know?"

Riley handed him a card. He took it without looking at it. "You from the Social?"

She almost smiled at the irony; here was a man who had brought pain and violence to people and he was frightened of a visit from the DSS. She became aware of movement along the open corridor to her right. "Look," she said quietly, "I'd like to talk to you. Can I come in?"

"No. What do you want?" His eyes began to look less vague, as if sensing there might be something he could gain from her presence.

"I want to talk to you about Bertrand Cage and John McKee."

"Who?"

"They're both dead. You used to work for them, didn't — "

"Fuck off!" As the door slammed in her face a stab of laughter drifted along the corridor. She hammered on the door again but Cook had obviously gone deaf.

As she walked downstairs the four kids appeared. A stringy boy in an oversized denim jacket pushed forward. "Cook's mad. You wanna watch him!" The others laughed, jostling for support and egging each other on.

"Why's that?" Riley asked.

"He talks to himself," put in a podgy girl with short, streaked hair. "And he's a perve." She grinned and nudged her nearest companion, a slender girl with coffee skin, eyes glinting beneath a tracksuit hood.

"Would be, if we let him," she muttered.

"Are you the filth?" a boy with a moon face demanded. He had an air of edgy tension about him that Riley had seen in kids where she had been born. Some grew out of it; some never lost it, ingrained from birth and carried through life like a badge.

"She's a snoop!" crowed the podgy girl. "I bet old Cookie's being watched by the Social!" She spat out a wad of chewing gum, deftly kicking it away just before it hit the ground.

"I'm not a snoop," said Riley. "Why do you say Cook's mad?"

"She's not the filth," said another, deeper voice. "But she ain't far off it."

The kids looked round, their mood changing instantly. Two older youths had joined them, appearing out of nowhere. The one who had spoken jerked a thumb sideways and the group melted away, their scuffed footsteps echoing off the walls.

Riley's mouth went dry. These two weren't that much older than the others, but it was time to leave.

"Why you calling on old Cook?" the first youth demanded. His stance was tense and full of aggression, and he had a painful-looking graze on one cheek. The other youth drifted off to one side, feigning disinterest. The move made the hairs bristle on Riley's neck. Both were dressed in baggy jeans, trainers and hooded jackets, brand names colourful splashes against the drabness. Old faces in young bodies.

"That's my business," Riley said flatly. She glanced around and saw no movement, no sign that anyone else was aware of events happening here.

The first youth scratched at the graze on his face. "Yeah? Like, his aunt's died and left him a fortune, right?" He was anywhere between fourteen and eighteen, with a thin, colourless face and a coarse crew cut. There was a crudely drawn tattoo of a bird on one side of his neck. He had maybe an inch of height over Riley, and did his best to stare down his nose at her. "Maybe we should have a chat about it." He leered sideways at his mate.

A scraping sound came from the end of the block and a man appeared dragging a dustbin. He didn't look at them but concentrated on tipping the contents into a large rubbish skip. The two youths shuffled their feet, caught momentarily off-guard.

It was enough to break the tension. Before they could say anything Riley stepped to one side and dashed past them. Surprisingly, they made no move to stop her, turning to watch her go with a look of amazement. The second youth scuffed over to join his companion, and she felt their eyes boring into her back as she hurried away.

Back in her car, Riley let out a deep breath and locked the doors before driving off. Her hands were shaking and she cursed herself for being so careless. For whatever reason she had got away without harm. Next time she might not be so lucky.

She mentally scratched Reginald Cook off her list. Even if he were willing to talk about Cage and McKee, his story would undoubtedly change with every new drink.

Her next call was as different from the flats as it was possible to get. Brambleside old peoples' home, set in leafy Kenton, had no brambles that she could see, and was new, fresh and serene.

A tall, imposing looking woman appeared within seconds of Riley ringing the bell. Starched in uniform and manner, she announced herself as Mrs Marsh, the matron, and asked Riley her business. She looked surprised when Riley explained the reason for her visit.

"Norman Page?" she echoed. "Goodness – it's ages since we had anyone asking for him. I didn't realise there was anybody. Are you a relative?"

"Not exactly," Riley confessed smoothly, letting a touch of Kensington slip into her voice. "My name's Riley Gavin. I'm a writer. You may have heard of my work? Well, I was hoping Mr Page might be able to give me some background material for some articles I'm writing. Would it be possible to have a quick word?"

Mrs Marsh retreated behind her matron's rulebook. "We normally expect at least two day's notice for visits. And then only from family. You're not family," she finished unnecessarily but with a smile, her tone clearly reflecting that this young woman was *obviously* well bred. Rules, however, were rules.

"Yes, I know, but—"

"And in any case, Mr Page is not allowed visits at the moment."

"Is he ill?"

The matron pursed her lips in an authoritarian huff. "If you must know he's been misbehaving again."

Riley killed the thoughts that entered her head. "Seriously?"

"Serious enough," the matron replied sourly. "We don't need to put up with his sort of carry on." She began to move backwards, the subject closed.

Riley took out her card, handing it to the woman. "Can I make an appointment to see him in a couple of days? I know I'm not family, but it is important."

"Well, perhaps," the woman considered carefully. "I'll have to discuss it first."

"Discuss it?"

The matron looked at Riley as if she'd developed horns. "With his solicitor. All our guests have solicitors. We don't just accept *anyone* here." With that she closed the door, rattling a security chain into place.

Riley drove home with a growing feeling of frustration. So far she had tried to interview two people, both of them at one time closely connected to Cage and McKee. One was beyond helping himself, while the other was beyond reach of anyone unless it was over the Dragon Lady's dead body. Both had been employed by the dead gangsters as toughs, ending up with Cook seemingly one short step away from the grave and Page in a home, with a solicitor making all his decisions for him.

As she stepped through the front door of her flat she heard a faint electronic beep from her answerphone. The neighbour's cat was curled up on the armchair and raised one eyelid before going back to sleep. Hard life for some.

Riley dropped her bag and rearranged a cushion on the sofa. She was about to press the message button when she felt a chill creep over her shoulders and down her back. Everything looked normal, but somehow wasn't. Then she noticed the lid of her laptop was slightly open.

And the cat. How had he got in? She distinctly recalled putting him out before leaving.

8

The silence in the flat drummed in her ears. She reversed
her car keys between her knuckles and quickly checked the
bedroom, kitchen and bathroom. Nothing. Yet all around
were minute signs of an intruder: a drawer slightly out
here, contents disturbed there; the laptop partially open;
the file from Brask and her notes from the library slightly
disarrayed. Things as she would not have left them. Yet
nothing was missing. She jumped when the phone rang.

"Yes?" She scooped up the handset and almost shouted
with relief.

"Miss Gavin?" A man's voice answered. "Frank Palmer.
You all right?"

"Oh, yes, I'm fine," she replied. "I just got in – I'm a bit
breathless from the stairs, that's all." She huffed a couple of
times, determined not to let Palmer know how wobbly she
was feeling.

"Uh-huh. Listen – could you come to the office, say,
tomorrow morning? I might have been a bit hasty turning
you down."

Brask must have persuaded him to reconsider. With this
latest shock, she wasn't about to argue, and promised to be
with him first thing.

She checked the flat again. In the kitchen she discovered
where the intruder had come in. The window was missing
a section of glass from one corner. Enough for a hand to
gain access to the sash. A faint scuff of dirt showed where
a foot had rested on the paintwork.

Yet still nothing seemed to be missing. Had they been

disturbed – perhaps by her return just now? Or had they been looking for something specific, like stuff they could readily turn into cash to buy drugs? If so, they had missed the blindingly obvious laptop. She dropped her car keys on the table and called the building's service department to arrange for the window to be mended. The manager wasn't happy about touching anything before the police had been called, until she persuaded him that she didn't want to spend the night waiting to see if the intruder would come back.

Lottie Grossman sat at her kitchen table shelling peas into a bowl. Across the table sat Gary, and alongside him John Mitcheson, listening on a mobile phone. He ended the call and switched off.

"That was McManus," he told the woman. "Someone's been asking questions about Cook and Page. Aren't they on that list?"

"They are," Lottie murmured. "So what?" She continued shelling the peas, her varnished fingernails ripping into the pods. The two men exchanged glances.

"The list shows anyone who could prove to be a link," Mitcheson pointed out. "I didn't expect anyone to get to them this quick – if at all. How much do they know?"

"Old men," Lottie said enigmatically. "Old men talk rubbish and nobody listens." She plucked a piece of broken pod out of the bowl and tossed it aside, the movement oddly birdlike. It bounced off the table and landed on the floor, and she looked pointedly at Gary, who reached down and retrieved it.

"So we ignore someone asking questions, then?" Mitcheson persisted. Her lack of concern was puzzling.

Lottie dropped the pod she was working on and glanced

at Gary. "Leave us a moment, would you, dear?"

When the door was closed Lottie turned to Mitcheson and stared at him, a faint pulse beating under one eye.

"My husband, Mr Mitcheson," she said with quiet venom, "would have your eyes out for taking that tone of voice with me. Especially in front of another employee." The pulse beat a little faster. "I suggest you remember that. Do you understand me?"

Mitcheson stared back at her and wondered why he was taking this. "My apologies," he murmured finally. "It won't happen again."

Lottie Grossman reached up and patted his cheek, her fingernails stopping at the corner of one eye. Mitcheson wanted to slap her hand away but restrained himself. He needed this job – for now, anyway. If it meant taking some shit from this woman for a while, then he could do it.

"Very well," she said quietly. "We won't mention it again. Don't worry about Cook and Page. McManus knows what to do. I suggest you see to the person doing the investigating. Today would be good." She turned back to the table and began to hum as she busied herself again with the bowl of peas.

Mitcheson slowly exhaled and left the kitchen, punching numbers into his mobile.

At Trinity Court a dark blue Toyota RAV4 slid quietly into a space between a battered transit van and a rubbish skip, and the driver cut the engine. He sat for a few minutes, occasionally checking his watch, then climbed out and walked across to stand under the overhang of the first floor balcony running the length of the building.

Ten minutes passed before footsteps echoed down a spiral stairway, and a familiar figure crossed the open space towards the RAV. The driver let out a pent-up breath through gritted teeth and stepped out to confront him.

"You're living dangerous, boy," he growled, making Leech spin round with a grunt of fear. He grabbed the youth by the arm, pulling him close. It was the first time he'd let him see his face. "You got a death wish or something?"

Leech went very still, eyes wary. "What's up?" he whispered.

"You're late. That's what's up. Carry on annoying me and you'll end up in the river. Got it?"

Leech nodded his understanding and the man relaxed his hold for a moment. He could always get the gun out and stick it up Leech's nose to reinforce the message.

"Has anyone else been snooping?" He nodded towards the first floor where Cook's flat was situated.

"No, honest," said Leech, shaking his head. "Just this chick." He scrabbled in his jeans pocket and handed the man a slip of card.

"Okay. Tell you what I want you to do. Take this heap of shit," he gestured to the Toyota, "and get rid of it. Up north along the river somewhere – and don't get caught."

Leech massaged his throat. "North?" The way he said it suggested crossing the Thames was like foreign travel, and the man wondered if Leech had ever been further than three streets away. Somehow he doubted it; the Leeches of this world didn't have the imagination.

"Yeah – north. You know – where all the shiny lights are and the rich people live?"

Leech stared at the car with a frown. "What's wrong with the motor? It looks new."

"I said lose it. That's all you need to know. Try palming it off on one of your scummy mates and I'll hear about it."

"What about my payment?" said Leech. "For watching Cook. You promised."

"Call me when you've got rid of the car. Now piss off."

Leech stalled the vehicle twice in his eagerness to get out of the car park, and the man shook his head in disgust. The sooner he finished with this loser the better. He knew Leech would offload the RAV without thinking twice, in spite of the warning. His kind couldn't help it. Not that it really mattered; it couldn't be traced back to anyone because it was already third-hand when he'd collected it and on its second change of plates. A favour for a favour. Now he'd done with it. When the car had gone he looked up at the block of windows and counted across from left to right. There was a light on. Easy-peasy.

Minutes later he was through the reinforced front door of the flat, holding his breath against the revolting smell. Jesus – didn't this old bastard ever wash?

He took a handgun from inside his jacket, checking the silencer. The extra length on the barrel made awkward handling in a confined space, but he doubted the flat's occupant would put up much resistance.

The blue light of a television flickered down the hall, and he could hear the build-up to the National Lottery show. No wonder it was so quiet everywhere – the whole block was probably waiting for their fortune to come up. Some hope. Especially for Cook.

He poked his head round the corner of the small living room and spotted Cook's scrawny figure stretched out on the settee, surrounded by crumpled beer cans and half-empty fast-food wrappings. He wore grubby, grey tracksuit trousers and a filthy vest discoloured by food stains. His eyes were half shut in the glow of the television screen. There was no one else in the room.

The intruder waited a moment until he was satisfied Cook was alone in his pigsty, then stepped around the doorway into the flickering half-light.

"Hey – Cook," the man whispered. When Cook's eyes opened the man raised his gun and snapped off two shots in quick succession. For one flickering moment Cook looked terrified, before he was slapped back into the settee under the impact of the two bullets.

The man counted to ten, watching for signs of life. Satisfied there were none he turned and left, gently closing the front door behind him. Once outside, he let out a lungful of air.

9

Riley didn't need to open the door this time to enter Palmer's office – there was no glass and very little door left. Through the hole she could see him in front of the window, calmly smoking a cigarette and staring out at the street. The place was a shambles, the remains of his computer spread over the office floor like electronic confetti.

"Earthquake?" she asked, glass crunching underfoot.

"Computer virus," he replied, turning to greet her. "One of the nasty ones."

"Ouch." She nodded at the mashed PC. "Did it cost much?"

Palmer shrugged. "Two days of trudging around after an air-conditioning salesman. His partner thought he was cheating on him. I managed to prove otherwise. The client couldn't pay me in cash in case the partner found out." When she looked blank, he explained, "They were partners in their private account, too."

Riley dusted off one of the chairs – remarkably, still in one piece – and sat down. She wondered how Palmer could be so calm amid this wreckage. She studied him for signs of injury, but there were none. "Were you here when this was done?"

"I had a ring-side seat. But I think that was the intention. It was called delivering a message."

"Who did it – an angry husband?"

Palmer sat too. "I was hoping you could tell me," he said, his greyish eyes boring into hers.

"I don't follow."

"Oh, did I forget to mention?" he said dryly. "There were two of them – both big, both with baseball bats. And they seemed to know you."

"But how? I've only been here once."

"Beats me. I figured it had to be you, because they referred to you as the pretty one – which, unless the guy was gay, lets me out. They also said to stop whatever we were looking into. Otherwise they'd come back and use my head as a baseball." He flicked at a piece of grey plastic on his desk. "Whatever you've been doing, you've seriously rattled somebody's cage."

Riley felt a finger of ice brush her neck, remembering the break-in at her flat.

Palmer must have noticed, because he said: "What?"

She told him about the disturbed items and the broken glass, then frowned. "But you're not involved in this – at least, not yet. And what's with the 'we' bit?"

"'You and your lady friend' were the words they used. That's pretty specific. Have you been bandying my name about?"

"Why would I?" Riley pointed out. "Didn't you tell them you'd refused the job?"

"We didn't really get that far." He turned to look out of the window again, revealing a piece of his computer attached to the tail of his jacket. Riley reached over and pulled it off.

He stared at it quizzically. "So that's where it got to. Hey, all I need now is some glue and I'm in business." He tossed the component across the room and bent down in the corner and plugged in a battered kettle. "At least this survived. Fancy one?"

"Why not? Black, no sugar, please."

"So. Want to brief me on what's happened so far?"

He spooned instant coffee into two cups. "So I can decide whether to help or not."

Riley recounted her activities of the last two days. Palmer's face showed little expression at the mention of the young thugs at the block of flats. He poured boiling water and handed Riley a cup. "About the break-in; you're sure there was nothing missing?"

"Not that I could see."

"Well, that rules out burglary; an opportunist would've grabbed your laptop on the way out. You said it was open, though."

"Yes. But I'd also made some paper notes to work from, and there was a file from Donald Brask. I'm pretty sure they had a look through them. I didn't really notice the order – they were mostly loose pages."

Palmer raised an eyebrow. "Would these pages have included my name and details?"

Riley opened her mouth to say no, then realised he was right; Donald Brask had given her the details on a slip of paper and she'd stuck it in the file for easy reference. She bit her lip. "Sorry."

He shrugged. "Doesn't matter. So, have you worked crime scenes before?"

"Yes. What about you?"

"Plenty. Crime in the army is pretty much the same as anywhere else." He stopped, frowning as if a thought had occurred. "Damn."

"What?"

"I thought there was something vaguely familiar about my two visitors. I've just realised what it was."

"You knew them?"

He shook his head. "Not personally...but I know the type." He blew on his coffee. "They were ex-squaddies."

They digested the statement between them for a moment. Then Riley asked: "Does this mean you'll help?"

He frowned, taking out another cigarette. "You're still going ahead with the job, then?"

"Of course. Why do you smoke so much? You never finish them."

He looked at the cigarette. "No idea. Nerves, probably. Why – is it a problem?"

"Only if we're going to be sharing the same breathing space."

He put the cigarette back in the pack. "Consider me hired. Do I get regular smoke and tea breaks?"

The phone interrupted Riley's reply. Palmer scooped it up and muttered his name. "Yes, she's here," he said, glancing at Riley. After a few moments he put it down without a word. "That was Brask," he explained. "The wires are humming all over London. He's getting calls from mates in the business and the Met. Another ex-villain's been shot. This one was late last night, south of the river. The dailies are starting to make connections."

"Where south of the river?" Riley queried.

"Near the Elephant and Castle. Bloke named Cook. Hey, wasn't he—?"

Riley nodded. "One of the men I visited."

Palmer pulled at his tie knot. "These boys don't hang about, do they? They find someone sniffing about and swing straight into action; burgle your flat, smash my office and kill a potential source – all within twelve hours. Looks like the body count's going up."

"And likely to go higher," said Riley. "If they haven't already called on Page, he must be the luckiest man in London." She reached for her mobile and dialled the nursing home. It was answered promptly by the matron.

"Hello, Mrs Marsh? It's Riley Gavin...I came by yesterday to see Norman Page. Is he okay..? Only I was wondering if anyone had been to visit him. You've seen him? I see...Thank you." She switched off her phone with a grimace and looked at Palmer.

"That didn't sound too positive," he said sympathetically.

"Basically, I can stick my request for a visit because he's as fit as a performing flea and how dare I question her integrity."

Palmer barely suppressed a laugh. "She sounds a real charmer. So what do you want to do?"

"What do you think? If he's got a pulse he can talk." She walked towards the door. "You coming?"

10

Mitcheson parked his BMW near Covent Garden and walked down to the Embankment, skirting groups of tourists and office workers. In spite of the cool breeze blowing off the Thames, there was already a heavy tang of exhaust fumes in the air, and he wondered why he wasn't somewhere far from here where the air was clean and pure.

He checked his back several times out of habit. By the time he was leaning on the embankment wall overlooking the grey waters, he was satisfied no one was following.

Moments later the man he knew as McManus approached and leaned on the wall alongside him, breathing noisily through his ex-boxer's nose. Big-boned and florid, he looked like a farmer in town for the day. Mitcheson didn't care for the man, but since he was Lottie Grossman's pet thug, he had little choice but to endure his brooding presence. Fortunately, he was brighter than he looked. Just.

McManus slapped a business card on the wall and pinned it down with a large finger so Mitcheson could read it. "That's the skirt doing the investigating."

Mitcheson read the name and felt as if someone had kicked him in the belly. Christ, it couldn't be...

"Are you sure?" he asked, staring at McManus. The big man was watching a seagull strut along the wall in search of food and had missed Mitcheson's look of surprise.

"Certain. She left a card with Cook before he gave her the elbow. I went round to her place for a quick look-see as soon as I got the call. She's a freelance reporter. I also found the name of a private snoop. I haven't had a chance to check further yet. I was lucky to get out of her place as it was – couple of minutes later and she would have caught me." He grinned dirtily, displaying a mouth full of false teeth. "That could have been fun, though."

Mitcheson rounded on him. "Knock it off. You didn't leave any trace, did you?"

"Do me a favour, soldier boy," McManus said softly, and stared back unflinchingly. "I don't leave traces. But I did pass the details to your two buddies. Talking of which, how did they do in Uxbridge? I hope *they* didn't leave any traces."

Mitcheson ignored the jibe. "I'll deal with the woman."

"Yeah? Like I dealt with Cook, you mean? I don't reckon you've got the balls." His expression was full of contempt.

Mitcheson felt a twist of distaste at the man's coldness. He was no stranger to killing, but had never killed helpless men who were too far gone mentally or physically to pose any kind of threat. He remembered Lottie Grossman's instructions to deal with the two old gang members, and felt a momentary self-contempt for having passed those instructions on to McManus in the first place.

"What about Page?' he asked.

"Page isn't your problem. Don't overreach yourself, soldier boy."

Mitcheson debated pushing it, but right here wasn't the time or the place. He left the man standing by the embankment wall and returned to his car. He might have to deal with McManus before long, otherwise his own position was going to be threatened. He didn't relish the prospect.

Mrs Marsh replaced the phone and stood for a while,

trying to overcome her sudden feeling of unease. Ever since Norman Page had arrived here, she had felt she was in some kind of limbo. She couldn't explain why. Maybe it was because most of her residents came from normal backgrounds, mundane and out of the ordinary, free of any mystery. But Page was different. He had arrived as arranged by his solicitor, and since then not a thing. No visitors, no calls, no history and only a couple of letters, since vanished. It was like he'd been put here in the shade to wither and die, unseen and unwanted.

She crossed the hallway towards the back stairs and frowned as her feet crackled through something on the carpet. For heaven's sake, she thought. How did leaves get in here? And in the kitchen, too. Someone must have left the back door open again. One of the temps no doubt, who didn't give a fig about health, safety or the heating bills. She bent and flicked the worst of them to one side where they wouldn't get trampled in any further. She'd get Mrs Donachy to see to it later.

Walking up the stairs, she thought about the call from the young woman – what was the name – Gavin? After so long with no contact and no interest from anybody, why should this woman suddenly be asking questions about Page?

She crossed the landing and peeped through the door of Page's room. She didn't go in because he was a light sleeper and woke at the slightest noise, then took ages to go back to sleep. One of his hands, she noticed, was clenched tight around the duvet, as if reacting to a sudden pain. A bad dream, perhaps.

She noticed the spare pillow had fallen on to the floor by the window. She could just see it beneath the bed. He obviously wasn't missing it. She'd pick it up later when she gave him his medicine.

11

They drove from Uxbridge to Kenton in silence. Palmer, ignoring Riley's rules, sat in the back and smoked, his head to the open window, contemplating the passing scenery as he blew smoke through the gap.

Riley drove as aggressively as traffic would allow, using the speed and agility of the Golf to counter her feelings of anxiety. Occasional glances in the rear-view mirror showed Palmer apparently unconcerned at the ride, and she wondered what the ex-army man was thinking. If he was worried about the attack on his office he seemed well able to conceal it. She wished she could share his air of calm. It wouldn't take the police long to spot the coincidence of a young woman visiting an old man like Cook shortly before his death; even the most junior traffic cop couldn't fail to fasten eagerly on that one.

"What are we going to do when we get there?" asked Palmer. "Kick the door in? Toss in a smoke grenade?" He flicked his cigarette through the window.

Riley forced her way between two lorries, drawing angry blasts from both vehicles. She caught Palmer's eye in the mirror. "I haven't thought that far yet. She's a bit of a tough nut. Any suggestions?"

"Sorry. Matrons aren't my strong point, ever since I puked up over one at junior school during a test for measles. I think it was the uniform that did it. I've never been able to date a nurse since."

"God, you're a big help," Riley muttered. But she found the imagery amusing enough to ease her tension and make her slow down. She pulled up outside Brambleside and turned off the engine. If there was anything happening inside, it was all taking place very quietly. There were no more than the usual cars parked along the kerb – all empty – and no signs of either ambulance or police in the drive-way. All very normal and suburban. Maybe Norman Page would be able to talk after all. As long as she could get inside and speak to him.

A tabby cat jumped down from a wall and ambled across to the car, where it turned its back and sprayed the front tyre, tail quivering like an antenna.

"Charming," Palmer muttered. "Fills you with confidence, doesn't it?"

"Where I come from," said Riley, "that's good luck."

The cat ducked through the fence in front of Brambleside, and disappeared from view, leaving a faint smell of ammonia drifting through the open car window.

"I'll go in," Riley announced. "You stay here and watch out for visitors. If you hear any screams, come and rescue me."

Palmer showed his teeth. "A piece of RMP advice: use maximum force and go in low. If that doesn't work, go to plan B."

"What's plan B?"

"Run like hell."

She left him in the car and walked to the front door. The doorbell sounded faintly from within the building and she listened for sounds of movement. Eventually the matron appeared in the doorway. The way she stared past Riley's shoulder to the road outside and the pallor of her face instantly told its own story.

"Mrs Marsh? What is it? What's happened?" Riley reached out and touched the woman's shoulder.

"What do you want?" she demanded in shrill voice. "I've already told you, you can't see anyone—" She began to close the door with a shaking hand.

But Riley stepped forward and blocked it. "He's dead, isn't he?" she said bluntly. "Tell me what happened."

Mrs Marsh's face seemed to fold in on itself and she backed away inside, letting go of the door. Her steely façade was crumbling before Riley's eyes. "You'd better come in," she muttered eventually. "But you can't stay long – the ambulance is on its way."

Mrs Marsh led the way into the kitchen, where she filled the kettle and switched it on. It was the routine of safety, the automatic response of someone in shock. She seemed content to fuss for a moment, moving things about on the work surface before turning to face Riley as the kettle began to hiss.

The kitchen was large enough to hold two large cookers and twin freezers, and an industrial-size dishwasher with its front door open revealing a full load of breakfast plates and cups and saucers waiting to be done. Everything was spotlessly clean, save for a few dried leaves nestling against the foot of one of the freezers.

The matron noticed Riley's glance and looked defensive. "The cleaner hasn't been yet. She takes care of that."

"What happened, Mrs Marsh?" Riley asked. She reached past the matron and switched off the kettle. Mrs Marsh stirred herself and began to make the tea.

"I just…found him," she said, replacing the teapot lid with a clatter. "After your call." Her eyes welled and Riley guessed she was terrified that she was going to be held professionally responsible for Page's death. She felt sorry for her – there was no accounting for one of your patients suddenly becoming a target on someone's death list.

"He was dead," she continued. "Just like that. No warning at all."

"Was there normally one – a warning, I mean?" Riley asked. For a moment she had a grisly image of inmates filling out a departure card before they could pass on to the next life.

Mrs March shook her head, turning to pour the tea.

"How healthy was he?" Riley asked.

"As fit as you or me," the matron said firmly, pushing a cup and saucer towards Riley. "He may have been confined to his room – voluntarily, I might add – but there was nothing really wrong with him. Physically, anyway."

"Physically?"

Mrs Marsh shrugged. "The problem was all up here." She tapped the side of her head. "And I don't mean the sex thing, either." She looked up at Riley and pulled a face. "Well, you know how some old men get."

Riley didn't, but she could guess.

"So what did he die of?"

Mrs Marsh held her cup and stared at the tiny bubbles moving slowly round on the surface. In the street a car horn sounded.

"What killed him, Mrs Marsh?" Riley repeated. There wasn't much time left.

Mrs Marsh's eyes suddenly filled with something other than professional concern, and she turned and placed the cup on the work-surface. She took a small handkerchief from her pocket and dabbed at her nose.

"Natural causes, of course," she replied defensively. "Mr Page wasn't unwell, but he wasn't strong, either." Her words sounded unconvincing.

"May I see him?"

The matron looked horrified at the idea. Then, to Riley's

surprise she nodded with something approaching eagerness. "Yes. I suppose so. But you mustn't touch anything."

Riley followed her from the kitchen past heavy pieces of utilitarian furniture dark with age and shiny with polishing. Up stairs lined with thick carpeting and lit by an art-deco window showing wan fairies hovering over large, colourful lupins. The air was musty and over-warm with a heady tang of air-freshener.

The room was cooler than Riley had expected, and if there was any smell lingering here, it was of aftershave. The furniture was simple and practical, and if Page had wanted any personal touches, his wishes had either been ignored; or he had no family, no interests and no artistic feelings. It was more of a cell than a home.

The form under the duvet was smaller than she had expected, too. Whatever Page had been in life, he had not been very imposing immediately before or after death.

Mrs Marsh lifted the duvet and revealed the dead man's face. It was little more than a mask, neither good looking nor evil. There was no obvious sign that his death had been anything but natural, and Riley felt a small twinge of disappointment.

"I came up after your call and checked on him," said Mrs Marsh quietly. "He was fine, I'm sure…apart from his pillow on the floor. I left it to go back down to get his medicine. He was such a light sleeper."

Riley looked down to where the pillow had fallen to the floor between the bed and the window. As she bent to pick it up she noticed a large indentation in the fabric. As she placed the pillow on the bed Riley felt the hairs move on the back of her neck. She held her hand above the pillow, fingers spread wide. The indentation was much bigger than her hand, but followed the same outline, with clear impressions of thumb and fingers.

She picked it up again, this time by sliding her hand beneath it. There was a damp patch in the centre on the other side. The old man must have drooled on it. Or coughed. The thought made her nauseous.

Mrs Marsh seemed unaware of anything, her eyes dull with shock. One thing Riley was sure of was that while the matron had followed instructions about restricting access to Page while he was alive, she had taken no part in his death.

"You're certain no one else has been in here?" she asked carefully. "In the last few hours, for example. When did you last see him alive – for certain?"

Mrs Marsh hesitated momentarily before shaking her head. "I'm not sure," she said honestly. "Probably last night, when I gave him his last dose. But those leaves you noticed downstairs? They were there when I woke up this morning…in the hallway. The back door must have been left open." She looked away guiltily.

Before Riley could say anything, a vehicle stopped outside.

12

"It's the ambulance," the matron explained. She glanced towards the door, stopping Riley before she could move. "The doors make a special sound…you get used to it in this job. You won't say anything, will you – about being in here? I could lose my job." Her eyes looked imploringly at Riley, desperate for the whole thing to go away. Yet even she must have known it was not as simple as that.

"I won't say anything, Mrs Marsh," Riley promised. "But I think you'll have to. They're bound to do a post-mortem."

Riley suspected that while Mrs Marsh might have taken some financial favours here and there to give special consideration to a resident, going against the law by covering up what she suspected to be a death from unnatural causes was beyond her.

She put a hand on the matron's arm. "Mrs Marsh. Were you expecting him to die?"

The woman shook her head. "No. He was weak, of course, but not terminally ill." She looked beseechingly at Riley. "Who could have done such a thing?"

Without waiting for a reply she left the room and went downstairs to admit the ambulance crew. The moment she was out of sight, Riley went through the bedside cabinet, but it was devoid of any papers save for some cheap books and magazines. Evidently anything of a personal nature had been cleared out. She checked the cabinet over the sink but that revealed no helpful clues, either. And no aftershave.

There wasn't time to get Palmer in here to take a look;

he'd have to rely on her observations. She followed Mrs Marsh downstairs. A private ambulance stood near the front door and one of the crew was just entering. Mrs Marsh's voice floated out from inside, giving directions, telling them to mind the furniture. She sounded more in control now she was on familiar ground.

Palmer was leaning against the car smoking, with the cat they had seen earlier winding its way round his ankles. When he saw Riley he flicked the cigarette into the hedge and shooed the cat away before sliding into the rear seat. "Any luck?"

Riley shook her head and tossed her shoulder bag into the back. "He's dead. The matron's terrified and thinks he was helped along. So do I." She explained about the indentations in the pillow and the leaves lying around inside.

"Convenient," Palmer muttered bluntly. "Any chance she deliberately left the door unlocked?"

Riley glanced in the mirror at him. "You've got a nasty mind, Frank Palmer. She may be open to the odd inducement, but our Mrs Marsh isn't the conspiracy sort – certainly not to murder. And the only reason I noticed the leaves was because the place is spotless."

Palmer nodded. "Sounds like somebody's doing a spot of clearing up of a different kind."

"Yes. I wonder if there are any more old associates like Page and Cook – ones I never found a mention of? If there are, they must be wondering who's going to be next on the list."

"You said there was a third man at the top of the tree – someone who ran things with Cage and McKee."

"There was. But no one knows who he was – or even if he's still alive. And Cage and McKee aren't telling."

Riley started the car and drove away. As they passed the driveway, Mrs Marsh was standing by the open rear doors of the ambulance, staring off into space.

Back at Palmer's office, Riley checked her mobile for messages. There was one. It was a familiar voice: "*Riley? John Mitcheson...Remember, we met on the plane? How about that dinner we talked about? Give me a call.*" His voice was calm and steady, as confident as she remembered from their talk on the plane. There was no hesitation when he had finished speaking, no repeated goodbye. He simply left a number and rang off.

"Will you go?" Palmer asked, when Riley explained about the message.

"Probably. Any reason why I shouldn't?"

"You tell me."

Riley caught his eye and reflected that Palmer wasn't as sleepy as he pretended. "I never gave him my mobile number."

"Well," Palmer commented, plugging in the kettle and scratching for tea bags in a drawer, "that's no big deal. If it was me that wanted to track down a hot babe I'd met on holiday, I'd drop a few euros down the hotel manager's shirtfront. Tea...coffee?"

"Nothing, thanks," Riley said, flushing at the thought that she had planned to do exactly what Palmer had just suggested. "But I didn't give the hotel my number, either. I never give it to anyone – not even my mother. It's strictly for outward use when I'm on the move. How could anyone trace it so quickly?"

Frank contemplated the ceiling, then said: "Maybe he's not just anyone."

13

The beaches between Malaga and Almeria were virtually deserted as a vicious breeze stung flesh with sand and sent beach balls and towels tumbling out of reach. The open-air cafes, usually busy throughout the day, were temporarily shuttered, with customers huddled inside waiting for the inevitable up-turn in the weather, while staff hurried to rescue sunshades and plastic chairs sent skittering across the promenades. Only the hardiest of tourists braved the drop in temperature and ventured on to the beaches, determination driving them to endure the unenjoyable come what may.

Even for these tough souls there was, initially, little to attract attention. A single boat moved on the water, approaching land from the south and sending up fans of spray as it bounced across the angry waves towards Torre del Mar. A boat like hundreds of others on this stretch of coastline, but at least it was moving and therefore watchable, unlike the dozens of others bouncing aimlessly at their moorings.

From the direction of the air force base in Malaga barely ten miles away, an AS 532 Super Puma helicopter with Spanish navy markings clattered over the villas and hotels, out across the expanse of beach and the white froth of the waves breaking on the shore. At the same time a powerful-looking launch surged round the headland, its stern flag snapping in the wind and announcing its origins with the Spanish Coastguard. Both craft seemed to be converging towards the small boat out at sea.

For several moments nothing changed, the three craft separate players in an unconnected drama on a blustery day. Then the incoming boat broke from its course, veering north and increasing speed to run parallel to the shore. The helicopter and launch adjusted their course to compensate. The incomer changed direction again, this time heading south, the creamy wake increasing at its stern as it put on speed. The other two craft did the same, giant sheepdogs herding their quarry toward the shore.

The helicopter reached its target first. Bearing down on the incomer and beginning to lose height, it sank to a point fifty feet above the waves in front of the speeding boat, while the Coastguard launch curved round to take up station out at sea. The small boat tried one final evasive manoeuvre, dashing like a terrier for a non-existent gap, then the nose sank as the engine was cut.

Lottie Grossman stared out over the rear garden where she had not long finished another bout of weeding, and heard the click of the disconnection from the phone in her hand. She waited a few seconds, then dialled an overseas number. After the news she had just heard, she was going to enjoy this, she decided. She was going to really enjoy it.

When the response came it was in bad Spanish. Lottie recognised the voice. The man on the other end was a small-time, low-level crooked ex-car dealer named Jerry Bignell. He had scuttled off to Spain several years previously when things had got too warm at home. Unable to lead any other life, he had set up a small drugs channel from Morocco with the help of some former London contacts. It wasn't a big operation, and hardly worth the Spanish anti-drug agencies or Customs wasting their time on. But the contacts across the Med were good and the product was high quality. In Lottie's opinion, it was time to step up a gear or two and make some changes.

"Your little boat has just been stopped by the Spanish Coastguard," she informed the man on the other end. "The crew are now under arrest. I hope you promised their families a pension."

"Who is this?" Bignell demanded, his voice flat and nasal with the tones of south London. He sounded drunk, which didn't surprise Lottie one bit.

"As of now," she continued, "your operation is dead. You don't have the money to buy fresh supplies – and the last I heard they don't accept Visa. You're busted."

"Cow!" the man screamed down the phone. "I'll have you for this!"

"No," Lottie said calmly, her voice curling down the phone like a snake. "You won't. If you try I'll send some-one round to see your daughter. Kensal Rise, she lives, doesn't she? Nice place…bit open to crime, though. But then, so is everywhere these days."

Bignell said nothing, but she could hear his laboured breathing as he struggled to keep his temper. He must know she wasn't bluffing.

"That's better. Now then, I'll pay you ten thousand pounds to forge a new link between my people and your contacts in Spain and Morocco. We'll call it an introduction and retirement fee."

"What?" Bignell spat incredulously. "Are you mad? You don't just buy into this like a fruit and veg stall down the Oval! They're not going to let you take my spot."

"Why should they care?" Lottie countered. "Money talks – especially if we offer to raise the stakes. Let's call it a change of management." She smiled down the phone and purred: "What else have you got going for you, Jerry?"

In the silence that followed, she knew she had him. Just as she had predicted. Like stealing off kids, really. "Good. I'll send my men round later today with the money. Get stupid and they'll be on the phone to London. After they've dealt with you, that is."

She dropped the phone and let out her breath in a rush. It had been a long time since she had experienced the thrill of sex – not that she had ever been over-fond of all that undignified grappling, anyway – but she reckoned this buzz more than made up for it.

She wondered where Mitcheson was. It was time he started earning his money. She hadn't seen McManus for a couple of days, either. But that wasn't too surprising; his loyalties always had been divided.

"Gary!" she called, and the young man appeared before her voice had ceased echoing round the hallway. "Find your boss and tell him we're going to Spain."

"I think he's gone out for the day, Mrs G," Gary said respectfully. He was not offering defence for Mitcheson, merely stating a fact.

Lottie shrugged indifferently. "Really? Well, that's all right. Everyone needs time off. Get a message to him, though, will you? His flight's tomorrow morning. Are those open tickets still good?"

"Yes, Mrs G."

"Right." She patted his shoulder. "You'd better get down the travel agents and have a chat with your girlfriend, hadn't you? Tell her it's the last time."

It was nearly eight before Riley arrived at Piccadilly Circus. Following John Mitcheson's directions, she turned south down Regent Street, leaving the bulk of the crowds behind. She checked her watch. Right on time.

The return conversation with Mitcheson had been brief and oddly formal, and she had forgotten to ask him how he had got her mobile number. She would do it as soon as she saw him. It might be easier face to face, anyway: no place for evasiveness.

It set her thinking about Frank Palmer, who seemed suspicious of everyone's motives. She felt no particular physical attraction for him, yet she'd found it comforting to have him around. And her instincts also told her Palmer was comfortable with the arrangement. They had gelled quickly after the initial coolness, and she hadn't felt for a moment that there was anything getting in the way.

She wondered where he was now. When they parted he had mentioned contacting one of his ex-army buddies for some information. Something to do with the two men who had destroyed his office.

Riley skirted a group of drunken Scandinavians spread across the pavement and ducked down towards Jermyn Street. As she turned the corner, she nearly collided with a large man walking the opposite way. He stepped aside with a balletic shuffle, eyes burning into her as she hurried by.

Unaccountably, she felt a chill settle across her back.

14

Frank Palmer took a sip of his pint and stared at the man opposite. He was surprised by the change in his former army colleague. His skin had the sallow air of one trapped in an office job, and tired eyes from staring too long at a computer screen. He was peering down into his pint of bitter with a sour expression, shaking his head ruefully.

They were in a smoky pub near Tottenham Court Road tube station.

"It's not like it used to be, Frank," the man sighed. "Not when we were in the regiment. These young fellas now, they're using the army like a career college. They're taking what they can of the training and selling it to the highest bidder. Some of them are earning fortunes in the security game...a few are even working on the black for HM Government, would you believe?"

Palmer looked mildly pained at his friend's criticism. "Steady, Charlie. I'm in the security game, too."

Charlie grinned. "Yeah, true. But you're not pulling down the sort of dough these fellas are. And as far as I know you never signed up for dodgy foreign governments who only need a bunch of men who can tell one end of an SA80 from another."

Palmer raised an eyebrow and felt a shiver of anticipation. His friend worked in military records in Whitehall. Men, women, serving and reserves, discharged and dishonoured, all came under his eye at some time or another. If there was anyone who could give him the information he needed, it was Charlie.

"You sound as though you're talking specifics."

Charlie shrugged. "Could be. Might not be the ones you're after though. I haven't had time to do a complete search, so it could be a wet noodle."

"I'll take that chance. What have you got?"

His friend produced a folded sheet of paper. He passed it across to Palmer and stood up with his empty glass. "Another one while you're reading?"

"No, let me," Palmer reached for some money, but Charlie waved a hand.

"Forget it. This is the most excitement I've had in weeks."

Palmer smiled in gratitude, studying the sheet while Charlie went to the bar. It was a hand-written list containing the names of half a dozen men.

Charles W Endby – Sgt. – 45 yrs – Royal Engineers
– Discharged 1/97

Malcolm Howard – Corporal – 35 yrs – Royal Marines
– Discharged 12/96

Mark J Appleton – Private – 22 yrs – Parachute Regiment
– Discharged 8/96

Alistair D G Duggan – Sgt – 36 yrs – Royal Marines
– Discharged 12/96

Gary Kepple – Corporal – 30 yrs – Royal Signals
– Discharged 1/97

John M Mitdasson Captain – 35 yrs – Royal Green Jackets
– Discharged 1/97

Palmer hadn't reached the end of the list before one of the names made an impact. Malcolm Howard. Was that 'Howie' – the one with the baseball bat? He was about the right age. If so, maybe his companion was on this list, too. It had to be someone accustomed to taking the lead; the man had possessed that air of easy authority.

He discounted Endby, unless he looked much younger

than his years, and Appleton who was too young. That left Duggan. And he had served in the same regiment as Howard. It was a tenuous link but, as Palmer was well aware, one not to be ignored.

Charlie deposited two fresh pints on the small table. "Any good?"

Palmer nodded. "Could be. What's this list from?"

Charlie smiled. "If I tell you that, I'll have to kill you after. Actually, it comes from the RMP computer in Chichester. It's a list of discharges for 'unspecified offences not carried forward to court martial'. That's modern army-speak for clearing out unwanted talent who were suspect but with insufficient evidence. In other words they didn't want a scandal."

"Suspect in what sense?"

Charlie shrugged. "Most of these chaps were doing jobs on the side. I can't recall which, but two of them were suspected of running drugs out of Cyprus. I think it was Kepple and Appleton. The others were mostly doing private security stuff while serving in Germany... close protection work and that. The MPs reckon they were raking it in standing guard for pop stars and media toffs while off-duty or on the sick. There was even some talk about one of them – Endby, I think it was – doing CP for one of the Serb warlords in Bosnia. He was supposed to be on holiday in England at the time. He was lucky they got to him before the other side did. Oh, and a couple of them also got caught bringing in souvenir weapons from Bosnia – stupid stuff like that."

"What about the officer – Mitdasson? Stealing from mess funds?"

Charlie frowned. "Mit-who?" He leaned across and took the list. "Oh, sorry. That's my writing. I had to do this on

68

the wing while the others were at lunch. You'd be amazed how closely everybody's watched these days. If I'd printed it all off on the inkjet, there's what they call an audit trail showing who's done what." He took out a pen and amended the name in capitals. "That's better." He grinned and handed the list back.

Palmer read the name and felt his gut tighten. "John Mitcheson?"

"Yes. Interesting chap. Did a bit of secret squirrel work a few years ago in Northern Ireland. Then he was seconded to a unit on loan to the Colombian Government. No secret about what he'd have been doing over there."

Palmer nodded, wondering if it wasn't a ghastly coincidence. Many members of HM forces had performed duties in Latin America over the years, mostly helping train the local police and army for operations against the drug cartels. Mitcheson must have been well thought of to have been selected for such a task. But that didn't explain what he was doing on this list, nor if there was any connection with the men who had smashed his office.

Charlie was still reciting from memory. "He came back in disgrace. He popped a local army corporal for shooting an unarmed civilian during a raid on a village. A young woman, apparently. Pregnant. She was trying to protect her home. There's no proof, but rumour has it Mitcheson took the guy behind a rubbish dump and snuffed him. He was lucky they had a chopper doing an evac, otherwise he'd never have come back. They threw him on a plane out of the country the same day. He spent some time in Bosnia with the UN, then got caught up in arms smuggling by a bunch of British Army NCOs. It all went sour after that and they decided to get rid. Pity – he was a good one, if his record is anything to go by. I'm not sure the smuggling thing was all it was made out to be, though."

"How do you mean?"

"Well, when you've worked around records long enough, you get a feel for reading between the lines. And I reckon there's more to Mitcheson's file than the records say. The other thing is – and I haven't been able to dig into it yet – some of the info on the files doesn't quite match... almost like it was written at two different times. You know what it's like when you have a first-hand account of a punch-up in a boozer, then another one written the following morning, when everyone's sober and feeling like shit? They don't quite tally."

"What about the others on the list?"

"KAs – known associates. Basically, that's why they're all together – they all came together at one time, most of them in the glass-house at Colchester before their discharge. Someone lumped them together on a file and cross-indexed them so I thought it was worth copying them all off."

"So you're saying Mitcheson knew Howard?"

"According to the file. Is it any good?"

Palmer nodded and drank some of his pint. "Could be. I owe you one for this."

Charlie waved a dismissive hand. "No problem. Like I said, it's been a bit of excitement." He glanced at his watch. "I'd better be off. I'll have another dig, and if I come across anything else, I'll be in touch. See you around, Frank. Eat that list before you leave."

Palmer watched his friend disappear through the crowd and felt a tinge of satisfaction. Now he had some names he felt a lot better. Except for one. He reckoned Riley could look after herself, but seeing John Mitcheson on the same list as someone who might have trashed his office wasn't good news. It meant Mitcheson, barring the most massive possible coincidence, had not contacted Riley Gavin by accident. And now they were together.

A waitress escorted Riley towards the back of the long, narrow restaurant. Most of the diners were couples, with the relaxed air of regular customers. The waitress stopped at a corner table where John Mitcheson was already seated.

He rose and smiled. "Riley. Good to see you again." He held a chair out for her, eyes brushing over her with an appreciative expression. He looked tanned and fit, and Riley felt other eyes watching them.

"You made it difficult to refuse," she told him.

They ordered drinks and exchanged pleasantries while studying the menu. The selection was limited but easy to choose from. Riley decided on soup and chicken, and Mitcheson went with her. When their drinks came, they toasted each other and exchanged looks over their glasses.

"So, was it worth coming back for?" Mitcheson asked.

For a moment Riley was lost. Then she remembered the call from Donald Brask that had broken into her holiday. "So far," she replied cautiously. "More work, is what it was. But maybe I'll get away somewhere later to make up for it."

He nodded. "Research, wasn't that what you said? You never said exactly what sort, though."

Riley remembered she'd been deliberately vague, citing details about research for magazines, conducting interviews and building reports for organisations and individuals. It had been close enough to the truth to be sufficient at the time.

"You never said how you managed to get my mobile number," she countered.

He pulled a face, looking guilty. "If I tell you I probably

71

broke the law, will you have me arrested?"

"I might. It depends which law."

"Well, you know I said I was a security consultant. That's true. I have a few friends, also in the business, who have…access to various sources of information – phone records being one. I got your home address from the apartment manager in Spain and the rest was easy." He held up both hands in surrender. "But that was all, I promise. I didn't do a credit check or ask if you had a history of unplanned violence towards men."

"Maybe you should have," she said. It sounded easily plausible and she knew there were people in the press with similar sources. It was how they fleshed out their information on news reports.

"Am I forgiven?" Mitcheson asked.

She shrugged. It really wasn't worth getting in a spin about. Anyway, was she really so annoyed, being here? "I can live with it. It's probably something I'd do myself, if I had to."

He nodded. "Now that sounds like you might almost be a journalist." He said it with a smile but suddenly there was a tension in the air between them. Riley wondered if her response would decide the course of the evening.

"Would that be so bad?" she countered. She felt a pulse begin to tick in her throat. Some people immediately put the shutters up when she mentioned what she did, as though they might appear next day splashed in lurid print across the country's tabloids. Mostly, it turned out, they had something to hide. She wondered if John Mitcheson had any such fears.

He shrugged. "Not at all. Not as bad as if you were, say… something more official."

"Police, you mean? God, give me a break – I haven't

worn black tights since I was at school."

"Actually, I was thinking Customs and Excise." He put his glass down and sat back as their soup arrived. He said nothing while the waitress served them. When she walked away, he continued, "The way you handled that squaddie at Gibraltar airport was pretty efficient. Showed a lot of confidence." He raised his glass and smiled with a show of sheepishness. "Proves how vivid my imagination can be, doesn't it?"

"Too right," she replied lightly with a raised eyebrow. "But why would my being in Customs be such a bad thing? Unless you're a secret drug-runner, of course?"

15

For a split second Mitcheson's smile faltered, then he chuckled. "If I was, I'd be taking you to dinner somewhere a bit more exotic than London."

Riley stared back at him, not sure if the sudden tension in the air was her imagination or not. "I guess so. Why don't you like Customs and Excise?"

He waved a dismissive hand. "Oh, nothing much. Call it professional wariness, if you like. They don't like private sector security operators for some reason. Probably think we're all VAT dodgers. So, where are you hoping to take your next holiday?"

The change of subject was smooth enough to be plausible but left Riley with a sense of unfinished business.

"You're not being evasive, are you?"

He looked at her, spoon hovering above his soup bowl. "I don't think so. Sorry – I have a bit of a grasshopper mind. I'm just curious about you, that's all. And I'd rather talk about you than me, any day."

Towards the end of the meal a phone buzzed and Mitcheson reached into an inside pocket and frowned.

"I'm really sorry," he sighed. "I thought I'd switched this thing off. Would you excuse me?"

He left the table and walked towards the washrooms at the back of the restaurant. Riley felt an odd sense of disappointment, as though he had suddenly confessed to a wife and children somewhere, or had revealed a harmless but unpleasant character trait. She dismissed it. She was being unfair. He probably had meant to switch the phone off, but it had genuinely slipped his mind.

When he returned moments later he was smiling. "I'm sorry about that. I hate it when people do that to me."

Riley shook her head. "That's all right. Not bad news, I hope?"

"No. Some business I have to attend to tomorrow."

Outside the restaurant a breeze skidded along the street, flicking litter against their legs. The sound of crowds and music from Piccadilly floated over the buildings, and one or two pedestrians hurried by, huddled against the chill. Riley shivered and Mitcheson put a hand on her shoulder. "Come on," he said. "I'll get you a taxi."

They reached the corner of the street and were just about to turn up towards Piccadilly when a shadow appeared in front of them. Riley looked up. It was the same large man she had nearly bumped into earlier. This time, the man held his ground and waited for her and Mitcheson to navigate around him. His eyes swept over them, and she could hear his breath hissing nasally as she passed him.

"Sorry," Mitcheson grunted, and guided Riley with a firm hand, placing himself between her and the big man.

As they left him behind, she commented: "Amazing how often that happens."

"Mmm?" Mitcheson's mind seemed far away as he glanced back towards the corner.

"Seeing the same person twice on the same day." She explained about seeing the big man on her way to the restaurant.

When she glanced up she could see the muscles in Mitcheson's jaw working. He spotted a taxi and whistled.

"Sorry, Riley," he said. "I have to go. Business calls. Can I ring you in a day or two?"

"Yes, all right. But why don't we share this taxi?"

He shook his head. "Can't, I'm afraid. It'll be quicker for me to take the underground. You go ahead."

"All right. Thank you for this evening."

He smiled briefly and opened the cab door for her. She'd barely climbed in when he waved and turned away as though distracted. She looked back to see him striding back towards the corner of Jermyn Street. The underground was in the opposite direction.

When Mitcheson reached the corner, he found the big man waiting for him a few yards away. McManus seemed unaffected by the wind and was standing by the window of a travel agent, outlined by the neon tubing. There was nobody else about.

"Well, soldier boy," he sneered. "Getting some pussy lined up? You're forgetting what you're being paid—"

Mitcheson stepped in and hit him. It sounded like a side of meat being beaten with a lump of wood. McManus dropped to the pavement, his breath leaving him in an explosive cough.

Mitcheson didn't wait for him to recover; once back on his feet, the big man was far too dangerous. He dropped a knee on to McManus's chest and grasped the lapels of his jacket with his hands crossed. McManus's breathing, already strained through his damaged nose, was now in danger of stopping altogether. In the dim light Mitcheson could see his face was darkening with the lack of oxygen.

He eased off the pressure, then bent and spoke into McManus's ear. "Why are you following her, McManus?" he demanded. "I said leave her to me."

McManus's eyes slowly lost their pained look and zeroed

in on Mitcheson's face. It was like having a particularly malevolent dog staring up at him. A dog that knew only how to kill.

Mitcheson shook him for a moment, then let him go and stood up. He wasn't going to get anything from this man; he was far too hard a nut to crack. All McManus understood was how to follow orders. Orders given by Lottie Grossman.

A noise made Mitcheson look along the street. A hundred yards away a pair of figures stepped out of a white van. There was mesh over the windows and the streetlights glinted off helmet badges. It was time to leave. McManus would have to wait.

As Mitcheson walked away, McManus levered himself up on one elbow and watched him go with an expression of loathing.

"I wasn't following her, soldier boy," he breathed. "I was following you."

16

Riley showered and ate breakfast in a mental fog, thinking about her dinner date with John Mitcheson. Sleep had not come easily when she got home, and she had repeatedly run over the bones of their conversation during the meal, trying to make some sense of how she felt. She'd found John Mitcheson engaging company, yet all the time she had been with him she had felt there was something in the atmosphere. It had been like sharing a cage with a tiger.

She shook off the thoughts and dressed, then went through her notes to get back on track. Four deaths and no clue as to motive or who might be responsible. Yet what were the chances of this many old ex-gangsters dying within days of each other? Whatever was happening to them was focussed and calculated...and personal. She went back to the brief that Donald Brask had provided. It wasn't likely to tell her much she hadn't already been over before, but it might give her a clue. Very often the information you needed was staring you in the face. All you had to do was recognise it for what it was.

Donald had included some details from the police investigation. There was a reference to Bertrand Cage's chauffeur, Peter Willis. He had discovered his employer's body when he had gone to collect him from the beach. According to their custom, Willis would drop Cage at the beach by car at about 08.30 in the morning, settle him in his deckchair, then return at 11.00 prior to driving him back to the house for lunch. Discounting illness, the routine never varied.

Which must have made it easy for the killer. No doubt Cage must have felt secure in his old age. How wrong he was.

Willis, the note went on to say, had been in Cage's employ for fifteen years. There followed some brief comments about his background, but little else about the man was known. The original silent retainer.

Riley dialled Willis's number again. Still no answer. She replaced the phone with a feeling of apprehension. Willis had either gone to ground after all the fuss surrounding Cage's death…or something much worse. She gathered her notes and mobile phone. A trip to Sussex, she thought. There was no way she was going to get any solid help from the police files, so she might as well drive down to see if she could trace Willis and have a quiet chat. Failing that, a talk with the neighbours was better than sitting here staring at the walls.

As she drove she called Donald Brask. The fat man had more contacts who owed him favours than anyone else she knew. He was also rightly proud of his database and the sources of information at his disposal, including some friendly reporters and a handful of police officers. He answered on the second ring.

"Donald," she said. "I need a favour."

Frederick Hyatt looked more like an academic than the head of a news bureau. Dressed in tweeds and a bow tie, he shuffled out into the foyer of the Charlwood Lodge hotel near Gatwick, blinking in the light after the gloom of the conference hall, and looked around urgently. When he spotted Riley waiting by the front desk, he nodded and crossed to greet her.

"You must be Miss Gavin. Donald always had an

accurate eye for description."

"Mr Hyatt." Riley checked his name badge and shook his hand. "Thank you for sparing me the time."

"No problem. He said it was urgent." He indicated a quiet corner of the foyer and led the way over. "I can only give you a few minutes, I'm afraid. I'm on next. The local Chamber of Commerce seems to think I can enthuse its members on the subject of modern media awareness." He smiled briefly. "As if they need it these days."

Riley took the hint and launched straight in. "Mr Hyatt, I believe you interviewed Peter Willis after Bertrand Cage's murder, is that right?"

"Yes. Only because he was fairly close by and I already knew about his job. We handled a profile about Cage a while back: local mystery man of substance and all that. It didn't go anywhere because Cage's lawyer stamped all over it and the story died. What about Willis?"

"I'd like to speak to him, but I can't raise him on the phone. I though you might know something before I go to his home."

Hyatt raised an eyebrow. "I'm not surprised he's gone under. Peter Willis and his wife are hardly media-savvy. They're an ordinary couple who've found themselves pitched into this thing without warning. I spoke to them before the main press arrived, just after the story broke. Unfortunately, they had a rough ride after that, especially when the television crews turned up. There's a big difference between a man with a recorder and a van bristling with antennae. In the end they'd had enough. What do you want from them?"

"I'm doing background on the two dead men," explained Riley. "And I'd like to track down any known associates of Cage and McKee. One of the most recent seems to be Peter Willis. I'm hoping he can give me some colour about their former activities."

"Such as?" Hyatt sounded cautious, his head tilted to one side.

"Such as what they did, who their friends were…their business partners. Why their past seems to have caught up with them the way it has."

Hyatt smiled and considered the pattern in the carpet. He nodded and pursed his lips as if making a decision, and it was obvious he'd had time to think about Riley's visit.

"Okay. Two things, Miss Gavin. You're assuming it was their past that has a bearing on their deaths. It wasn't – at least, not in the sense you mean. These men had no past because they had never fully left it behind. All they had was what they had done last. Oh, they might not have been as fully active as they used to be – they were old men, after all – but that didn't mean they were no longer involved."

"They were still running things, then?"

"To an extent. It doesn't take muscle to own shares, Miss Gavin. All the front work is undoubtedly being carried out by professional managers. From what I could determine, Cage, at least, still had revenue coming in from a variety of enterprises, channelled through a network of holding companies. McKee would have been the same." He smiled crookedly. "I tried to join the same golf club as McKee once. When I told my wife what the membership fee was, she threatened to divorce me."

"Do you know who these holding companies are?"

"Well, I could get the names for you, but unless you're a corporate or tax expert it won't do you much good. Most of them are perfectly respectable. It's not like it was back in the fifties and sixties, you know, when criminals acted as if they were untouchable. A few of them – the Cages and the

McKees of this world – learned to take their business seriously and moved with the times."

Riley looked doubtful. "Well, if their deaths are anything to go by, someone seems to have stuck with tradition."

Hyatt shrugged apologetically and glanced at his watch as a volley of applause leaked out from the direction of the conference hall. "I'm sorry, Miss Gavin, that sounds like my spot coming up." He reached into his pocket and took out a slip of paper. "Donald vouches for you, so I'm willing to go with him. This is the hotel where the Willises are staying. It's just down the road from here. They're booked in under the name of Watson. I can't guarantee they'll give you much, but they have agreed to talk."

"I appreciate that."

He leaned forward suddenly. "Also, I don't know how much longer they'll be there before someone else finds them."

"What do you mean?" Riley felt a shiver at the sudden change in his tone.

Hyatt looked cautious. "It might be nothing. I had a call first thing this morning from someone claiming to be from one of the broadsheets wanting background on Willis. Address, phone number, stuff like that."

"And?"

"It didn't sound right. I know most of the personnel. The dailies have gathered all the local background colour they want – and they certainly know where Willis lives. This one didn't want to give his name so I gave him the brush-off and called head office. They haven't got anyone else down here other than their normal man, so why they would need to send another body doesn't make sense."

Riley found she was holding her breath. If the mystery caller was the killer, and he had managed to find where

Willis was hiding, there was little hope of reaching the chauffeur in time. One thing she had learned about these people was that they didn't waste time.

"Thank you for warning me. Does Peter Willis know?"

"I called him immediately." He gave her a stern look. "Please be kind to them. They're not really a part of this – I'd put money on it."

Riley followed Hyatt's directions to a neat, anonymous hotel just off the A34 south of Crawley. She went inside and asked to speak to Mr Watson. After a brief call, the receptionist gave her the room number and directed her to the first floor.

A man answered the door, opening it a small way and peering past her shoulder down the corridor. "Can I see some identity?" he murmured quietly, sliding his hand out through the gap.

Riley handed over her passport. He took it and studied it carefully before standing back to let her in. Seeing him properly, she recognised him from the photo in the newspaper library, although he now looked thinner and somehow smaller. He wore a dark blazer and highly polished shoes, and looked ready to go out. Just inside the door were two suitcases.

"Mr Hyatt said you'd be round," he said, closing the door softly behind her. He sounded nervous, and clamped his lips shut at the end of the words as if trying to hold in a burgeoning sense of panic. In spite of that, his tone was polite, and Riley felt a momentary surprise. She had expected a degree of annoyance or aggression after what they must have been through.

His wife was a different problem. She stood by the window, hands clasped in front of her in a manner that was plainly hostile. She was plump and homely and wearing a print dress and summer sandals, but there was no warmth in her expression. Riley felt a faint stirring of guilt; she was hardly helping matters by turning up here.

"You know why I'm here?" said Riley quickly, glancing at the suitcases. "Do you have time to talk?"

"No." Mrs Willis answered immediately, throwing her husband a defiant look. Plainly, agreement to this meeting had not been unanimous.

But Willis nodded, trying to smile reassuringly back at his wife. "It's okay. Mr Hyatt explained. We've decided to take a short break," he said, intercepting Riley's look at the luggage. "Get a little sun after all this...business." He indicated a club chair by the television and sat on the double bed, neat in his blazer and shiny shoes, while his wife stood her ground by the window. "Actually, our flight's been delayed. Overbooking or something. They said they'd call, but it could be quite a while."

"I still think we'd be better waiting at the airport." Mrs Willis bit out the words, meaning the airport would be an effective barrier against having to talk to people like Riley.

"How can we help?" Peter Willis said quietly.

Riley asked him if he had known Cook and Page. He looked blankly back at her, shaking his head. "In that case," she continued, "do you know anything about a third man who used to be an associate of Bertrand Cage years ago – probably in the clubs."

Willis considered it for a moment, then shrugged. "I didn't know anything about Mr Cage's business. I only worked for him after he retired. The previous chap died and Mr Cage needed a chauffeur. He couldn't get around easily, you see; he had bad arthritis and some other problems. I got the job through an agency. What he did before was none of my business."

"But you know what he was – what business he was in?"

Willis looked defensive, jutting his chin forward. "I know what he used to be. But he was always good to me."

"Did you meet any of the others?"

"McKee, mostly," Willis said shortly, with a look of distaste. "I didn't rate him. No finesse. Mr Cage couldn't stand him, either. Not that he ever said as much. They were more like associates than friends."

"Did they meet often?"

Willis shrugged. "Fairly regular – maybe every three months. But always at the house. They argued sometimes."

"Violently?" She watched Willis's eyes for reaction, but he looked back at her without any sign of concern.

"Not worth killing over. The police asked the same question."

Riley nodded. "Do you have any idea who might have killed him?"

"I wish I did." Willis said emphatically. "At first I thought it might have been McKee, but it couldn't have been, could it?"

While Peter Willis had been speaking, Riley had been aware of his wife, shuffling her feet in the background, her mouth opening and closing as if about to say something. Riley took it as an opening and turned to the older woman.

"How about you, Mrs Willis? Any ideas?"

Mrs Willis looked surprised to be consulted, wavering for a moment as if regretting drawing attention to herself. Then she drew herself up with a forceful shrug of her shoulders as if determination had won the debate. "Peter lost his job over this," she said in a fierce rush. "There wasn't a pension, although Mr Cage did see us right."

She glanced at her husband. "Peter's too…loyal to say what he really thinks, so I'll have to say it for him." She lifted her shoulders before continuing. "I used to clean at Mr Cage's house a long time ago. I didn't know him any better than Peter did, and I only heard him argue with someone the once. He was a very quiet man, you see… not given to raising his voice. Then, about five years ago, I suppose, I heard him arguing. I was in the kitchen. It was a real blazing row and the language was… well, not what you'd call nice, if you see what I mean. Mr Cage was almost shouting – which was very unusual."

"Was this face to face or over the phone?"

"Face to face," Mrs Willis confirmed. "The other man had come to the house and demanded to see him. Peter had let him in, but only after Mr Cage said it was all right." She glanced at her husband. "It was Peter's job to look after him, you see."

Riley looked at Willis, who was smiling at his wife. "You were his minder?"

Willis nodded. "It came with the job. I used to be Regimental Provost when I was in the army; that's how I got on an agency list. Good line of work when I was younger." His expression mourned the passing of youth and its associated work.

"So who was this other man?"

"Gross by name, gross by nature," Mrs Willis muttered bitterly. She nodded, glancing for confirmation at her husband. "Now there was a man could kill someone without blinking."

17

In the silence that followed, Riley felt a tingle in her shoulders. "Gross?" she asked carefully. "That was his name?"

"Grossman." Peter Willis stirred and looked at Riley. "Ray Grossman. This was years ago. Grossman could be dead by now. He wasn't well, even then. Big man, he was. Overweight and soft looking. Like he'd been a couch potato all his life."

"Where did he come from?"

"The Smoke, I think. I only met him that one time." His expression made it clear that once had been enough.

Riley nodded. She'd ask Donald Brask to delve into his files. "I suppose there wouldn't be anything at the house, would there – information about this Grossman?"

Willis gave her a flinty look and she dismissed that as an avenue to explore. There were obviously limits on the amount of help he was prepared to give.

"The police will have cleaned it out already if they're doing their job right," he said stiffly. When he stood up, Riley took the hint. The interview was over.

"Thanks for your help. I'm sorry I descended on you so abruptly. Are you going anywhere nice?"

"All over, really," Willis replied vaguely, walking her to the door. "Nowhere for long. We like driving…moving around." He opened the door and briefly checked the corridor, then stood back to let her pass. She turned to shake hands, but he was already closing the door firmly behind her.

*

"So we have a name." It was three hours later and Frank Palmer was behind his desk, fiddling with a retractable ruler. He'd listened in silence to Riley's account of her meetings with Hyatt and the Willises, occasionally making a note on a small pad at his elbow, but seemed to have something else on his mind.

"It's a start," Riley replied. "I gave Grossman's name to Donald. He said he'd have a trawl through his files to see if it means anything. How about you and your army friend? Any luck?"

Palmer gave Riley a strange look and stood up. He walked over to the kettle on the floor and plugged it in, then busied himself spooning coffee into mugs with agonising deliberation. When he showed no signs of replying, she went across and glared at his back. "Did I just speak in Swahili or something?"

"Sorry," he said, pouring water and handing her a mug. "Brain's in overdrive at the moment." He wandered to the window and stared out, blowing on his coffee. Almost as an aside he asked: "Apart from that, how did your evening out go?"

"My evening?" Riley was surprised by the sudden change of direction. "It went very well, thank you. But what's that got to do with this – or you?"

"Did he tell you how he managed to get your phone number?" He smiled to soften the question. "Just concerned, that's all."

"Yes, he did," Riley replied. She realised she was being unfair after her concerns the previous day and owed him an explanation. "He said he had friends in the security industry who could access that sort of thing. It seemed reasonable, and it would have been – I don't know –

churlish to object if all he wanted was to go out with me." She described the events of the evening, finishing with the large man she had seen twice near the restaurant, although she wasn't sure why she remembered that.

Palmer looked round, suddenly interested. "Can you describe him?"

"Big – maybe six-four. Forty-ish, thinning brown hair. Looked like an ex-boxer. Or a heavy. Why are you asking? You still haven't told me what you got up to in the last couple of days. You were going to see if you could identify the two men who smashed up your office."

Palmer puffed out his lips and took a sheet of paper from under a folder on his desk. "My mate in Whitehall," he said, "works in a section of the Ministry of Defence that deals with military personnel records. They have a database down there that houses the name of every person who has served or is serving in the forces. It only goes back to about 1960 at the moment." He flapped the paper in the air. "But he managed to come up with a few names." He explained Charlie's findings after feeding in the name of Howie, and the possibility that he was Malcolm Howard, late of the Royal Marines.

"God, Palmer, that's remote," Riley pointed out. "Howie could be a nickname for all sorts of reasons. This Malcolm Howard could be an anorexic weakling with a pot-belly and flat feet – too feeble to even *lift* a baseball bat."

"Unlikely," said Palmer, "if he was in the Marines. Same with Duggan, the other one. I'd lay good money they were the two who trashed my office. They have the right background: military training, accustomed to giving orders and not frightened to chuck their weight around. On the other hand, clever enough to know when beating the crap out of me wasn't necessary."

Riley had to admit Palmer was probably right. She held out her hand. "Can I see?"

Palmer looked up. "Pardon?"

"You said he came up with a few names. Can I see the others?"

Palmer pushed the sheet of paper across the desk. "You're really not going to like this..."

18

John Mitcheson spent the short drive from Malaga airport to Almeria in the back seat with his eyes closed, trying to quell a looming headache. He'd already seen this stretch of coast road more than once, and the way he was feeling, the sun was far too bright. At least the cream Mercedes had air-conditioning and floated along with barely a shudder. After being stranded at Barcelona for two hours due to air traffic problems, he knew he was in for a hard time for being late.

Gary, neat as a pin as usual, was at the wheel. He occasionally glanced at his passenger in the mirror, but apart from that spent most of the journey with his eyes on the road.

"Who's at the villa?" asked Mitcheson. The call to his mobile the previous evening had instructed him to get on a flight to Malaga the following morning without fail. Gary would be there to meet him.

"Not sure, boss," Gary replied. "Doug and Howie, of course…they've been dealing with the other bunch, getting them out of the picture."

"Any problems?"

Gary gave a sharp grin. "Not much. Bignell pulled in some hired help from Malaga, but they didn't amount to much. Pity, really – I was looking forward to some action."

Mitcheson nodded in sympathy. After years of active service, the sudden inactivity after leaving the army was a problem many men had difficulty adjusting to. It wasn't hard for him, but he knew men like Gary, Doug and

Howie still hankered after the release of action. It was why they had been taken on: Mitcheson to do the organising and them to be the blunt face of the hammer. When that skill wasn't used, they became restless.

Unfortunately, what had seemed a straightforward exercise in a show of strength was turning into something darker. They had all been prepared to do whatever was asked of them – disposing of McKee, Cage and the others – although Mitcheson doubted the last two had been necessary. But Lottie Grossman's emergence as psychotic queen bee and her instructions for Bignell's disposal had changed the game.

The car slowed and turned up a side road, the surface becoming uneven as they headed inland. After two hundred yards, they passed through some orange groves and turned through an imposing gateway. A gravel drive led through a parade of trees and ended before a long, ranch-style, single-storey villa gleaming white in the morning sun. Two other vehicles, a Land Cruiser and another Mercedes, stood in the shade of some trees to one side.

As Mitcheson emerged from the car he heard a low growl and a rottweiler padded out from the porch. It must have weighed as much as a man and he wondered how you trained such a beast not to eat your friends instead of your enemies.

"Fuck off, Bonzo," he snarled, and stepped past the quivering animal into the front entrance. He was the only one who could get away with it, and was amazed Doug and Howie, not renowned for their tolerance, hadn't put a bullet in the dog's pea-sized brain by now.

The smell of air freshener and soap assailed his senses. The aroma reminded him of a couple of military hospitals he'd stayed in. He crossed the large tiled hallway and noted a large vase of what he thought vaguely might be dahlias. He wondered if they'd been brought over from England, a touch of home garden for ex-pats. He entered the living room.

There were five men present. He knew four of them.

Doug and Howie were lounging on a settee near the window, looking tanned and fit. They nodded, Doug flicking his eyes towards the towering figure of McManus, who was standing behind a slim, swarthy individual sprawled in an armchair. This man, in his early fifties, was flashily dressed, with a heavy gold chain on one wrist. He was staring into space and blowing smoke-rings from a large cigar as if he hadn't a care in the world, yet there was something about his manner that was entirely false.

Mitcheson looked back at Doug who shrugged and raised his eyebrows.

He was puzzled by McManus's presence. He wondered how the man had got here; he evidently hadn't had the same problems with flights that had affected his own journey. He looked towards the fifth occupant of the room, hunched in a chair near an open set of patio doors. Beyond was the blue glint of a swimming pool. The man's frame indicated he had once been broad across the shoulders, and Mitcheson knew that in his younger days the man had allegedly been a dangerous person to cross. Now he was shrunken and frail, with a pallor that seemed at odds with the hot sun outside.

"Ray," Mitcheson said with a nod.

There was something still menacing about Ray Grossman, in spite of his obvious incapacity, and Mitcheson knew that behind the half-closed eyelids lurked a mind that was still sharp and deadly.

"Glad you could make it," Ray slurred, his voice dry as

gravel. "Enjoy your night out, did you?" There was no mistaking the implied rebuke. One characteristic the man shared with his wife was a mania about position and respect. Mitcheson had rarely met anyone in the army so insecure, and he still found it odd that these people set so much store by pecking order.

He glanced at McManus, who seemed to have found something to smile about, and decided to ignore the bait. He walked across the room and sat down in another armchair.

"I was told to take this morning's flight," he explained. "I ran into problems getting out here." The last thing he wanted was to get into a war of words with Grossman. It wasn't worth it and would only serve to give McManus an excuse to drive a wedge between them.

Gary appeared in the doorway. Behind him came the plump, heavily made-up figure of Lottie Grossman.

Mitcheson shot a steely look at Gary for not warning him. The younger man returned it, unperturbed, then set his eyes set rigidly in front. Mitcheson made a mental note to speak to him afterwards; he had an uneasy feeling Lottie had been working on his sense of duty behind Mitcheson's back.

More interesting, however, was Ray Grossman's reaction. He seemed to shrink into his chair with a sour expression, and there was a palpable feeling in the air of a transfer of authority.

Lottie Grossman advanced into the room while Gary shut the door and leant against it, hands crossed in front of him. The signal was clear; no one was leaving.

"Now then, Jerry," Lottie said softly, as if continuing a conversation that had been interrupted earlier. The man in the armchair brought his attention back to the room and tensed, the cigar forgotten. "You don't want to go ahead with our plan, is that right? What's the problem – our money not good enough for you?"

A clock ticked in the silence and Mitcheson looked at Doug and Howie for a clue, but they seemed as puzzled as he was.

"I don't— " The man choked on his cigar smoke and sat forward, his eyes dark and angry. He looked hard at Ray Grossman, who was staring into his lap, then back at Lottie. As he moved, McManus stepped slightly closer, one hand resting on the back of the man's armchair. "You're robbing us blind, Lottie," Jerry protested with a whine. His eyes flicked towards the huge man at his shoulder. "We had a good thing going, you know…it worked. You can't just walk in and take it!"

Lottie Grossman's expression was ice cold. "I think we just have, Jerry," she muttered. She picked up a mobile phone from a table nearby and toyed with it. "We made a good offer: ready cash in return for your business. No paperwork, no tax, no contracts…just let us get on with it and everyone'll be happy. But you don't like our terms, do you, Jerry? It seems your partners don't share your point of view, though. They've just boarded a flight to Miami. Going on holiday, are they?"

Jerry stared at Lottie and shook his head. He swallowed and looked round the room at the others. "You're having me on."

Lottie studied her nails and said: "Of course, they *might* have gone to get some help. What do you think?" She fluttered a manicured hand at McManus, who leaned forward and took the cigar from the man's fingers, then crushed it out in an ashtray.

Mitcheson leaned forward, chest thumping with the

tension. "What's this about?"

For the first time, Ray Grossman made a move to join in the conversation. He glared at Mitcheson and pointed a bony finger. "Sit tight, you," he grated. "You're too late. If you'd been here when I wanted you, this would never have happened." With that, he staggered to his feet and moved with difficulty out on to the patio, where he slumped into a plastic chair overlooking the pool. Gary looked to Lottie for a moment, and when she nodded, went over and closed the doors behind the old man.

Everyone's attention swung back to Lottie.

Satisfied she had their full concentration, she turned and nodded to McManus, who stepped out from behind the armchair, a tight grin on his face. In one meaty hand he carried a large, black automatic pistol. Before the hapless Jerry could react – before any of them could – he turned and shot him in the chest, the crash of the shot deafening in the room. Jerry was slammed into the back of the chair and a faint smell of burning drifted in the air as his shirt smouldered. Nobody rushed to put it out.

McManus turned, the pistol swinging round to cover Doug, Howie, Gary and, most pointedly, Mitcheson. They all sat very still.

"And that, gentlemen," Lottie Grossman smiled, "is what happens to people who don't do what they're told." She flicked a hand towards McManus and Gary. "Get rid of that mess. The rest of you – we've got business to discuss."

19

A fly buzzed in Palmer's office as Riley scanned the piece of paper he had given her. When she saw the last name on the list, she went pale.

"What the hell is this?" she asked softly. "Why is this name on here?"

"I asked Charlie to pull out any name approximating Howie. He came up with just the one – Howard – who seemed to fit the age range. The others are all listed as KAs – known associates. Mitcheson's name came out with them. The connection was made by the database, not me."

"How efficient." Her voice was coldly matter-of-fact.

Palmer calmly returned her look. "I'm sorry, Riley."

"Really, Frank? But something tells me you're not surprised." She was furious, but knew he had done the right thing. Not that it helped her presence of mind or the fact that she felt so foolish.

Palmer shrugged. "Surprised, no. He got hold of your phone number far too easily – whatever mates he might have. Hot dates don't do that."

"So you're my moral guardian, now, are you?" her voice stopped short of anger, but the gap was slim. "What have you been doing – taking tips from my mother?" She threw the list on the desk. "You'll be asking me if I've slept with him next!"

She paced up and down while her anger subsided. It didn't take long; she was nothing if not pragmatic and knew that given similar circumstances she would have done the same. It was what investigation work was all about.

"Okay," she said finally, putting both hands up. "So we have a number of men – all ex-military and all connected – who seem to be involved with whatever is going on here. But that doesn't tell us what it is. Nor why all those old gangsters were killed off. It wasn't because they forgot to pay their golf club fees."

Palmer nodded. "If we accept for the moment that Howard and Duggan are the two baseball fans *and* they appear to know Mitcheson, who happens to have got your mobile number by foul means, it seems more than just coincidence."

"We know how he got it."

Palmer pulled a face. "I've been thinking about that. There is another, simpler way he could have got it: the same way the baseball fans got my name."

Riley thought about it. There was only one answer. "From my flat."

"I doubt it was him," Palmer said. "Mitcheson was in Intelligence in Northern Ireland but it wouldn't necessarily make him a candidate for cat-burglary. He could have got someone else to do it, though."

They sat and contemplated what they knew so far. It wasn't much but the path was extending all the time.

"What about Ray Grossman?" said Riley. "Can we track him down?"

Palmer ducked his hand in a drawer, pulling out a slip of paper. "I rang an old contact in the Met. He's retired now, but he's got the memory of an elephant. He remembered Grossman, but he thought he'd died last year. Cancer."

"Did he have any form?"

"Not officially. He was reckoned to be a top dog but they could never prove it."

"It must be worth checking, though. How about an address?"

Palmer grinned. "Done it. There's only one Grossman that fits that age range. Wrong sex but it could be a lead. She lives out in Buckinghamshire." He handed her a piece of paper with an address on it. *Pantiles, Jordans, Bucks.*

Riley gave him a cool look tinged with a smile. "For a bodyguard you're not a bad investigator. How about we check on her?"

"Suits me." He glanced at his watch. "I'll buy you a cream tea if we can find somewhere on the way."

"You're on. I haven't eaten anything today."

Palmer hesitated. "There's one other piece of information my friend came up with."

"Go on."

"I ran the McKee and Cage names past him."

"And?"

"He thought they and Grossman were linked. They were into clubs in a quite a big way back in the fifties and sixties. Nothing really heavy, but their turnover was good. Drinking dens, a bit of gambling, some girls…low overheads, high profits. Mostly in London but there were a couple down on the south coast, too. Rumour had it they sold out in the mid-sixties."

Riley recalled what Hyatt had said about the two men. "But that's not necessarily the case?"

Palmer shook his head. "No. Think about it; the sixties were all about expansion. Gaming. Money. Kids with cash looking for kicks…sex…drugs. Everything was on the up after years of austerity. The Met was cracking down on organised crime with some of the biggest names in the underworld either dead or banged up, and even the main bulk of the opposition was suddenly dropping out of the picture. For someone not under scrutiny it must have been like being handed a monopoly on a plate and being told you had a clear field to play in. Would you sell out when you were coming to the crest of a wave?"

"I wouldn't know," Riley said. "I'm not a gangster – and I don't remember the sixties." She narrowed her eyes for a moment. "But you're right – it doesn't sound likely." She walked over to the window, looking out. "Based on what Willis told me, the arguments he heard sounded like on-going business differences. If so, they weren't as inactive as everyone thinks."

Palmer nodded. "Why let someone else have all the cream when you can continue pulling it in yourself?"

"But your man said Grossman died last year. That leaves us none the wiser." Riley hesitated and turned towards him. "Unless he left an heir to the throne."

20

They took Riley's Golf, following Frank's directions out towards the A413 and the Chalfonts. He sat in the back, smoking, while she concentrated on negotiating the late afternoon traffic.

Suburban concrete became a brief stretch of uninspiring countryside, with a few horses cropping in scruffy fields, before entering the twilight zone of plush stockbroker housing and small, select estates. Main roads gave way to narrow, twisting lanes lined with lush hedges and leafy trees, where BMWs and Range Rovers parked in the curving, gravelled drives were the norm.

Riley slowed at Palmer's direction. He flipped his cigarette out the window and sat forward.

"Should be somewhere in this area," he said. "They probably don't use anything as common as house numbers in this kind of place, so we'll have to hope Mrs Grossman has a nice, ostentatious sign outside her gaff."

They entered a narrow lane with houses on one side, spaced well apart, past a dog barking at them from a drive-way, and an elderly man mowing his front verge to snooker-table neatness. Large trees towered overhead, their topmost branches meeting and creating dark pools of shadow.

A woman appeared out of a gateway some distance ahead. She mounted a bike and pedalled towards them. Riley slowed the car and flashed a white envelope through the open window. The woman stopped alongside the car.

She was in her early thirties, with a careworn look that spoke of too much work and too little time to do it in. In a basket on the front of her bike were a plastic bag and an overall.

"Excuse me, love." Riley's voice took on a beseeching tone. "I wonder if you could tell me where the Grossman house is – I'm afraid the office didn't give terribly good directions. I've been driving for ages trying to find the place."

The woman looked cautiously at Riley, then at Palmer relaxing in the back seat. Evidently satisfied they weren't about to firebomb the area, she turned her head and pointed towards the gateway she had just left. "It's about a hundred yards down on the right. Big place with a curved roof and white shutters. There's a couple of willows out front." She looked at the envelope. "I can take that if you want. I do cleaning for them."

Riley smiled and dropped the envelope on the seat beside her. "No, that's all right, thanks. I'm supposed to deliver this in person under pain of death, and maybe get some measurements." She put on an annoyed expression and sighed. "Not that it looks likely today. They promised someone would be in, too. Oh, well…I'm only a Pee Bee Ee."

"You what?"

"Poor bloody employee, sweetie. Do what I'm told – know what I mean? Do you know when Mrs Grossman will be back?"

The cleaner shook her head. "Couldn't say, love. Might be tonight, could be tomorrow. I've worked here six months but they never tell me what they're doing."

"They?"

For a moment the woman seemed to have doubts about

talking. But then she shrugged and said: "Well, Mrs G and them men that come and go all the time." There was a note of disapproval in her voice mixed with a flash of relish at being able to confide in someone.

Riley managed to hide an instinctive surge of excitement and put on an understanding smirk. "Mmm...the old devil. Young, are they?"

The woman gave a tired smile. "Yeah, but it's not like that. They work for Mrs G and sometimes stay at the house."

"What do they do?"

"Beats me, love. They're young enough to do anything. But like I said, they don't tell me what they get up to. It's like it's all a big secret."

"Are they the only men in the house?"

"Yes, thank God," the woman said with feeling. "There was an old man but I think he died years ago. Her trouble is, she can spot if I've missed something at a hundred yards. Mind, there's one of them that does a better job of cleaning than I do. Bloody man's a bit strange, if you ask me...especially with all the training he does."

"Training?"

"Yeah. Out in the garden every day. Jogging, press-ups, sit-ups...my husband reckons he must be a keep-fit fanatic. I think he's ex-army, myself – my dad was in REME. This bloke Gary jumps to it every time Mrs G so much as opens her mouth. Proper little poodle. My husband reckons he's after my job, but that's silly."

"Maybe not," Riley suggested casually. "If he's ex-army, he'd be very good at cleaning. What else does he do?"

The woman looked surprised at the notion and her mouth dropped at the corners as she considered it. "I hadn't thought of that. He also does her driving when she goes out,

103

and makes sure everything's working. He's what my husband calls a gopher." She shook her head as the idea Riley had implanted began to sink in. "Christ, I knew it..!"

"And they're all out?" said Riley quickly, before the woman could move on.

"Yes. Somewhere in Spain. Mrs G has a villa over there." She sighed. "All right for some, isn't it? Never asks me if I want a bit of sun." She looked at Riley again and blushed. "Sorry, love. What was it you said you wanted?"

"Something else they haven't told you," Riley said sympathetically. "She's putting the house on the market. She wants a valuation. This envelope holds the contract. Maybe she'll give you a good reference."

"Oh. I suppose." The woman's voice was faint at the prospect and she shook her head. "In that case maybe I can show you in... so you can measure up." She peered into the car. "You do have a card, though? Some identification?"

"Of course." Riley fished in her glove box and handed her a business card. "That's really sweet of you, um..?"

"Marion," the woman replied, and turned her bike round. "You follow me, then, and I'll let you in. I'll have to switch off the alarm first."

As Marion pedalled away, Riley caught Palmer's eye in the mirror. "Looks like we're estate agents."

Palmer nodded. "I've never been an estate agent before. Do I have to do unctuous as well?"

"If you do, I'll kick you. There's a clipboard and tape in the boot."

She followed Marion down the short drive and parked in front of the house. As they got out she glanced around instinctively. There were no houses in direct line of sight, so more for Marion's sake than any onlookers, she stood and looked at the house for a few seconds, pointing and chatting to Palmer about the exterior and briefing him on the measurements they needed.

"How the rich live," Palmer observed, looking down a path between the house and a double garage, to where they could see part of a patio. Beyond chequered ochre and grey paving slabs, the garden extended downwards in stepped layers, across a vast expanse of immaculate lawn dotted with flowerbeds, into a border of bushes and trees. Bird song echoed through the treetops, while a lawn-mower chattered away on an adjacent property.

"Money," Riley agreed. "Whatever they do – or did – it had to involve lots of cash."

When Marion told them she had switched off the alarm, they followed her to a small side gate and were ushered into the kitchen.

"Shall I leave you to it?" said Marion. "There's things I can be doing upstairs. I'll make coffee in a bit, if you like."

"We're fine, thanks," said Riley. "This is really sweet of you."

As soon as Marion disappeared, Riley began a quick search of the ground floor while Palmer left her with the tape and clipboard and went back outside to look at the garage.

The kitchen was a shade smaller than vast, with quarry tiles covering the floor and elegant, hand-made Italian tiles running from floor to ceiling. State-of-the-art gadgets were everywhere, and she got the impression that the house might have been designed around this one room. Evidently Mrs Grossman liked entertaining or cooking.

She walked across the kitchen into a large hallway. A circular table big enough to seat eight people in comfort stood against one wall with a large vase of dried flowers in the centre. A smaller one holding a telephone and a directory stood against another. To her right was a stair-case with polished mahogany banisters; to the left were two doors. One led to the sitting room at the rear of the house. She tried the other and found a walk-in clothes cupboard fitted with shelves, drawers and hanging space for coats. On the hooks hung a variety of coats, macs and jackets. Recalling what the cleaner had said about the keep-fit fanatic, Riley tried all the pockets. Nothing.

She spotted a large laundry-type bag in one corner and flipped it open. Inside was a crumpled tracksuit, still sweat-stained. She pulled it out and checked the pockets. In the jacket was a scribbled note, limp with dampness. The writing was barely legible, but she could just make out the words 'Bentley's. Tickets'.

The other pockets yielded nothing of interest, so she prowled the rest of the ground floor looking for clues. Photos on the cabinets caught her eye. They were mostly family snaps at various celebrations. The same man and woman appeared in several of the shots, smiling cheesily at the camera. They were both expensively dressed, the man in suits with a flash of a large ring on his left hand and an opulent wristwatch clearly visible at his cuff, while the woman varied from an exotic sweep of hair and large drop earrings to a more severe bob cut and a display of gold chains at her neck.

To Riley, for all their cosy, middle-aged smiles, neither looked the sort she would like to share living space with. She guessed the man must be the late Mr Grossman.

Interestingly, none of the photos included children.

She drifted quickly up the carpeted stairs and into the bedrooms. She could hear Marion opening and shutting drawers at the other end of the landing. Two small rooms were full of toiletries and clothes, clearly belonging to younger men. Neither gave any clues to their occupants' names, and she realised they had been expertly cleaned of all means of identification.

The largest bedroom overlooked the sweep of stepped lawns, and was bigger than most living rooms. There were no signs of a man's effects in evidence, nor any jewellery. Odd, she thought. Every woman in creation has *something* of value lying around.

She discovered why when she moved aside some dresses in the wardrobe; a small, steel door with a central dial gleamed in the dark recess. She was tempted to try the dial but decided against it; the house alarm would be off but the safe might not be.

Back downstairs she looked through the kitchen drawers. Kitchens were where people spent most of their time, and all the bits of paper that concerned daily life found their way tucked into drawers or clips, pending being moved to a better place.

Her search yielded two items of interest. One was an instruction booklet for a motorised wheelchair. On the back page were a guarantee and the manufacturer's address. The second was a small brochure for a private airfield near Rickmansworth. Inside were details about hangar facilities and membership fees. She pocketed both and went back into the hallway, where she found a telephone directory on the smaller of the two tables. Bentley's turned out to be a local travel agent. That made sense, since the note in the tracksuit jacket had mentioned tickets. She noted the address and phone number and went in search of Marion, to say they had all the information they needed.

Two minutes later, Riley was taking them at speed back along the road.

21

"I thought you said you'd buy me a cream tea, you cheapskate."

Riley stared at the battered decor in the cafe off the North Circular, and at the heavy tan liquid that passed for tea. Outside, evening rush-hour traffic crawled past in a welter of exhaust fumes.

Apart from the owner, the place was deserted. Palmer set two plates down on the table, each bearing a solid-looking currant bun of indeterminate vintage.

"Sorry," he said. "No cream, no jam, strawberries are off. Champagne isn't quite chilled enough for the wine waiter's liking."

Riley stabbed her bun with a battered knife. It was solid and unyielding. She sighed, pushing the plate away. "Okay, so what have we got?"

Palmer picked up his bun and bit into the crust. He chewed thoughtfully for a moment, then put it down and drank some tea.

"We have a house of some size, owned by an elderly woman, possibly the widow of an old, bad man who never got caught. Whatever – there's money in there somewhere. We have at least one very fit man – possibly ex-army – who lives in, who may or may not be strange."

"Toy-boy?" Riley ventured. But even as she said it, she couldn't summon up much enthusiasm for the idea.

Palmer looked sceptical. "If there was any hanky-panky going on I reckon Marion would have known. She seemed the observant sort. There are no obvious signs of children, so that does away with the heirs inheriting the club empire bit. But other than that, we have nothing else that makes any sense." He sighed and prodded the bun as though it might stir into life. "All in all, I've never seen a house with less clues about it. Almost like it's been swept clean by experts."

"If it's the right place," Riley observed. "The only link we have is your friend knowing the address of Ray Grossman – who's probably dead, anyway. For all we know this Mrs Grossman could be a sweet old cousin with the same name."

"I bet she isn't," Palmer agreed cynically. He chewed another piece of bun.

After leaving the Grossman house, they had driven to the nearby town centre and found the travel agents. It was a small family firm and the young girl behind the desk looked bored with the lack of business.

Riley had plunged straight in. "I don't suppose you handled the Grossman party tickets, did you, sweetie?" she'd asked. She wanted to present the picture of someone in a jam, but not about to forget other wage slaves with too much to do.

"We handle all Mrs Grossman's travel arrangements," the girl replied formally, as though she'd been reading from a prepared script. "How can I help you?"

Riley explained about the house being about to go on the market with her agency, and that an urgent buyer had popped up. "Problem is," Riley continued, "Mrs G didn't leave us her number in Spain. We didn't expect to have anything until she got back, you see."

The girl continued to look bored and Riley had seized on a sudden flash of inspiration. "Gary was supposed to give it to us before he left, but I think he had other things on his mind." She raised an eyebrow and gave the girl a knowing look. "I wonder what that could have been."

The girl blushed. Evidently tickets were not the only things Gary got at this travel agency. "I'm not sure," the girl said, glancing towards the back office. She pulled a note-pad towards her and copied a number from a file, then passed the piece of paper to Riley. "I don't have the address," she said softly. "Only Gary said he was driving from Malaga up the coast towards Almeria. If you see him, will you get him to call me?"

Riley smiled. "Of course. But I bet you'll be seeing him soon."

The girl shook her head. "I don't think so. We probably won't be handling their account any more."

"Why do you say that?"

"Because Mrs Grossman's bought a private plane. Gary said these tickets would be the last ones."

Riley had taken one last chance and nudged the girl a bit further. "You couldn't tell us who they were for, could you?"

The girl had stared up at her, before shrugging and tapping at her keyboard. "They were for a Mr Duggan, a Mr Howard and…" She'd paused and glanced anxiously at Riley as if teetering on the edge of changing her mind about giving out confidential details. "… and a Mr Mitcheson."

Riley had turned and walked out, leaving Palmer to thank the girl for her help. She'd been stabbing out a number on her mobile when he'd joined her on the pavement, her face pale and tight. She'd spoken briefly before listening, then switching off.

"Riley—" Palmer had begun, but she'd cut him off with a raised hand.

"Don't, Frank." She'd glanced at him, her face softening a little, but the muscles in her jaw were bunched with

110

tension. "Please don't say a word. That was the International Operator. She couldn't put the number any closer than Malaga – which doesn't help us. Come on. How about some tea."

Now, in the quiet of the café, she pulled out the other two bits of information she'd found in the kitchen drawer. One was the leaflet about the airfield at Rickmansworth, the other was the motorised wheelchair brochure. "All we've got is these."

"Interesting," Palmer commented, studying the wheelchair details. "I wouldn't have thought this would be very practical around all those terraced bits of garden, would you? I didn't see any ramps." He reached for her mobile and dialled a number. While he was doing that, Riley stood up and went to the washroom. When she came back he was sitting with two fresh cups of tea looking very pleased with himself. On the brochure he had written an address. *Villa Almedina, Moharras.* In brackets he had written the word *Nerja.*

"Are you going to tell me how you did that?" Riley asked coolly. "Or are you just going to sit there all day looking smug?"

"I told them I'd been asked to fit ramps for a wheelchair at the Grossman house, and could they give me some measurements. They told me it was being delivered anytime now – but by special instructions to this place in Spain." He grinned. "Easy when you know how."

"Don't be a smart-arse. What about the airfield?"

He handed her the phone. "That's more an insurance thing, I reckon."

"I see." Riley gave him a flinty look. "And playing the insurance role is a girlie kind of thing." She snatched the

111

phone and dialled the number on the leaflet, asking to be put through to the airfield manager.

"Hi, General Accident here," she announced smoothly. "We're just checking details of a group of policies on behalf of a client. Could you confirm the location of a private plane?" Riley fought for the name of a likely model. " ... a Beechcraft, I believe, with secure facilities at the airfield? Mrs Grossman is the owner. Thanks, I'll wait."

The manager came back moments later. "Yes, we have a plane owned by Mrs Grossman, but it's a Cessna Titan."

"That's great," Riley intoned. "If we need to inspect the aircraft, would that be possible? It's only a formality."

"It would, normally," the manager told her. "But the plane's not here. The pilot filed a flight plan for Spain, I think, coming back in a day or two." He hesitated. "Why are General Accident involved? The plane's already insured. We checked all that out."

Riley clicked the off button and turned to Palmer. "Well, we know they – whoever they are – are in Spain, and they've got a Cessna Titan. The question is, who is the wheelchair user?"

Palmer shrugged. "Whoever they are, they've got plenty of money. Motorised wheelchair delivered to Spain, a Cessna, a tasty house, a live-in odd-job man and a team of former military gophers...you don't get all that on a company pension."

Riley chewed her lip and tapped the address on the wheelchair brochure. "Spain. That's where I first saw Mitcheson, before we met at Gibraltar airport. If this villa is near Malaga, it makes it only a couple of hours from Gibraltar – three at most."

A shadow loomed over the table and the proprietor cleared the cups and plates. "This ain't the boardroom of

Microsoft, you know," he muttered bluntly. "You two gonna sit here all day, or what?"

Riley smiled sweetly and stood up. "Thanks, but no. I'm not sure all my jabs are up to date."

They went outside where Palmer looked up at the grey sky, and stretched. He turned to Riley. "How important is this assignment to you?"

"Important? I don't follow."

"Well, the investigation. Would it matter if you dropped it here and now?"

Riley looked at him, her eyes narrowing. "I took this assignment on," she said with quiet resolve, "and that means I have to see it through. And time is getting short. Are you suggesting I quit?"

"No." Palmer shook his head, unfazed by her reaction. "I just want to know if you're sure about this, that's all." He held up a hand to forestall her objections. "Frankly, I reckon the only way of getting more information is to follow the band."

"You mean to Spain?"

"Can you afford it?"

Riley nodded with certainty. "If this story is worth anything, it'll lead on to other things. I'm prepared to take a punt on it. How about you?"

"Sure, why not? I could do with a spot of sun."

Riley nodded. "I was just thinking the same. I hope your passport's up to date."

Palmer patted his breast pocket. "Never travel without it. Shall I book tickets and rooms in the name of Mr and Mrs Palmer?"

Riley gave him a withering look. "In your dreams."

22

In the villa at Moharras, Mitcheson sat across the living room from Lottie Grossman. Alongside him sat Doug and Howie. Gary and McManus hadn't yet returned from disposing of Bignell's corpse.

Outside, the sun was sinking over the hills behind the villa, lending a soft, heavy appearance to the landscape. To the front, overlooking the sea a mile away, a fast boat carved a pale scar across the flat surface of the water, and closer inshore, two jet skis sent up fantails of spray. On the patio Ray Grossman sat in a new, motorised wheelchair, idly toying with the controls. An instruction manual lay on the ground.

Lottie glanced at her watch and put her cup down. "Well, I can't wait all day for the others. As you know," she said, looking at each of them in turn, "our first priority was to take over the controlling interest in three night-clubs – two in London and one in Brighton. This has been accomplished, and the managers are now happy to be reporting to a single owner rather than three. Business is good, but we'll be making adjustments where necessary to reflect the change of…shall we say, emphasis." The woman smiled coldly behind her glasses, oblivious to the lack of response from the three ex-soldiers. "We're now moving into the next phase, which means improving turnover in this part of the world. And I've decided to make some changes."

They all looked at her and she smiled with evident satisfaction. Mitcheson gritted his teeth at the school-marmish manner and wondered how he had ever managed to get embroiled with this madwoman.

"Shipping more drugs, you mean?" he said bluntly.

Lottie turned her eyes towards him. "I prefer to call it 'the product', Mr Mitcheson."

"So where is this product going?"

"I think that's obvious, isn't it?"

"Through the clubs."

"What's the matter, Mr Mitcheson? Don't you approve?" She glanced at the others, who looked bored by the whole discussion. Then she sprang a surprise. "The drugs are just a sideline. I've decided to move into a different product line altogether. We're going into the people business."

When nobody said anything, she seemed unmoved and continued: "I've been doing some research. There's a high-value end of the people trade just like any other. Wealthy families prepared to pay extremely good money to get sons or daughters into any EU country – but especially Britain. They want them to have a new start in life and are ready to pay accordingly. In exchange for the fee, we get them into the UK and supplied with a full set of papers."

"Illegal immigrants?" said Howie. "Bit risky, isn't it, with all the fences and detection systems."

"Not for the people we're aiming at, Mr Howard. I'm not talking about backs of lorries or inside shipping containers. We'll ship one in for the same price as half a dozen would normally pay to go through somewhere obvious like Calais. They can afford it, so why not? We'll use top quality papers and take our time, and we'll never use the same entry route twice. That way we avoid coming to the attention of the police or customs. If we do it right, word will start to spread. As it does, the price goes up." She smiled. "Two or three a month maximum will bring in a great deal of money and with far less risk than drugs."

Mitcheson was stunned. She had obviously thought this through, and it was daring enough to work, given the right handling. But he had severe misgivings. "You never said anything about illegal immigrants when you took us on."

"Because there was nothing to say. Since then I've gone to a great deal of trouble to set up the right people. People who can supply the documentation we'll need." She smiled archly. "You'd be surprised how many civil servants we get as regulars in our clubs. And debt is such a cruel burden, isn't it?"

"So what now?"

"Now we need to make it happen, before we lose momentum. I want to move forward. The clubs were dying – and had been for years. McKee was getting old and comfortable, and Cage was senile. My husband has not enjoyed the best of health, and there was no one capable of taking over the running of the clubs the way I wanted." She smiled grimly. "Basically, we needed a new product line under new management. It's done every day in the City of London and nobody turns a hair."

It was the first time Mitcheson had heard anyone admit that Ray Grossman was no longer in control. He wondered if her husband knew. After the way the old man had left the room just before Bignell was shot, he probably did but was powerless to stop her. Maybe this villa and the fancy new wheelchair was his payoff.

"Anyway," Lottie waved a dismissive hand, "where I need your particular skills is making sure there are no problems with this end of the operation…in particular with our new friends across the water in Morocco, who will also source our new product. They're bound to be suspicious at first, but I'm sure we'll win them round as soon as turnover increases substantially."

"Won't they kick up at Bignell being dumped?" Doug asked, finally taking an interest.

"They might," Lottie replied coolly, "but I doubt it. Bignell was never going to amount to anything significant. He was a minnow who thought he was big-time." She sniffed with contempt. "He was happy making peanuts. I'm after much bigger rewards. And anyone who works with me will share in those rewards."

Mitcheson said nothing. He had no wish to be involved in drugs or illegal immigrants at any level, but you couldn't always choose the path you trod. At least this way offered a chance of getting some money together until he decided what else he could turn his hand to. Unbidden, a vision of Riley crept into his head, sitting alongside the swimming pool. He shook his head to dismiss the image. That was over. For now, anyway. Maybe he could meet up with her sometime.

"All right," he said. "So what's the next move?"

Lottie Grossman smiled. "I've called a meeting," she announced. "Here, tomorrow afternoon at four-thirty. The Moroccans are sending a representative over. His name's Andre Segassa. I want absolute security in place."

Mitcheson was surprised. "You want the meeting here? That's risky. They might try something once they know the layout."

"What else do you suggest?"

He shrugged. "Better to use a hotel – somewhere big where they wouldn't want to try anything. That way you don't compromise your base."

Lottie nodded. "Of course. You're thinking like a soldier, aren't you? Quite right. But I may decide to get rid of this place, anyway. It's probably too small for future needs in any case. We may have occasional…guests to accommodate for a day or two. Besides…" She plucked a sugar lump from the tea tray beside her and popped it in her mouth. "I want them to see a show of strength. So it's all hands on deck, please – and as much hardware as you can bring."

Mitcheson nodded. "Fine. Anything else?"

"Yes. I want Gary to go back to check the house in Jordans for me."

Mitcheson checked his watch. "I doubt we'll get him on a flight in time this evening. Doing a round trip tomorrow is cutting it fine if there are any delays."

Lottie stood up, signifying the meeting was over. "That's not a problem – he can take the plane."

They all looked at her. "Plane?"

She turned at the door. "Oh, didn't I tell you? I've bought a plane. McManus and I flew over in it this morning from England. The previous owner went bust and needed a quick sale. The pilot's on standby at Malaga. He can fly Gary over this evening and back tomorrow morning. See to it, would you?"

A battered builder's van coughed to a stop outside the gates of a small villa on the outskirts of Malaga. The two men inside sat for a few moments, listening and watching while the engine ticked as it cooled down. Cicadas filled the air with their endless clicking as the evening closed in, and a moped buzzed frantically in an adjacent street. Further along the pavement was the building site for a medium-size hotel. A huge crane towered overhead and the dying sun outlined the skeletal structure of the scaffolding and framework for the concrete shell. Outside the wooden fence a bedraggled dog, tongue lolling in the heat, rolled over in the shade.

Gary climbed down from the driver's seat and opened the

gates of the villa, while McManus went to the front door and pressed the bell. Both men wore gardening gloves, with baseball caps pulled down over their eyes. They could hear the bell ringing somewhere in the depths of the villa, but it had the melancholy sound of an empty space.

They eyed the buildings nearby. Satisfied no one was watching, Gary went back to the van and drove it into the small courtyard, while McManus closed the gates behind him.

Using the van as cover, they took a heavy roll of carpet from the back of the van and carried it to a side door. McManus fished in his pockets and took out some keys and opened the door, which led into a kitchen and utility room.

Gary wrinkled his nose in disgust. Rubbish was piled high in a bin in one corner and overflowing on to the floor, a mix of empty wine bottles, cans and food-wrappers from take-way restaurants. The living area was a mess of crumpled UK newspapers – mostly national dailies – and soft-porn magazines.

The men wrestled the carpet upstairs and dropped it on the double bed in the main bedroom. McManus unravelled it. He peeled away the plastic bin-liners covering Jerry Bignell's body and carefully rolled them up inside the carpet.

"Welcome home, Jerry," he laughed softly. "Sleep well, you loser."

Gary went through the drawers, taking anything of value and liberally spreading the contents on the floor. When someone did finally check on Bignell – if they ever did – it would be written up as a burglary gone wrong.

The two men did the same downstairs, emptying out the contents of a bureau and desk. Then they took the carpet out to the van and drove away.

23

"I feel like a Goth at a white wedding, sitting out here," Riley muttered darkly, sliding down further in her seat. She and Palmer were in a hired Peugeot 306 just along the road from the Villa Almedina. A large pine tree threw dappled shadow over the car, providing some relief from the hot sun. Palmer had assured her it would also provide camouflage should anyone exit or enter the gate to the villa and cast a glance their way. The nearest house was two hundred metres away, with all its windows shuttered, and traffic on this road was nearly non-existent. The only danger was that a member of the local police might take an interest, although Palmer thought that unlikely. Anyway, they were tourists, with a hotel booking just outside Malaga to prove it. Tourists did strange things like sitting in cars instead of on beaches. English tourists being the strangest of all.

"Cars in the shade are commonplace," he told her confidently. "No one's going to pay any attention."

Riley glanced at her watch. It was just after midday. They had caught an early flight to Malaga and picked up the hire car to drive the thirty-odd miles to Moharras. The road – like the airport – had been busy with tourist traffic, and they had been glad of the air-conditioning in the small car. On the way, Palmer had popped into a small supermarket, returning with a cold-box filled with drinks and sandwiches.

"An army marches on its stomach," he'd announced. "I hope you like ham and cheese – it's all they'd got."

"Thanks, Palmer," Riley said, peeling back one of the wrappings to reveal two slices of bread surrounding a thick slice of yellow cheese and a slab of pallid meat. "I see you've never heard of cholesterol and heart disease." She dumped the sandwich back in the box and took a can of cola instead. It was already too hot for picnics, anyway.

Palmer swooped on the sandwich with a grin. "After some of the field rations I've had, this is luxury."

"Why am I not surprised."

She was halfway through the drink when a Land Cruiser nosed out from the entrance to the Villa Almedina. Sun flashed on the windscreen, obscuring the occupants, but Riley counted three men inside. The vehicle paused briefly before heading towards the coast, a swirl of dust in its wake.

Palmer let out a long sigh. "Didn't get any detail. You?"

Riley shook her head. "No. But I had a feeling the people inside might have."

He nodded. "Let's hope they're not observant."

Riley got out of the car. "How about a stroll, Palmer? Fancy a bit of sun and fresh air?" She stepped out from the shade of the tree and the heat weighed down on her, drawing the air from her lungs. A thin taste of dust from the disappearing Land Cruiser touched her lips and she reached into the car for a bottle of water to rinse her mouth.

"Where we going, boss?" Palmer asked, levering himself out of the car.

Riley settled her sunglasses in place, then set off along the road away from the entrance to the villa. With her tan shorts and T-shirt, and a pair of lightweight walking boots, she could have been from any one of several hotels and villas in the area.

Palmer followed, pausing to clap a panama hat on his head. In the burst of direct heat, his chinos stuck to his legs and a thin ridge of hot skin began to itch around his neck. Uxbridge and its chilly pavements suddenly seemed a universe away.

If they were spotted by anyone from the villa, Palmer hoped they would pass as tourists who had fancied a stroll off the beaten track. Just as long as they didn't meet the men he knew as Doug and Howie. The memory of the debris that had once been his office was still fresh in his mind.

They followed the curve of the narrow road past a thin belt of pine trees forming a natural boundary to the Villa Almedina. Through the tangle of branches they caught glimpses of the single-storey building, and flashes of reflected sunlight from the windows. There was a faint sound of running water, with the occasional hiss of a high-pressure lawn sprinkler, and a dog barked twice with a short, flat coughing noise.

Riley veered off the road and angled towards the trees, with Palmer following and watching their backs. Soon they were out of sight of the road.

They stopped before a low, dry-stone wall overgrown with a covering of dry grass and old pine needles. Beyond the wall they had a fairly clear view of the back of the villa showing a length of patio and a splash of blue swimming pool. The sound of running water was louder now, augmented by the gentle buzz of a generator.

"Nice place," said Riley.

"Apart from the dog," said Palmer, his voice tight. A large rottweiler was standing near the house looking towards them. As they watched, the dog bunched its powerful muscles and shot towards the trees. Just as Riley and Palmer were ready to turn and run, the dog skidded to a halt on the edge of the patio as a seagull launched into the air from the lawn where it had been toying with a stray flap of paper. The dog stared up in frustration before turning and trotting back to the house, where it flopped down in the shade of a table, oblivious to their presence.

Riley felt the tension flow out of her. "I never thought I'd be grateful for seagulls," she whispered.

Palmer nodded. "As soon as we get back I'm joining the RSPB."

The patio door opened and a woman emerged. Dressed in a sundress and high-heeled sandals she was large and pale-skinned, and from this distance they could see she wasn't young. She called to the dog, slapping her hand against her ample hip. The rottweiler lifted its head, then stood up and padded over to her. They couldn't hear the words but the tone was sharp, biting. The dog obediently lowered its head and sank to the floor and the woman walked away, leaving it panting in the open heat of the sun.

"Lottie Grossman?" Palmer asked. He was counting on Riley recognising the woman from the photographs she'd seen in the house.

"That's her," Riley confirmed.

The patio door opened again and a figure in a wheel-chair appeared, the buzz of an electric motor drifting across to them.

"Well, well," Palmer hissed. "Look what we have here."

They watched as the man drove the wheelchair in a jerky fashion across the tiled surface to within a few feet of the pool, where he sat staring into its depths. The woman watched his progress until he stopped, then began deadheading some flowers in tubs by the house.

"He was in the photos," Riley said. "At least, I think it

was him. He looks smaller and thinner."

"Ray Grossman," Palmer guessed.

"But your friend in the Met—"

Palmer nodded. "I know. But he only *thought* he was dead. Could be Grossman simply dropped out of sight and rumour did the rest."

The rottweiler climbed to its feet and walked slowly back to the shelter of the table, its large head swinging towards Lottie Grossman. The manoeuvre failed. The woman turned her head and shouted at the animal, then she picked up a long-poled skim-net used for cleaning the swimming pool and, with a darting movement surprisingly quick for a woman of her size and age, was upon the dog. She beat it three times with the handle end of the net, each stroke on the rottweiler's flanks echoing across the garden. The dog cowered, trying to avoid the pole, then moved back to the centre of the patio, where it lay down again and licked its side.

The man in the wheelchair didn't look round.

Riley and Palmer exchanged a glance.

"Bloody Nora," Palmer breathed. "I wouldn't want to change places with that dog."

"If you do, I'd take a suicide pill with you," Riley replied. "Come on – I've seen enough."

They walked back towards the car. As they approached the edge of the trees, Palmer held out a hand to stop Riley and motioned her down.

He edged forward until he had a clearer view through the branches, and swore silently. The Land Cruiser was parked alongside the Peugeot and two men were peering into its windows. A third figure sat in the driver's seat, watching.

Palmer felt a movement behind him as Riley squatted down and peered over his shoulder. He was about to suggest she go back when she glared at him. "Don't even think it, Palmer," she warned him. "I don't do helpless female."

He let it go and nodded towards the car. "Recognise anyone?"

"The driver, maybe...could be Mitcheson. But not the other two. How about you?"

Palmer nodded. "They're the baseball fans who junked my office."

24

"What d'you reckon?" Doug was standing alongside the Land Cruiser looking at Mitcheson. Howie was studying the contents of the Peugeot.

"Anything inside?"

"Picnic stuff. Sandwich wrappers...cold-box...couple of empty coke tins. A local map on the dash. Could be tourists." He looked back towards where the road curved out of sight alongside the villa grounds. "Probably gone walkies – or a bit of fun in the trees." He grinned and looked as if he might take a walk along the road to find out, when a mobile phone buzzed in the Land Cruiser. Mitcheson picked it up and listened. Seconds later he dropped it and shook his head.

"Forget it," he called. "Gary's just called from the airport – he's on his way in. Problems, apparently." He started the engine.

"What about this?" Doug asked, jerking a thumb at the car.

"We'll check later. If it's still there in an hour, we'll scout the perimeter and flush them out."

He drove back down the drive to the villa and parked in the shade. Doug took a heavy canvas sports bag from the back and followed the other two to the front door. As he did so, the rottweiler appeared at the corner of the building.

Howie threw it a nasty look. "I'm gonna slot that brute," he said quietly. There was a look about the dog that didn't seem right. They had all seen Lottie Grossman's method of treatment, and were all convinced that one day the animal

126

would lose it and turn on her – and on anyone else around at the time.

"Cool it," Mitcheson warned him. "If he senses a threat, he'll have you marked down first. Let's keep him primed for real trouble – if it comes."

Lottie Grossman met them in the cool of the hallway.

"Problems?" she asked.

Mitcheson inclined his head. "A car parked along the road. Could be tourists. Could be someone having a snoop. Segassa's people, maybe."

Lottie nodded and took a phone from the wall nearby. "I'll call my friend the chief of police. Did you get the registration?"

Mitcheson gave it to her. She dialled a number and spoke briefly, then replaced the receiver. She watched as Doug placed the sports bag on the floor and opened the top. Inside, under a tracksuit and towel, were four hand-guns and boxes of ammunition, along with silencers and a nondescript cardboard box.

"What's that?" Lottie asked, pointing at the box.

"Image intensifier," Doug replied. "Useless piece of second-hand kit, but it was all we could get at short notice. Might be useful later, you never know."

She nodded and walked through to the living room, gesturing for the men to take chairs. She appeared cool and relaxed, but a faint bead of perspiration shone on her forehead, and her heavy make-up had smudged in the corner of one eye.

"Gary and McManus should be here soon," she informed them. "They've just got back from Jordans."

"They?" Mitcheson thought only Gary had gone back to check the house. He'd been wondering where Lottie's tame dinosaur was hiding. Now he knew. The news made him uneasy. McManus was a stray bullet looking for a target; having him wandering about uncontrolled gave him an itchy feeling in the middle of his back. "Why McManus?"

"He had a couple of things to take care of." The words came out flat and final, and Mitcheson's unease grew even more. What couple of things? Maybe he'd find out from Gary. "What did he say?"

"There have been visitors at the house. My cleaner was questioned by a man and a woman, supposedly estate agents. Stupid woman even let them look around the place. Not that there's anything they could find. McManus says the description fits the woman making enquiries about Cook and Page." She looked at Mitcheson, a pulse flickering at her temple. From outside they could hear the sound of the rottweiler's relentless pacing. "I thought you were dealing with her. Why is she still bothering us?"

Mitcheson felt the other two staring at him and returned the woman's look as calmly as possible. He wondered how long it would be before Doug and Howie joined Gary in his gradual drift across the floor to the Grossman camp. If this continued, he was in danger of losing what control he had over them to a woman being carried away by a rush of power to the head.

He took a deep breath. He had no idea what McManus had told Lottie about his findings in Riley's flat, but it was safe to assume he hadn't left anything out – including their fight near Piccadilly. He spoke calmly. "She's a freelance reporter named Riley Gavin. She doesn't have an inside track on what's going on, but by the sounds of it she's managed to trace your address. But that's all. She doesn't know about the villa, and there's no way she can find out – unless there were any clues at the house."

"Don't take me for a fool, Mr Mitcheson," Lottie said

softly, her hand beating double-time on her thigh. "Of course there are no clues – I spent weeks stripping the place of anything like that."

Mitcheson shrugged. "Then there's nothing to worry about, is there?" He returned her stare, irritated by her obsession with position. "The reason I didn't take steps against her, or—" he paused meaningfully, "let McManus anywhere near her, was because we can't go round getting rid of everyone as casually as swatting flies."

The silence was broken by the sound of a car pulling up outside. The rottweiler growled and trotted away to investigate.

Lottie said nothing, which to Mitcheson, was the most worrying of all.

From the hire car under the tree, Palmer and Riley watched as the dust settled from the cream Mercedes that had just passed through the gate. They had caught a brief glimpse of the driver and passenger, and Riley had felt a jolt at recognising the big man she had seen in Piccadilly.

"Seems like Grossman's gathering his forces," Palmer said.

"I wish we could get inside," said Riley. "Perhaps we can come back later."

"Maybe." Palmer had his doubts; these people were trained soldiers. "For now, though, I think we'd better move. Those latest two may have spotted us as well. If we hang about they could be swarming all over us."

He started the engine and drove quietly away down the road towards the coast.

Ten minutes later, Doug and Howie stepped out from the trees not far from where the hire car had been parked. They both carried handguns and had made their way silently all the way round the villa, checking bushes and undergrowth.

Howie spoke into his mobile: "The car's gone. Could have been tourists."

"Check the perimeter again, anyway," Mitcheson's voice came back. There was a click as he cut the connection.

"Can somebody stop that noise?" A detective of the Malaga Criminal Investigation Unit spoke loudly enough to attract everyone's attention while he stared at the body of Jerry Bignell. Downstairs a cleaning woman was wailing like an air-raid siren which she'd been doing since she first arrived and made her discovery. While a uniformed officer went down to attend to the woman, the detective sighed and wondered why these English criminals were littering his country with their rubbish. He'd long suspected what Bignell was up to, but hadn't yet got round to reeling him in. Now there was no need. He couldn't see the man's death was any great loss.

He winced at the smell fouling the air, swatting at the flies buzzing around the body. If they left it much longer this place would be a serious health hazard. He went downstairs to call for assistance and see what the wailing woman had to say.

25

"I'm going for a walk," Palmer said, poking his head round the doorway of Riley's room. "You want anything?"

They had booked into a small hotel along the coast road outside Malaga. It was sandwiched between a new development of half-built holiday apartments and a shopping complex bright with multi-coloured lights and gaudy adverts for suntan oil and Ray-Ban sunglasses.

After hanging around the garden behind the hotel for a while, discussing their next move and subconsciously waiting for dusk to fall, they had returned to their rooms to catch up on the sleep they had missed during their flight from England.

Riley looked up from the bed, where she was hunched over her laptop. "Nothing, thanks," she said. She had been indulging in some mind-mapping, randomly jotting down thoughts about the investigation. The names of Cook, Page, McKee and the others were dotted about the screen, joined by a series of lines, arrows and exclamation marks. She had just added John Mitcheson's name with a question mark and another line to Ray Grossman and his wife.

She listened as Palmer's footsteps echoed down the tiled stairs towards the lobby, and wondered if she shouldn't have tagged along with him. It might be better than sitting here uselessly staring at her screen getting eye-strain, her thoughts jumbled like scattered pieces of a puzzle. The inactivity was beginning to get to her and she desperately wanted to have another look at the villa. But Palmer would throw a fit if she went without him.

Half an hour later, when he had still not returned, she closed the laptop and drove back along the coast road. She knew it was risky, but she really couldn't take the waiting any longer. Besides, it would hardly be the first time she had gone snooping alone.

She turned on to the road leading to the Villa Almedina and drove past it into open countryside. In spite of the falling light there was still a remnant of heat-haze in the distance over the fields, and a line of trees danced like chorus girls along the brow of a hill. There was little other movement, save for two men with deeply weathered faces scuffing wearily along the road. Both were dressed in faded work-clothes and carried tool-bags over their shoulders. One wore a scruffy baseball cap with a Coca-Cola logo, and the other fanned himself with a battered straw hat that had seen better days. They stared as Riley drove by, but didn't pause in their measured tread.

After half a mile she turned the car round and drove slowly back. There was no sign of the two men, so she cut the engine and coasted into the side of the road just before reaching the villa. She climbed out to the sound of a turgid breeze in the trees and the distant hum of an electric motor.

She took a bottle of water and locked the car, then walked along the verge until she reached the stone wall where she and Palmer had stood earlier. The dry undergrowth crackled beneath her boots, and she tried to banish all thoughts of snakes. The atmosphere here was cooler, with a strong smell of sap hanging in the air. She wormed her way into the trees and squatted down to watch the rear of the villa, focusing on the patio and pool.

She sipped sparingly from the water bottle but soon began to wish she'd used the bathroom before coming out.

It wouldn't take long for the thought to become intense and nagging. It's easy for men on this kind of job, she thought. All they have to do is unzip where they stand and no one gives it a thought.

A twig snapped off to her left. She resisted the impulse to spin round and turned her head slowly, her breathing stopped. A flash of movement caught her eye. When it wasn't repeated she decided it must have been a bird and settled back on her heels to wait.

Ten minutes later still nothing had happened around the villa. She wondered what Palmer was doing. Probably propping up a bar listening to the gossip, knowing him. Not that she thought he was idle; in fact there was something about Palmer that told her once he took on a job, he was the type never to be off duty. Her opinion of the private detective had risen considerably since she had first met him, and she realised his laid-back aura of weariness was little more than an act. She felt guilty at having come out here without him, but it was too late now.

A car engine sounded nearby and she saw a flash of light off paintwork towards the front of the house. Doors slammed and voices drifted through the branches, then silence. More members of the household, or visitors?

There was a scuff of movement to her left. Again she turned her head but couldn't see anything. Then she heard a low growl to her front. She looked towards the sound and realised that what she had first taken to be a dark patch of tree trunk was now moving.

The rottweiler was standing barely twenty feet away, looking right at her.

The yellow eyes stayed on her as the animal approached. Its pupils contained pale flecks, and there was a line of dried white saliva around the dog's jaws. Riley could see the muscle bunched around the beast's shoulders, and her mouth went dry as she realised trying to run would be hopeless; this animal would be on her before she got to her feet.

Another snap sounded to her left and someone muttered a low curse. The effect on the dog was instantaneous. It stopped dead, its head turning like the muzzle of a gun.

The result was dramatic. A man rose from the undergrowth thirty feet away and stared at the dog with a look of terror. His face was deeply tanned, and he wore a familiar baseball cap bearing a Coca-Cola motif. It was one of the workmen Riley had seen earlier along the road.

It explained why she hadn't seen the two men on her way back. So this was where they had gone, to catch some sleep under the trees. Now one of them had woken up and disturbed the rottweiler.

It was then she realised that the man was holding a handgun.

The dog saw it in the same instant and launched itself forward through the trees like an arrow, a deep rumbling coming from its chest. There was a crash of trampled undergrowth as the man stumbled backwards, then the sound of a thick branch snapping, and the dog gave a howl.

Voices called from the direction of the villa, and Riley decided it was time to go. She turned and hopped over the wall, running along the verge to the car. Behind her she heard shouting and more snapping sounds from among the trees.

She fumbled with the car keys, perspiration making them slippery. Finally the door opened and she skidded off the grass verge on to the road, a billowing cloud of dust building behind her, masking her from the view of anyone coming out of the trees.

At the end of the road she pulled out on to the main coastal highway. Her nerves were screaming at her close brush with disaster. Palmer would throw a fit if he found out. She shivered again at the thought of the dog, and thanked the gods that its attention had been diverted by the man in the cap.

As she accelerated in the direction of the hotel, a figure in a dark uniform stepped out from the side of the road a hundred yards ahead. She instantly felt a leaden feeling in her stomach. He was pointing at her and waving her down. Behind him stood a police car, its blue light flashing.

26

Frank Palmer knocked at Riley's bedroom door. He'd already tried once but there was no reply. Was she asleep? He glanced at his watch. Surely she couldn't be that tired?

He walked over to the rear windows and peered down into the car park. The car was gone. He ran downstairs and asked the desk clerk if he knew where Miss Gavin had gone. The man shrugged.

"Do you have a courtesy car I can use?"

"Sorry, no," the clerk replied carefully. "It takes one hour and I can arrange one for you."

Palmer spotted a small Fiat parked outside. "Who does that belong to?" he asked.

The clerk smiled proudly. "Is mine."

"Great." Palmer took a fistful of notes from his pocket. "I want to hire your car for an hour or so." He figured it was more than the clerk earned in two day's work.

"But, sir – I cannot…"

"You can," Palmer urged. "I've got to collect a friend from the airport – a business contact. If I don't get there, I'm in deep shit – you understand?" He added more notes. "Come on – you've got my passport."

Avarice won. The clerk handed Palmer his keys and watched as the Englishman hurried out of the car park and down the road. He wondered if the man realised he was heading the wrong way for the airport.

Palmer drove the small Fiat fast along the coast road, wondering what the hell Riley was up to. He'd had a bad feeling about the men they had seen at the villa. The two who had visited his office had let him off without a beating then, but he doubted they would do so again.

He saw a blue flashing light up ahead and slowed down. No sense in him getting into trouble for speeding. As he crawled by on the tail of a van in front, he saw the reason for the hold-up was: Riley being escorted into a police car, as a second policeman climbed behind the wheel of her hire car.

He drove on until he saw a convenient turning, then spun the wheel and headed back towards Malaga. Within minutes he'd caught up and settled in behind them.

"What happened?" Mitcheson asked, squatting down beside Doug. Both men carried handguns. They were in the trees near the villa, and Doug was checking through the pockets of a body lying on the ground. A bright splash of blood stained the throat and chest, and the remnants of the man's shirt hung in tatters. Nearby was a baseball cap.

"The mutt got him." Doug gestured to where the rottweiler lay dead. Flies were already buzzing about their heads, attracted by the blood. "And he got the mutt."

Mitcheson swore softly. "Christ – what with?"

Howie stepped up alongside them and scooped a handgun from the ground. "Star 9mm," he said. "Cheap and cheerful version – most likely a copy."

"Was he alone?"

"I counted three," said Doug. "Two of them ran, then a car took off down the road."

"Okay. Let's get him inside. Bring the dog as well."

Mitcheson and Howie lifted the man's body and threaded their way through the trees, while Doug brought the dog. Gary was waiting on the patio with his gun drawn, while inside, McManus stood guard by the hallway.

In one armchair in the living room sat a slim, dark-skinned man in his mid-forties. He was expensively dressed in a lightweight silk suit and cotton shirt. Facing him were Lottie Grossman in another chair, and Ray Grossman scowling from his wheelchair.

Mitcheson and Howie dumped the body in the doorway. The man in the armchair glanced down but said nothing. His liquid eyes were glued to the firepower in the room, and he couldn't have failed to be impressed by the speed with which the men had responded to the intruders.

"Know him, Mr Segassa?" Mitcheson asked. He gestured at the gun in Howie's hand. "We found this near the body. Two others got away."

Segassa looked surprised for an instant, then waved a dismissive hand. "I have never seen him before. There are many criminals in this area." He stared at the surrounding faces and added dryly: "Mostly English."

"All right, Andre," Lottie Grossman said softly. "Now that little matter is out of the way, we can talk terms for the first delivery." She spoke as though nothing had happened, yet her tone left the man in no doubt that he had just witnessed the power of the group of men she commanded.

Frank Palmer pulled up across the street from the police station and watched as the car carrying Riley turned through a guarded gateway, followed by the hire car. He wondered why Riley had chosen to go off alone. Whatever the reason, she had fallen foul of the law and needed extracting.

He returned to the hotel and handed the keys back to the clerk and asked him to call a taxi. If he also got picked up, he didn't want the clerk involved through his car number. He had the taxi drop him a block away from the police station and walked the rest of the way deep in thought. This latest development was an added complication. Had Lottie and her group called the cops? Or had Riley simply been unlucky and infringed a local traffic regulation? The third possibility was more worrying, the local cops might have acted in co-ordination with the Grossmans.

He stood outside for a moment, considering his options, then took a deep breath and walked up the steps and through the front doors. Nothing like a frontal attack, he figured, for upsetting the enemy.

The inside of the reception area was like police stations anywhere: the walls lined with lurid posters requesting information about offences committed and warning of the dangers of drugs and drinking.

Palmer filtered his way through a group of distressed German tourists in sun hats and shorts and arrived at the desk, where a stressed-looking sergeant was issuing orders to subordinates and hurling sheets of paper through a hatch in the back wall. Palmer flashed his passport. "I've been told you have a friend of mine under arrest," he said politely. "She was picked up at Moharras. I wonder if you would be kind enough to give me some details?" He gave Riley's name.

The desk sergeant disappeared, then returned a few minutes later and motioned him to sit down and wait. The minutes ticked away with grinding slowness. Palmer sat and half-listened as the German tourists told in angry detail how they had been the target of pickpockets on the beach.

Two other men emerged from the back office and stood nearby talking in low tones. The one doing most of the talking was Spanish, and plainly a policeman. The other was English and dressed in a dusty suit and scuffed brown shoes with frayed, red laces. He had a beaten, ingratiating manner, and was scribbling in a battered notebook while constantly nudging the policeman for more information. Eventually, the detective managed to make his escape and retreated through the door.

The desk sergeant interrupted Palmer's eavesdropping and motioned him through a side door. He led him down a corridor and knocked on a blank door at the end.

The office was sparse and lacked any personal touches. Behind the bare desk sat a captain in uniform, his cigarette smoke drawn upwards by a large ceiling fan. He stood up as Palmer walked in and dismissed the desk sergeant with a wave of his hand.

"I have already spoken to Mrs Grossman," the captain said without preamble. "I did not expect anyone to come so soon."

Palmer kept his expression blank and shrugged. He didn't know where this was going, but it seemed already to have escaped him. He also had half his mind on the conversation he'd overheard out in the reception area.

The captain shrugged, too. "Well, it is of no consequence. The young lady will be charged under our traffic laws and sent home." He clapped his hands lightly together in a washing motion. "I understand she is English. You know her name?"

"Yes," Palmer replied. "We know her." He took out his wallet. "I will, of course," he said, "pay any...traffic fines your courts would normally apply."

The officer nodded and wrote a figure on a piece of paper, which he slid across the desk for Palmer to see. It was a lot of money, but there was no other method of getting Riley out of Lottie Grossman's way. He counted out the notes and slid them across the desk. The officer nodded, slipped them in the desk drawer and locked it.

He picked up the phone and spoke rapidly, then replaced it and said, "The lady will be brought out immediately. I am sorry we could not bring her to Villa Almedina, but there are limits to what I can arrange." He puffed on his cigarette and blew out a thick cloud of pungent smoke. "She was speeding," he continued, as if sensing some justification was needed in exchange for the money. "My men were merely doing their job, of course."

"I understand," Palmer said. "Excellent work, captain." Evidently Lottie Grossman liked to take extra precautions to protect her privacy. He felt a growing admiration for the woman; she certainly believed in good organisation. He wondered how much she was paying this officer for his discreet help.

There was a knock at the door and a squat, dour-looking woman in uniform appeared. Riley was close behind her, looking as if she could spit nails. She looked stunned to see Palmer and he shook his head to warn her not to say anything.

The officer ground out his cigarette and stood up. He muttered briefly to the policewoman who departed immediately, before ushering Palmer out into the corridor. Past the desk, they threaded their way through the group of German tourists and out on to the front steps. Palmer had never been so pleased to taste fresh air.

The officer indicated Riley's car, which was now parked at the front kerb. "You may go. I strongly suggest you leave on the next plane." He turned to Palmer, his look intense. "Both of you. This is not a good time to be here unless you are on holiday." With that he turned on his heels and walked back inside.

There was a dangerous glint in Lottie Grossman's eyes when she dropped the phone back on its hook, and a pulse began to beat in her throat as she turned to stare at Mitcheson. She had just finished talking to a contact at the police station to see if anyone suspicious had been seen in the area near the villa.

"That was the captain at the central station. He just released a woman his men stopped earlier along the coast road near here. She was driving the Peugeot you saw outside. He says one of my men just called in to pay a fine for her release."

Mitcheson frowned. They had been out-manoeuvred, although he couldn't help but feel relieved. "Did either of them have names?"

"The captain can't remember," Lottie Grossman said, her voice heavy with disbelief. "He says he ordered them to leave the country immediately. How convenient." She rasped her painted fingernails together. "He'll regret that. But so will the woman."

27

"I can't believe that bunch of fuckwits!" Riley swore roundly and threw the last of her clothing into her bag. She was still outraged by her arrest and her expulsion from the country. "And those people...they had guns, Palmer – and that monster of a dog. What in hell are they up to?"

She shivered and wrapped her arms around herself.

Palmer took a miniature of brandy from the mini-bar, and tipped the contents into a glass.

"Get that down you," he said, handing her the glass. "Medicinal only – I don't need you going into shock on me. Then we'd better move to another hotel. The police might just check this place – or let Grossman's people do it."

Riley blinked at the roughness in his voice and realised he was right on both counts. If she let this thing get to her she was going to be useless, and if the police found her still here, they'd be in worse trouble. She drank the contents in one go, wincing as it burned her throat.

"God – what do they make that from?" she asked.

Palmer smiled. Protest was a good sign. He excused himself and went along to his room to make a phone call. When he returned, he was carrying a slim newspaper and his bag. Riley was just putting her mobile down.

"Ready?" he asked.

"I've just checked my messages," she said nodding at the phone. "John Mitcheson wants to talk. It was timed thirty minutes ago."

"If he's out at the villa, he'll know it was you the police picked up."

Riley walked across to the window. "He left a mobile number to leave a message. He said it was urgent."

Palmer looked sceptical. "And you're going to call?"

"It could be a step forward. Why not?"

"Because," Palmer said with quiet logic, "it could also be a trap. He may not be the worst of the bunch, but someone in that group has done the killing. If it wasn't him, it was one of his men. How do you know it isn't a set-up?"

"I don't. I agreed to leave the country just to keep that police captain happy, but I never said I was giving up on the assignment. After what we've seen, I can't give up." She sat back on the bed. "You can go back if you want. I'll pay you up to date."

Palmer ignored her and dropped the newspaper on the bed. It was an English-language paper for local residents. "Something I didn't tell you. While I was waiting to spring you from the nick, I heard a detective briefing a local reporter on a murder they discovered today in Malaga. An Englishman named Bignell was shot dead in his house. They say it was drug-related, and that Bignell was a local distributor. They'd been watching him for some time and were getting ready to make an arrest. Someone beat them to it."

"How does that involve us? There are loads of Brits living around here. Some of them are bound to be bent."

Palmer tapped the paper on the bed. "It was their reporter I overheard being briefed at the station. His name's Benson. I rang him just now and asked if he could give me the bare bones. He told me it'll be in tomorrow's edition. All he would say was, a kid saw two men delivering a carpet at Bignell's house yesterday evening, and they didn't look Spanish. Benson reckoned Bignell was well known for making regular trips across to

144

Morocco – and he wasn't the type to go for the sand or the scenery."

"Does that mean there's a connection with Grossman?"

"I didn't ask him," Palmer said honestly. "I've got a meeting with Benson tomorrow morning to see if he'll tell me more. He asked what was in it for him. I said we'd see him right."

"What does that mean?"

He grinned enigmatically. "You'll see."

"You're pushing your luck, Palmer," said Riley grudgingly.

"Yeah – but it's all part of my innate charm. Are we on?"

"Okay. But I'm still going to call John Mitcheson. Something tells me his reasons for wanting to talk aren't merely social."

Palmer stood up and walked to the door. "That's what I was afraid of. Come on – I've booked us into another place along the coast. This place feels too exposed now you've gone and got yourself a criminal record."

Breakfast next morning was on the patio behind their new hotel. The Ascona was a rambling three-storey complex of rooms and small apartments catering predominantly to English guests and a scattering of Germans and Scandinavians. While it wasn't full, it provided sufficient noise and colour to give them a level of cover that would endure all but the most detailed examination.

Palmer tucked into the buffet bar with a healthy appetite, while Riley stirred her coffee absent-mindedly. The latest edition of the local English-language newspaper lay on the table between them. They had dissected the front page, which was splashed with headlines about the murder of the Englishman, Jerry Bignell, but the story contained little more than guesswork backed up with brief details about Bignell's history in the Malaga area. The reporter had skirted carefully round any direct accusation that Bignell was one of the local criminal imports, but the implications were clear for any readers wishing to indulge in a bit of speculation. A grainy head and shoulders photo showed a sour man in his late fifties, his blotchy face apparently suffering a bad case of sunburn.

"Not hungry?" Palmer asked her, pushing away his plate and lighting a cigarette.

"Not very," she replied. "When are we meeting this reporter?"

Palmer looked at his watch. "In about thirty minutes at a beachfront bar called the Oasis. Don't come if you don't feel up to it." He regretted the words the moment he uttered them, then added: "He may know nothing... and he's no oil painting."

"Don't relegate me to the position of wee girlie, Palmer," Riley warned him. "I'm coming to see if this reporter actually knows anything or whether he's just punting a line of guesswork to sell more papers. And what the hell do looks have to do with it?"

Palmer raised his hands in defence and smiled. "Hey – I was only thinking of you. This getting arrested lark can be quite draining on the emotions – or so I'm led to believe. You're probably feeling quite traumatised and don't realise it."

Riley smiled in spite of herself. After a night of tossing and turning in the sticky atmosphere of her room, her head buzzing with images of the scene among the trees at the Villa Almedina, having to face a bright-eyed and cheerful Frank Palmer across the breakfast table did little to help her frame of mind. But he was right; she had better be alert if they were going to get anywhere with what information they had.

"I called Mitcheson last night," she told him. "He wants to meet me at two this afternoon in Malaga. He suggested the Hotel Palacio in the centre."

"So he knows you're still here, then."

She ignored the slight dig. "He sounded...I don't know...cautious."

Palmer nodded and blew smoke towards the ceiling. "So would I if I had Lottie Grossman ready to bite me in the neck." He looked her in the eye and continued: "Okay. But I'm coming with you."

"Forget it." Riley shot him a bleak look. "I only want you to watch my back, Palmer, not hold my hand like a little girl. Anyway, you need to keep an eye on the villa, in case something blows up there."

He held up a hand to signal defeat. "Okay. You're the boss. But just so you know, I don't trust this guy. If it looks dicey, get out of there."

"Agreed. Now, are we going to see this reporter?"

They left the hotel thirty minutes later and Riley drove them along the coast road until they saw a large, garish sign pointing to the Oasis bar and restaurant. It was a low-slung building sandwiched between two gleaming white tourist palaces and facing out to sea. Extensive stretches of tinted glass bore brightly-coloured but unconvincing coconut palms, and unlit neon signs proclaimed nightly live music and Happy Hours. The main car park contained a single car – a sorry-looking Volkswagen Beetle – while a delivery lorry unloaded crates of beer through a set of double doors at the side. It was evidently too early for the morning trade to have begun in earnest.

"My, Palmer," Riley remarked as they pushed through a double set of swing doors, to be greeted by a heady smell of stale beer, fried food and cigarette smoke. "I'm really glad you didn't choose somewhere down-market for this meeting."

"Don't knock it," he replied cheerfully. "Most of my best work has been done in dives like this one."

"Really? You should get out more."

28

There was a single customer, the man Palmer had seen in the police station. He was alone near a window overlooking the beach, staring into a coffee cup. Behind the bar a young man in a white shirt and black waistcoat polished a stack of saucers, with a row of cups on the top waiting to be cleaned.

Palmer led Riley over to the table, signalling to the barman for two coffees on the way.

"Mr Benson?"

Benson looked up and tried to look surprised. He gave a faltering grin which didn't quite come off either, and waved a hand instead. "That's me. Take a seat."

He nodded slowly and watched as Riley slid into the bench seat across from him, then turned towards the bar and raised his hand again. "What c'n I get you?" he offered. His voice sounded shaky and Palmer and Riley exchanged a glance. If this man had slept indoors last night, it must have been in a cement warehouse, because his clothes were covered in fine grains of grey powder and his shirt collar was crumpled and grubby.

"I've ordered coffee, thanks," said Palmer. He looked across at the connecting table, where an empty glass stood in the middle with a wet smear track running from near Benson's elbow. "What was it – brandy?"

Riley turned to Palmer, her mouth dropping open. But he ignored her, staring at Benson without expression until the local reporter licked his lips and nodded.

"Thanks. That'd be good." His voice broke and he tried

another smile. "Whatever gets the day going, right?" He stared down at his hands, then seemed to notice his frayed cuffs and dropped them into his lap.

When the barman brought their coffees, Palmer said: "And a brandy, please."

The barman glanced at Benson, then back at Palmer. "Spanish or French?"

"Spanish. Make it a good one."

The barman shrugged and walked away, flapping his tea towel at a fly on the next table before scooping up the empty glass.

"That's decent of you," said Benson. "Very under-estimated, Spanish brandies. So who's your lady colleague?" He eyed Riley with surprise, as though he had never seen a woman in the place so early before.

"I'm Riley Gavin." Riley began to reach across to shake his hand, but he sat back and closed his eyes briefly, as if overtaken by a sudden bout of tiredness. She threw Palmer a filthy look that said 'What the hell are we doing here?' and dropped her hand.

Benson up close surpassed Palmer's description earlier. He was reed-thin and angular, with bony hands and wrists. His fingers were coarse-looking, with bitten-down nails and ancient scar tissue across the knuckles as if he might have once been a fighter who'd fallen down a lot. His face was narrow and in need of a shave, with long sideboards and a curl of lank, grey hair hanging behind each ear. A widow's peak gave him the appearance of a pantomime Dracula, encouraged by a flash of yellowing, uneven teeth between bloodless lips.

"So, what can I do for you?" he asked, opening his eyes.

"We're gathering general background information," said Palmer, taking the lead. "It's a piece we're thinking of doing on London firms who've moved out here."

Benson looked back at him, his eyes suddenly rat-like. "By firms I take it you don't mean B&Q or John Lewis." When they said nothing, he continued with a shrug: "Just checking. You should know the criminal element's been done to death already, and the last exposé was in the *Mirror* a couple of months back. The journo who covered it got his knees broken for naming names."

"Is that why you didn't go into too much detail about Bignell's death?" Riley asked him.

If Benson was annoyed at this slur on his professional courage, he didn't show it. "You don't know the type," he countered evenly. "Upset them and it's not just you they come after; it's your family...friends – anybody."

"I'm sorry."

The barman arrived with a glass of brandy and set it down carefully in front of Benson. His expression said clearly that this was a waste of good liquor.

"No worries," Benson said matter-of-factly. "It's a fact of life, that's all." He sipped his brandy almost daintily and winked gnome-like at Palmer in appreciation. "Couldn't rush this if I tried." He put the glass down and sat back. "Now, what is it you want to know about Mr Jerry Bignell?"

"Why he died. Who killed him. Stuff like that," said Palmer. He took out his wallet and left it on the table in front of him. In the background came the squeak of the barman's polishing cloth.

Benson sipped his drink, then stood up. "Excuse me," he said politely. "Just be a second." Then he walked away towards the back of the club, with the exaggerated gait of someone who actually wanted to lie down.

Riley turned on Palmer with a furious look. "What the

bloody hell are you doing, Palmer? That man's a raging lush and you're pouring drink down his throat! We'll be lucky to get any sense out of him when he comes back. *If* he comes back."

Palmer nodded towards the coffee cup Benson had been looking into when they arrived. "You think that was his? It's dried out. He took it off the bar for local colour. The glass on the next table was his – he heard us come in and got rid of it."

Benson returned and slid into his seat. "Sorry 'bout that. Where were we – oh, yes, Bignell. Well, what's to say? He was a crook and he got killed. Happens all the time." He sipped more of the brandy and sighed.

"We'd like to know who his friends were," said Riley.

Benson smirked. "Easy. He never had any. The ones he thought were his mates all bunked off just before he got killed."

"They were warned off."

"Most likely."

Palmer lifted his wallet and riffled through some notes inside. "By?"

Benson licked his lips and shifted in his seat. "You said you wanted some info on Bignell." He looked suddenly nervous, but his eyes were on the money.

"We're more interested in who killed him. Aren't you?"

"No." Benson began to rise but Palmer put a hand on his wrist.

"Listen, I hate to come out with a well-worn cliché, Mr Benson," he said, "but you help us and we'll make it worth your while."

"Why should I? These are dangerous people."

"Because you're not going anywhere with this story, that's why. If there was anything harder to report or more

152

money to make out of it, you'd have done it already."

Benson sat down again with a resigned sigh. He picked up the glass, drained it in one, then pushed it across the table. "Go on, then."

He waited until the fresh drink arrived, then twirled it around before continuing. "Bignell was nothing. He ran a small operation because his boat could get lost among all the other traffic in the area and the Spanish police had more important targets to chase, like property scams and organised crime. He wanted to be bigger but hadn't got the balls or the money." He grinned, showing his yellowed teeth. "Drugs are like any other business; you need capital to set up a decent deal. Bignell hadn't got it." He shrugged. "Then somebody fingered him to the local police and they had to act. They stopped his boat."

"By somebody," said Riley, "you don't mean a concerned citizen."

"You got it." Benson looked at Palmer. "Look, you were right, okay. I wasn't going anywhere with this because it wasn't worth the grief. But if I tell you anything else, I could still be in deep shit." He glanced at Riley. "Sorry."

Palmer took out some notes from his wallet and put them on the table. "How about that?"

Benson nodded. "I'll need to get away straight after."

"Won't the paper object?" said Riley. "You leaving it like this?"

But Benson shook his head. "There is no paper. I'm strictly freelance." The look he gave her showed what the admission had cost him, and that their respective ideas of freelance work were worlds apart.

Palmer added a few more notes to the pile. "That's it." He closed his wallet and put it away.

Benson shrugged, then dipped his finger in his brandy

and licked it. "Okay. Word is, after Bignell got pulled, the locals wanted to charge him, but were out-voted by UDYCOS – that's the Drugs and Organised Crime Unit. They wanted to roll up his contacts in Morocco. Unfortunately, someone else got to him first." He picked at a patch of grot in one eye. "And before you ask, no, I don't have any thoughts about police corruption. Bignell then started saying he'd been fitted up by some new firm moving in. I spoke to him a couple of days ago, and he gave me a name. Said this bloke has moved in locally and used to be something back in England years ago. Now he's out here looking to set up in Bignell's place…only bigger."

Riley leaned forward. "The name?"

But Benson wasn't ready yet. "He said he'd had threats against his family. Then his mates pulled out and left him holding the limp end. He was scared witless, you ask me. Bignell was no hero, but he wasn't a rabbit, either." He shifted in his seat again, then said softly: "Grossman. Ray Grossman. That's all I know." He fished a piece of card from his top pocket and placed it on the table. It held a name and phone number. "This is one of Bignell's mates. He's in Miami. Jerry said he knew Grossman from way back." He finished his drink and smiled grimly, holding the glass. "On your way out..?"

Palmer stopped at the bar to settle the bill, and asked the barman to take a fresh glass across to the table. Then he followed Riley to the door. On the way they stepped aside as two men entered, carrying jackets. They looked like local labourers, both deeply tanned and wearing cheap, lightweight clothing, their shoes dusty and worn. One of them held the door open for Riley before going inside.

They were ten minutes along the road to Malaga when

Palmer sat up in his seat and slapped his knee. "Christ – turn round!"

Riley looked startled. "Why? What's up?"

"Those two men we passed on the way out. Did you see their car?"

Riley began to brake and look for a place to turn. "No. Yes…it was something big, wasn't it? I didn't really notice." Then she realised. "Oh, no."

Palmer pointed. "Turn here, quick. The car was too big and they didn't look right. Foot down." He drummed his hand on the side of the door, which was the most agitated Riley had ever seen him. She pulled the car round in a long turn and slammed her foot down, heading back towards the Oasis.

When they arrived, the car park still held the old VW Beetle, but no other vehicle. Palmer leapt from the car and ran inside, slamming through the sets of swing doors.

The bar was empty. On the table where they had left Benson was a glass.

It was still half-full.

29

They left the Oasis bar, with no sign of Benson anywhere, and headed back to their hotel. On the way, they changed their hire car, since the police, and by implication, Lottie Grossman's men, now had its description. They chose a nondescript blue saloon and parked it along the street from the hotel in a public lot, then walked along to another agency and hired a second car in case they needed to switch vehicles or split up.

"You've done this before, haven't you?" said Riley, as Palmer pocketed the keys of the second vehicle. She needed to talk to keep her mind off thinking about what may have happened to the reporter.

Palmer nodded. "Standard procedure in SIB operations. But we didn't have to pay for the wheels."

Back in her room Riley dialled the number Benson had given them. The only name she had was Warren. It was answered by a male voice with a throaty English accent. Riley beckoned Palmer across to listen in.

"Is Warren there?" Riley said.

"Who wants him?" The man sounded as though he was struggling to wake up.

"I'm calling about Jerry Bignell. He's had an accident."

There was a silence broken by the sound of heavy breathing on the other end. Then the voice said: "I'm Warren. Who's this?" He sounded suddenly wide awake and Riley thought she heard springs groaning as he swung out of bed. There was the rasp of a cigarette lighter and an intake of breath.

Without giving her name, Riley told the man she was a journalist working locally and had been put on the story after Bignell was discovered murdered in Malaga.

"Yeah? Why should that bother me?"

"Because Jerry gave me your name."

"Okay." There was a pause. "What's the gossip?"

She told him the barest details as related by Benson. "Before he was killed," she continued, "Jerry said you knew who was heading up the group who'd moved in from London and taken over your set-up. Is that right?"

"Jerry talked too bloody much."

"But you do know?"

"Maybe."

"I spoke to Jerry a couple of nights before he was killed. He said you knew these people from way back." Riley glanced at Palmer, wondering if she had pushed it too far. "This won't come back on you. I just need to know. Is it Ray Grossman?"

There was another intake of breath and a lengthy pause, then the man said: "Ray used to be big years ago, raking it in from some clubs he bought into back in the sixties with a couple of other guys. They recently fell out but still ran the business between 'em. Then a few days ago both the other guys got topped and Grossman was left holding the reins. I still can't believe it."

"Why not?"

"Because it wasn't his style, that's why. Ray was hard, but he never went in for this stuff – not unless he was forced."

"Perhaps he's changed."

"Yeah, right.'" Warren sounded sceptical. "What would be the point, in his condition?"

"I don't follow."

"Christ, you ain't dug far, have you? Ray's dying of

cancer, that's why. Such a shame." Warren's voice was coldly unsympathetic.

Riley exchanged a look with Palmer, who looked blank. "Why didn't you hang around, then?"

"Because I didn't want to die. Ray might not be up to much any longer, but his missus is something else. She's real poison. Her and her thugs."

"So you're saying—"

"That's all I'm saying," the man said. "This number's changing as of now. Don't call again." The phone went dead.

Riley switched off the phone and looked at Palmer. "So the lady's in charge."

Palmer nodded. "There's a turn-up. I wonder if Mitcheson knows that."

"He must do. But there's only one way to find out." Riley stood up and collected her car keys. "I'll see you at the villa." She gave him a warning look. "I mean it, Frank: don't play big brother. I can handle this." She left before Palmer could argue.

At the Hotel Palacio she ordered an iced tea in the lounge. The air was cool and smelled of something floral, a proper oasis after the Oasis. She tried not to think about it, or of the possibility that Mitcheson might have ordered Benson to be snatched. Yet how could he have found out Benson was meeting them at the bar? Unless Benson himself had been careless.

"Miss Gavin?" It was the waiter. "A phone call for you." He gestured towards the reception desk.

The receptionist indicated a courtesy phone lying on the end of the counter and Riley picked it up. It was John Mitcheson.

"If you look in the mirror behind the counter," he said

without greeting, "you'll see a pale Merc parked in the street outside."

Riley looked. By the kerb was a large cream Mercedes, and she could just make out a figure sitting at the wheel, arm outside the car and fingers drumming on the roof. With the press of passing pedestrians, she couldn't make out if Mitcheson was looking her way or not.

"I see it," she confirmed. "What's the matter – are you frightened of being seen in hotels with strange women? I'll come out to you."

"Don't do that." Mitcheson's voice was urgent. "The man in the car is called McManus. He's the one you saw in Piccadilly the other night. Remember?"

Riley felt the hairs move on the back of her neck. She instinctively turned away, shielding her face. "What does he want?"

Mitcheson didn't speak for a few seconds. Then his voice came flat and unemotional. "He's been told to kill you."

Riley felt a chill touch her shoulders. She was shocked by the contrast between the tone and conversation of Mitcheson's voice compared with the other night.

"Is that why you suggested meeting here?" she asked coldly. "To finger me?"

"Don't be bloody silly. McManus doesn't even know you're here. If he did he'd already be out of the car. He's on his way back to London to look for you. I got caught into giving him a lift to the airport – he's taking a private plane back to the UK." He paused. "I checked you were here in Spain because I figured it would be safer than London."

Riley took a deep breath. "Okay – I'm sorry. Can we meet?"

"Give me half an hour, then go to room 1221. I'll be

along as quick as I can. Stay off the street." The line went dead.

Riley thought about telling Palmer. They hadn't arranged any method of contact other than by mobile, so she dialled his number. There was no answer. She broke the connection and walked back to the bar, selecting a chair set back out of sight of the reception area. Thirty minutes was going to seem like a lifetime.

At the Villa Almedina, a large, black Lexus purred through the gates. As the car slowed and turned to face back down the drive, the front door of the villa opened and Gary emerged. At the same time, Doug and Howie appeared at the corners of the house and stood watching as the vehicle crunched to a stop.

A slim, darkly tanned man emerged smoothly from the front passenger seat, his eyes settling bleakly for a moment on the thin belt of trees near the road where the man and dog had died. Andre Segassa followed moments later from the rear of the vehicle and nodded to the three men in turn. Professional to professional.

Gary held the door open and gestured for the new arrivals to go inside.

"Mr Segassa," Lottie Grossman greeted the drug-dealer. She shook his hand and indicated that they should follow her. As they passed across the hallway, Segassa glanced to one side and saw a man sitting hunched in a wheelchair at the end of a tiled corridor. He paused momentarily, then walked through the front room and out on to the patio, noting as he did so that the two men he now knew as Doug and Howie had followed them from the front and were watching him and his companion.

"So," Lottie smiled, pouring soft drinks from a vacuum

jug into tall glasses. "Can we begin negotiations?"

Segassa nodded and took a glass. "Of course, Mrs Grossman. As long as all the terms are satisfactory, my colleagues are happy to talk with you. I will act as intermediary."

"I'm so pleased." Lottie took a sip of her juice and tapped a painted fingernail on the side of her glass. "Such a pity about your man's accident with my dog. Did I tell you I have another one on order?"

Segassa was momentarily taken aback by the bleakness of her words. Where he came from, life was cheap and liable to be snatched away on the whim of man or nature. Yet he could not recall having ever come across a woman before who seemed to value a dog higher than a man... and in the end rate neither of them as anything more than a commodity to be replaced like a broken light-bulb.

He sipped his juice and wondered if it was all an act. Fear sometimes made weak people puff themselves out like cockerels. Yet there was something different about this woman. Something indefinable. Maybe she was just crazy. Crazy people, in his experience, were the very worst to deal with.

"Hello, John." Riley walked past Mitcheson into the room, wondering if this had been a good idea. She wasn't expecting any heavies to leap out of the wardrobe, but she knew Palmer was partly right in his suspicions, and that Mitcheson was more involved than she would have liked.

"Riley." He closed the door behind her. "Care for a drink?"

His eyes briefly scanned her figure in the sun-dress she had put on before leaving the hotel, and she remembered with a warm blush that he had seen in her in much less.

She sat down in a club chair away from the window. It seemed safer somehow, even this far above the street. "Please." She watched him pour two glasses of white wine. He had an economy of movement, as if he didn't wish to waste energy without good reason. He handed her a glass and lifted his own.

"Are we celebrating something?" she asked.

He shook his head. "I wish we were. But it's not like that. I…" He gestured with a vague wave of his hand and ran out of words.

"So why don't you tell me how it is, then?" Riley was surprised by her own calmness. Was it foolishness on her part or did she feel deep down that this man meant her no harm? "Like, why has this man – McManus? – been told to kill me?" Her voice stuttered on the final words. She hadn't realised how difficult it would be to say it.

"Because you got involved, and the business in London."

"What business?"

"McManus was the one who broke into your flat. He'd picked up your business card from one of the men you visited. Cook, was it? Anyway, he must have seen a photo of you. When he saw us together he started to make connections. He couldn't be sure if you and I were working together, so he made do with putting the poison in with his bosses. I tried to head them off, but they weren't having it. They tend to see things in black and white."

"They?"

"Lottie Grossman and her husband, Ray. And McManus himself." He stared into his glass. "I think one of my men has been dragged in, too. Maybe all of them."

"Your men?"

He shrugged. "It's a long story. It'll keep."

162

"So what are they getting into? Drugs? Is that why Bignell was murdered – to get him out of the way so they can take over?"

Mitcheson put his glass down and walked across to the window, shaking his head. "You've got to stay out of this, Riley," he said quietly. "It's dangerous and getting worse… and not just from the Grossmans. There are others involved now."

"What others? Bignell's Moroccan contacts?"

He turned and looked at her, plainly shocked by how much she knew. But he didn't deny it, she noticed.

"McManus will soon find out you're not in London, and when he does he'll come back looking for you. He's no Einstein, believe me, but he's got strong instincts and he uses them. It makes him very good at what he does."

"And what's that?"

"He hurts people. Kills them if he has to."

Riley felt a shiver of apprehension. "Like that rottweiler." Riley could have bitten her lip the moment she uttered the words, but Mitcheson didn't react. He must have already worked out that she'd been there.

"Like the rottweiler," he agreed eventually, with an expression of distaste. "The only difference is, I don't think the dog enjoyed its job quite as much."

30

He spoke of the dog in the past tense, Riley noted, and she hoped it had managed to get a bite or two in before the gunman had killed it. What with Lottie Grossman as its owner, the poor animal hadn't had much of a life.

"What do they hope to gain by the killings?" Riley asked. "Most people would know it would draw too much attention."

Mitcheson turned back to the window and shrugged. "Normal rules don't apply," he said grimly. "And they're hardly most people. There's so much money out there waiting to be grabbed, and they want their share. In fact, the way they see it, they need it."

"What for?"

"Ray Grossman's very ill. I don't know how he's hung on so long. They were advised to get him to a warmer climate, which is why they bought the villa. But with a visiting nurse and the medicines, they need more money to keep him out here. If he goes home he'll be dead within weeks."

Riley's mouth was dry. She felt he wasn't telling her everything, but trying to force the issue probably wouldn't work. Instead she changed tack. "What about you?" she asked coolly. "You could get out. Leave them to it."

"I can't do that. Not yet." He spoke with an air of finality.

"Why? What do you owe them?" She stood and walked across the room. "And what do you mean, not yet? John, why are you even involved with these people? I can't understand it. Something tells me this isn't you...not the real you, anyway."

He swung round, the movement bringing them within inches of each other. Riley was so close she could see her own reflection in the depth of his eyes, like a portrait in miniature looking up at him.

"I can't explain," he said simply. "It's…it doesn't make much sense to a—"

"To a what? A woman? Oh, please."

"To an outsider." He looked away from her, shaking his head. "I feel a… a responsibility to the men."

Riley stared up at him. "You're right – I don't understand. They're men, that's all. Grown men at that. They can think for themselves, can't they?" Then she realised what he was hinting at: they were all ex-army. "*Honour?* Is that what you're saying? You feel you'd be betraying them if you pulled out? For heaven's sake, John, that's insane!" She put out her hand and rested her fingertips on his chest, instantly aware of the beat of his heart and the warmth of his body through the thin shirt. Suddenly he was holding her, and she swallowed and closed her eyes, finally giving in and moving against him. Their bodies touched and she heard a brief moan as their lips met. She responded, her body moving hungrily against his.

Mitcheson's hands pressed against her bare back where the sun-dress was cut low, and she felt his fingers spread wide across her skin. One hand slid lower, caressing the swell of her buttocks, while his other hand moved up to her ribcage, sliding up and round with a whisper against the fabric of the dress until he was gently cupping her breast. She felt herself respond to his touch.

Then, as the last vestiges of her resistance began to slip away, her mind flashed back to the image of the man in the trees, and the dog, followed by the snapping of branches. In that instant, the moment was gone, the passion and hunger draining away to be replaced by the shocking reminder of what this man was involved in. She pulled away, her hands flat against his chest. "No!" she said sharply, pushing his arms down. "John, no."

He looked surprised as she stepped away, his hands reaching for her. For a second he seemed about to protest, then his eyes cleared.

"I'm sorry," he said quietly, his words slurred with passion. "I thought you— " He shrugged helplessly.

"Me, too," Riley whispered, and walked past him to the door. She felt guilty for having succumbed briefly to the temptation, but oddly, felt even worse for pulling back. "But this is impossible."

"Only if you let it be." His voice was bleak.

"It's just...all those deaths." Then she remembered Benson's sudden disappearance that morning. "Did your men take Benson away and kill him, too?"

Mitcheson looked blank. "Benson? I don't know any Benson." He shook his head. "If it's any consolation," he continued, "none of the ones who've died were nice people."

"Maybe not," she said. "But doesn't it bother you that so casually getting rid of people who are in the way has an inevitable outcome?"

His eyes flickered for a moment. "What's that?"

"That it might not be long before someone decides it's your turn..."

Frank Palmer stood in the gloom of a laundry room at the end of the corridor and watched as Riley stepped outside and closed the door of room 1221 behind her. He breathed with relief as she walked away and disappeared down the stairs. She seemed to have come to no harm, although she appeared flushed. Maybe Mitcheson had tried something

166

on and she'd had to knee-drop him on to the carpet. The thought brought a smile to his face. Serves the bastard right for sending those two goons to smash up my computer...

He heard the clank of a cleaning trolley and decided it was time to go before a maid found him in here and screamed the place down. If Riley knew he'd been here watching over her instead of at the villa, she'd throw seven kinds of a fit. He stepped out of the laundry room and walked along the corridor towards the emergency stairs at the far end. As he did so, the door to room 1221 opened and Mitcheson emerged. Palmer instantly fought down a wild instinct to turn back, and hoped the ex-soldier still didn't know what he looked like.

Their eyes met briefly and Palmer felt himself being scanned and noted. But if Mitcheson saw anything in his face he didn't show it. Palmer heard the lift button being thumbed impatiently behind him and grinned to himself. Definitely a case of a knee-drop. That must have put a serious kink in his plans.

He passed through the emergency door and ran down the bare concrete stairs to the ground floor, where he emerged through a single door into the reception area. If he drove like a maniac, he might just get to the villa before Riley. If not, he was going to have some explaining to do. As he stepped into the hothouse atmosphere of the street, he saw the Mercedes pull away from the kerb and accelerate through the traffic. Mitcheson. He tugged his car keys from his pocket and ran for his car, pointing the nose towards an alternative route which might bring him ahead of Mitcheson if he was lucky. If it brought him ahead of Riley, too, it would be a miracle, but he firmly believed that good things happened to nice people.

As he reached the suburbs close to the coast road,

dog-legging through an area of small, low commercial units and houses, Palmer saw a flashing blue light ahead. His bowels constricted as he remembered Riley's arrest, and he slowed down, looking for a side turning. But he was now locked in traffic and already saw a policeman striding along the line of cars, waving them to move on.

As he neared the police car, Palmer saw it was parked alongside a large builder's skip between two small warehouses. A crowd had gathered and were being pushed back by a uniformed motorcycle cop who was trying to pull a strip of bright tape across the gap between the buildings to form a barrier.

Another police car arrived and bullied its way across the road, forcing Palmer to slow even further. As he inched past the scene, he looked down and saw what had drawn the crowd. A body lay behind the skip, the legs twisted awkwardly in an ungainly pose that only came with an absence of life. What caught his eye specifically, was that the crumpled trousers covering the legs ended in a familiar pair of scuffed brown shoes with frayed, red laces.

31

Riley was angry with herself as she left Malaga behind and
headed out north on to the coast road. She was trying to
blot out what had happened in the room at the Hotel
Palacio. Well, nearly happened. She was even angrier with
Mitcheson. With herself for losing control and with him
for being the person he was and doing the job he claimed
not to be able to walk away from.

Now she needed to absorb herself in the assignment,
partly as a salve against her damaged feelings, but partly,
she realised, to bring it to an end. Quite how she was going
to do that, she didn't know. Maybe she would have to hand
what she had to the local police, although if they were so
easily swayed by the Grossmans, it might be tougher than
it looked to get them on side. There was, of course, the
local anti-drugs squad – UDYCOS, as Benson had called
them – but she knew even less about them or how to
contact them. There was also the question of proof. All she
had so far was a vague collection of allegations, which
wouldn't fly far. She needed more facts.

She turned on to the road that led past the villa and
coasted to a stop just past the bend, near where the dog
had attacked the gunman. She frowned. There was no sign
of Palmer's car.

She pulled a pair of chinos and a T-shirt from a bag
behind the seat and quickly squirmed out of her dress. If a
local farmer happened to come by now, she reflected, he
was going to get one hell of an eyeful. On the other hand,
if it were a policeman, she'd end up back in a cell – and this

time Palmer wouldn't get her out again so easily.

She locked the car and slipped over the wall into the trees, creeping forward until she had a clear view of the rear of the villa. A cloth-covered table bore the remains of a buffet, and she recognised all but two of the people clustered around the patio. The two men Palmer had described as the baseball fans stood at either corner of the house, while a third patrolled the paved area between the house and the pool. He was shorter than his companions, with a neat, compact build, and looked very fit. Riley couldn't see any guns, but she had no doubt they were there.

Another man sat in the shade with his back to the villa, and she thought she recognised him as one of the two men she had seen walking along the road near here yesterday, only minutes before his companion had appeared among the trees.

She concentrated on the two other people seated at a table with a large parasol fluttering above their heads. One was Lottie Grossman; the other was a slim, swarthy man in a cream suit and gold-framed sunglasses. He didn't appear to be saying much. He looked more at ease in this setting than the others, and Riley wondered if he was one of the late Jerry Bignell's Moroccan contacts.

The woman's voice suddenly echoed sharply across the lawn, and Riley realised she was using a mobile phone. She slammed the phone on the table and said something to the slim man opposite. He pushed back from the table and stood up, angrily flicking down the cuffs of his jacket. In an instant the man seated near the house was on his feet and the three bodyguards tensed.

Another short exchange and Lottie Grossman levered herself up from her seat and approached the slim man, her hand patting him on the arm in a placatory manner. He nodded twice and shrugged, then returned to the table and sat down. His companion did the same and the scene was restored.

Minutes ticked by, during which the slim man made two calls on the mobile. During each one he conferred with Lottie Grossman with his hand over the receiver. Riley guessed they were in the middle of some negotiations, with the dark man acting as go-between. At the end of the call he sat back and Lottie Grossman did most of the talking.

A car approached with a crunch of tyres on the gravel drive at the front of the villa. One of the baseball fans disappeared to investigate, and returned moments later followed by John Mitcheson.

Riley felt a jolt at seeing him again. She ducked further down into the cover of the trees, glad she had thought to change her clothes.

From behind her came the noise of another engine and tyres on the road. She wriggled backwards, risking a quick peek. It was Palmer. He got out of the car and hopped over the wall to squat beside her.

"Where the hell have you been?" she grated. "I thought you'd already be here."

"I fancied an ice-cream," he told her breezily. Then his expression became sombre. "Benson's dead." He explained what he had seen, leaving out the fact that it had been in Malaga.

Riley didn't respond for a few moments. Then she said: "I asked Mitcheson about him, but he didn't seem to know the name." She shook her head. "Christ, what a mess."

"Maybe Mitcheson was telling the truth," Palmer suggested. "Left hand and right, I expect. What's going on here?"

"Another meeting. Looks like some high-level horse-trading is going on with the man in the cream suit. I think that's his minder against the house. Mitcheson said they're trying to raise money from drugs to keep Grossman out here. My guess is, that's where cream suit comes in."

"Drugs." Palmer wiped a bead of perspiration off his cheek. "Hell of a way to fund a retirement plan."

"The cream suit and Lottie G had a set-to earlier on. He looked ready to walk but they seem to have patched it up. By the way the Black Widow smarmed all over him, she must have realised she'd come close to losing it."

"Good. Shows they're desperate."

Whatever had been agreed or not, the talking seemed finally to have ended. The man in the cream suit stood up and shook hands with Lottie, nodded at Mitcheson, then beckoned to his bodyguard. With Lottie leading, the three disappeared through the house, while the baseball fans and the third man drifted out of sight towards the front.

Left by himself, Mitcheson stood by the edge of the pool staring out across the lawn. For a second Riley could have sworn their eyes met. She froze, her breathing suspended. Then his gaze moved on, inspecting the tree-line foot by foot, before turning and walking into the house.

"Jesus…" Palmer breathed, and Riley realised he, too, thought they had been seen.

"Come on," she said, moving backwards towards the wall. "I need to find out who these people are and where they're based."

Palmer followed, trying not to look at her bottom in the chinos. Before reaching their cars, they agreed to switch positions periodically, with Palmer going first to get ahead of the Moroccans' vehicle. Riley waited until the Lexus nosed out of the gate, then set off in pursuit. As the

Lexus drew up at the junction with the main coast road and signalled to turn right towards Malaga, Riley spotted Palmer's car parked outside a shop near the corner. There was no sign of him and she wondered what he was playing at.

In a sudden change of manoeuvre, the Lexus turned left and surged into the traffic heading east towards Almeria. Riley, already indicating right, was caught out as a small delivery van rattled alongside on her left, blocking her path.

Just then Palmer stepped out of the shop doorway, eating an apple. He signalled with a flattened palm movement for Riley to hold it where she was and climbed unhurriedly into his own car. Then he set off after the Lexus.

Riley waited until both cars were out of sight. She wasn't sure if the sudden change of direction by the Lexus was because she had been spotted or whether the Moroccans had genuinely decided to go elsewhere. She decided not to risk getting too close, and let three cars similar to her own go by before easing out and following Palmer.

32

Three cars back from the Lexus, Palmer chewed on his apple and wondered where they were going. He glanced in the wing mirror, spotting Riley some distance behind. Luckily she had caught his delaying signal and had not immediately given chase.

Forty minutes later the road began to veer inland as it approached the small town of Motril. The Lexus signalled left and disappeared up a narrow road. Palmer waited until he was sure another car was still between them, then followed.

The road passed through an area of uninspired, dusty houses and emerged into a development of small, neat villas set back amid landscaped gardens. With fewer cars about, Palmer was beginning to feel very conspicuous.

He had done a lot of surveillance and pursuit exercises, but had never quite lost the feeling of vulnerability that came over him whenever circumstances brought him too close to his quarry. It was difficult not to imagine the driver in front peering into his rear-view mirror and knowing precisely what you were up to. He tapped his brakes as the car between him and the Lexus – a rickety Datsun with puffy grey smoke blowing from the exhaust – slowed and pulled into the side of the road. As he steered round it, a trio of children burst out of the rear door and raced across the pavement towards an elderly couple waiting at a gate to a small villa.

The Lexus was now ahead of him, but had slowed dramatically, and Palmer could see the driver looking in his rear-view mirror. Damn, it, he'd been spotted. All his instincts cried out to make an instantaneous decision and abort the chase. He did the only thing he could think of: he signalled and pulled in just ahead of the Datsun.

Ignoring the Lexus, Palmer hopped out of his car and raised both arms to the couple outside the villa. He strolled back to the Datsun and thrust his hand out to the male driver, who automatically responded, although clearly puzzled. From the corner of his eye Palmer saw Riley drive by. The Lexus had now reached a corner a hundred yards away, but was moving slowly. Maybe they had been convinced by his little role-play.

"Am I in Motril?" Palmer asked the driver. At short notice it was the first thing he could think of saying.

The man's wife understood and pointed towards the east, in the direction where the Lexus and Riley had gone. "Si. Motril…one kilometre."

As he turned back to the car, another vehicle passed by. It was a dusty Seat with two male passengers in dark glasses, their attention on the road ahead. A car like so many others in the area, except that, with a cold feeling in his gut, Palmer sensed their interest was focused specifically on Riley Gavin.

He jumped into his car and took out his mobile, keying Riley's number. But the screen remained blank. Bloody things; never a signal when you wanted one. He turned the ignition and screamed away from the kerb, tyres spinning.

As the Lexus turned a corner and headed back towards the coast road, Riley dropped a gear and followed. She hoped Palmer's quick thinking had dropped him out of the frame. Now all she had to do was avoid being detected herself. Following the car too quickly round a blind corner risked finding it waiting to see who was on its tail, but it was a chance worth taking if she could find out who these people were.

Another sharp turn and the Lexus disappeared. Riley spun the wheel and followed, and knew instantly that she'd made a mistake. She was on an unpaved track between housing developments, and the Lexus was parked just fifty yards away, waiting.

She braked hard, the tyres losing traction in the dust of the track. Before she could hit reverse gear, the doors of the Lexus opened and out stepped the two men from the villa. The man in the cream suit walked almost casually along the track towards her, while his minder took the other side. Neither man seemed in a hurry.

The minder was carrying a handgun.

Palmer was stunned. Ahead of him was a line of stationary traffic, temporarily held up by a broken-down truck that was being pushed out of the way by a group of building workers. At the tail of the queue he recognised the dusty Seat which had been following Riley, but there was no sign of her or the Lexus. They must have turned off down a side road somewhere. He did a noisy three-point turn and retraced his route. This wasn't looking good.

Half a minute later he noticed a turning between two building sites. He took it…then stood on the brakes when he saw a man waiting on the track ahead of him. Riley's car was in the background, her silhouette at the wheel.

Riley sat very still with her hands on the wheel, while the man in the cream suit stopped by the car, his feet crunching in the rough surface. Through the open window she could hear a cement mixer grinding off to one side.

"You wish to buy my nice car?" the man said dryly in lightly-accented English. "Is that why you are following me?" He smiled genially, although with no real humour, and studied his fingernails. "My colleague remembered you from the trees outside the villa Almedina. Is that so?"

Riley nodded. She had a feeling that denying she had been there wouldn't help.

"A sad business. You were fortunate it was not you." He brushed a speck of something from his sleeve, then looked up as another vehicle approached. In her mirror, Riley saw Palmer's car come to a stop in a cloud of dust. The man issued an instruction to his colleague, who used his gun to signal Palmer to stay put. Then he turned back to Riley. "What is your interest in this matter?"

Riley wondered what to tell him, then decided on the truth. It was as good as anything else in the absence of a downright and believable lie. "I'm a reporter," she said. "I'm investigating the deaths of some criminals in England."

"Ah. Another reporter." The man nodded. "Always looking for information to buy…or sell. Why have you come to Spain?"

"Because the Grossmans are responsible." She looked at him and added very deliberately: "I'm not interested in anyone else."

The man smiled. "I am pleased to hear it. The Grossmans. They kill so…casually." He shook his head. "So stupid. What will you do with your story?"

"I'll publish it and they'll probably be arrested."

"Of course. And what of…any other people?" His eyes were disturbingly intense, and Riley felt a cold realisation that what she said next could very well alter her whole life. And Palmer's, too.

"Like I said, I'm not interested in anyone else. Just the Grossmans."

The man seemed to consider that for a moment. He nodded. "In that case, go home, young lady. Publish your story. But, a warning…" His eyes became suddenly more bleak than she could have believed possible. "If you talk of me or my colleagues, Miss Riley Gavin, I will arrange for something very unpleasant to happen to your friend, Mr Frank Palmer." He smiled coldly. "Not tomorrow, not the day after. But one day." With that he turned on his heel and walked back to the Lexus.

Riley was stunned. She watched the Lexus purr past and disappear out on to the main road, and found her hands were shaking on the steering wheel. She fought to calm herself. *He knew their names. But how?*

At the Villa Almedina Ray Grossman sat slumped in his wheelchair and glared impotently at his wife. They were in the single bedroom where he spent increasing amounts of his time, and Lottie was looking down at him with stone-faced implacability.

"You stupid, stupid bloody cow!" Ray gasped, his breathing tortured and noisy. A small trickle of saliva had escaped from his mouth and was glistening on his chin. He struggled to lift one hand to beat on the arm of the wheelchair, a frail and fumbled tattoo of frustration. "How can…do this? Can't…never get away with it. Why don't… just listen to me…fer Christ's sake?"

His wife struggled to hide a look of contempt, but it came out as a coldly patronising smile. It was as ugly as Ray Grossman had ever seen in his life, and he felt unbearably sad at the way things had turned out.

"You're upsetting yourself," Lottie said matter-of-factly.

She could have been commenting on the state of the garden or the weather outside. Another cause for sadness, Grossman thought; any trace of true compassion had long since disappeared.

"Upset? Of course…upset, f'God's sake!" Grossman breathed agonisingly, the pain in his chest increasing and choking off his words. "Don't see, do you? You…you're way out your league. These Moroccans'll eat you up…spit you out." He collapsed back against the seat and groped for the plastic mask hanging by his side. As he sucked in oxygen the blood stopped pounding in his head, the pain receded and his chest settled to a slower, rhythmic pattern. He closed his eyes, his thin lids fluttering.

Lottie watched him, unmoving.

When his breathing was back to normal, she stared down at her fingernails and said: "You never did listen to me, did you, Ray? I was always ready to fix you up after you'd had problems, or listen to you going on about the other two skimming off the top. But you never gave me credit for any ideas, did you? You always thought I was a brainless little slapper like all the other little tarts. Well, things have changed. You agreed to us taking control of the clubs…and you knew people would get hurt in the process."

Her husband snatched away the mask, his eyes furious pinpoints of light. "I never said to kill them! Bleeding Jesus, Lottie – you've gone over the top!"

"Do me a favour," she spat contemptuously. "You may have been happy to sit by while McKee and Cage cleaned us out, but I wasn't."

"But we could have bought 'em out!" he insisted. "They wanted out, anyway. And the other two were beyond it." He took another pull at the mask. "Same with Jerry

Bignell…he'd have gone away in the end. You didn't have to set McManus on him. Where is McManus, anyway – he's never here when I want him."

Lottie walked towards the door, then turned to look at her husband, her face cold and unyielding. "McManus is in England," she said coldly. "Doing what he should have done a long time ago."

"What? Who said he should do anything?"

"I sent him there, the same way I send him other places." She gave him a pitying smile. "News update, Ray: McManus doesn't take orders from you anymore. He answers to me from now on. All right?"

She closed the door behind her, and Ray Grossman, who had never done time in his life, suddenly knew what it felt like to be a prisoner.

In the front room, Lottie found Gary holding the phone in his hand.

"McManus, Mrs G," he said. "The Gavin woman's not been around for two or three days. Same with Palmer – his office has been shut tight. It must have been her the local police picked up down the road."

"Has he done the other thing?"

"Yes."

"Good. Tell him to get back here fast. Where's Mitcheson and the other two?"

"Outside checking the perimeter."

Lottie looked at her watch. "Get them in here. I want to discuss tomorrow's plan of action. And get on to our police captain…find out where that damned woman is staying."

Riley powered up her laptop and logged on to check for emails, her mind still on what had happened earlier. The incident with the Moroccan had changed everything.

She still wanted to find out who he was, but not at the risk of having Palmer's life on her conscience. And if she was certain of anything, it was that the man had meant every word he'd said.

"It was my fault," Palmer had said, after the Lexus had gone and he'd gone to check Riley was okay. He'd been as stunned as she to discover the Moroccan knew their names.

"He said something about reporters buying and selling information," she'd told him. "I think he was referring to Benson."

"I agree. Benson was the only one who knew our names. He must have tried to make a deal with them." He'd looked angry with himself. "I'm sorry – I got careless."

"Forget it," she'd replied. "You couldn't have known. At least we know he doesn't trust Lottie Grossman any further than he can throw her." Then she'd told him about the Moroccan's threat. "I really don't think he was bluffing."

Palmer had shrugged philosophically. "Maybe. Maybe not. Come on, let's get back to the hotel."

Riley turned to fleshing out and updating the notes she had made so far. The report was beginning to take shape and she needed to email something to Brask.

Palmer was on the balcony, blowing smoke-rings into the evening air. He was on his second brandy sour and looking calmer after the shock confrontation with the Moroccans.

Riley stopped typing as her laptop beeped to indicate an incoming message, and stared at the screen in dismay. "Oh, no."

"What is it?" Palmer got up and came inside.

She spun the screen towards him. It was a message from Donald Brask:

Hyatt called. Peter Willis and his wife missing.
Luggage still at hotel and tickets unused. Suggest you
watch your backs.
Donald

Riley felt sick at the idea that any harm had come to the couple. What if she had been responsible for the discovery of their whereabouts? She said as much to Palmer.

"Forget it," he said flatly. "It's not as if they were that well hidden. Don't forget, even the airline knew where they were."

Riley closed the laptop and stared into the distance. He was right. But this was beginning to ripple outwards. The question was, who else was going to be touched by it?

"Where to now?" Palmer asked. "Back to London?"

Riley shook her head, now more resolved than ever. "Are you kidding? We haven't caught them doing anything yet. We can't prove they killed Bignell, nor that they've set up a deal to bring in anything more harmless than dried dates and camel hats."

Palmer raised an eyebrow. "Now why don't I like the sound of this?"

"Because," Riley told him, "I need proof. And the only way to get that is through John Mitcheson." She picked up her mobile and dialled his number.

33

Breakfast at the Villa Almedina the following morning was a subdued affair. While Doug, Gary and Howie checked the villa's perimeters and cleaned their weapons, Mitcheson, Lottie Grossman and McManus were on the patio. McManus had arrived earlier in the Cessna via Malaga, and was in a sour mood. His anger at not being able to find Riley Gavin was aimed openly at John Mitcheson.

"Seems to me she was tipped the wink," he growled, ripping open a bread roll and spreading it thickly with red jam.

Mitcheson said nothing. There was little to be gained by having an argument with the man, and even Lottie Grossman seemed irritated by McManus's constant sniping on the subject. She had also made it clear he no longer answered to her ailing husband. He had taken the news with ill grace, but said nothing. Even he must have known Ray Grossman was no longer capable of running things.

Mitcheson also knew that Lottie Grossman was capable of swinging suddenly and violently against himself, and he didn't need that kind of aggravation just yet; she'd simply set McManus on him without warning.

What she said next, however, came as a shock.

"When you've finished your breakfast," she told McManus pointedly, pushing a slip of folded paper across the table towards him, "that's the hotel the Gavin woman gave when she was arrested. Go get her."

"Where is it?" Mitcheson was appalled but casually held

out his hand. He could feel the heat in his temples and wondered how he could stop this happening. McManus had only one way of dealing with a person, and it didn't involve much in the way of talk.

"You don't need to know," snapped Lottie. "He's quite capable."

McManus tucked the slip of paper into his breast pocket, flicking a snide smile at Mitcheson. "Easy-peasy," he breathed. Coming from his lips, the childish comment seemed to take on an obscene tone Mitcheson had never known before.

"Find somewhere to keep her out of sight, then let us know you've got her, you understand?" Lottie instructed him. "And don't do anything else. I don't want anything rebounding on us back here."

"I can lose her for good if you want," McManus countered. "Like Bignell."

"No." Lottie was adamant. "Bignell was a one-off. This isn't our turf and now's not the time to take chances. Just keep her out of our way until I decide what to do with her."

"We could bring her back here and talk to her," suggested Mitcheson.

"No." Lottie pushed her cup away and impatiently brushed crumbs off her fingers. "Just neutralise her. Isn't that the term you use?"

Mitcheson shrugged as McManus drained his coffee cup and left, wiping his mouth on his hand.

Lottie Grossman watched him go and turned to look at Mitcheson. "He's an unpleasant, uncultured slob," she said to him. "But he's given good service to my husband. A bit like that rottweiler the Moroccans killed." She smiled thinly. "I don't want you two busting each other's balls all the time, do you understand me?"

He decided the safest way of getting through the day without throttling this old witch was to play along with her, so he nodded agreement and asked: "What's on the cards for today?"

"Another meeting with Segassa. This time in Malaga – and with someone who can negotiate directly." She smiled and patted Mitcheson's hand, her earlier anger forgotten as though it had never occurred. "We don't do middle-men anymore. Especially now they've seen what my men can do."

Mitcheson felt a momentary irritation at how his men had suddenly become hers, but said nothing. He doubted Doug, Howie or Gary would care much who they reported to as long as they got paid. Where it might backfire was if this woman expected too much of them without realising the possible consequences. They were good but they weren't fireproof.

"Where do you want it to happen?"

"I hear the Hotel Palacio's good for meetings," Lottie said.

Mitcheson glanced at her to see if there was any significance in her choice of words, but her head was angled so the sun reflected off her glasses, giving no hint of the expression in her eyes. He chose to believe it was just coincidence and nodded calmly.

"I've already had Gary arrange it," Lottie continued, "for just after lunch. I want everyone there, but keep two of your men outside in reserve." She looked at him. "I don't trust those Moroccans, even in a public place."

McManus watched them from inside the villa and scowled. His suspicions about Mitcheson were increasing all the time, not least fuelled by bitterness at his changing role in the Grossman organisation. There was a time when the only other person they included in their plans was himself. But that was in the days when Ray Grossman was in charge…when there was a proper respect for him. The sort of respect that meant he never had to pick up a bill, never had to fight for a parking space, never had to sit at home wondering what to do for entertainment.

Now this soldier boy and his mates had their feet under the table and his resentment and bitterness bubbled up like a poison.

His thoughts turned to the Gavin woman and what he would do when he found her. He knew Lottie would have his balls if he overstepped instructions, so he'd have to be careful. But that didn't mean he couldn't have a bit of fun.

He recalled the photos he'd found in her flat. Ripe looking woman. Looked like she'd strip down well. Maybe fight a bit, too, if he was lucky.

The sooner he picked her up the better. First he had to think of somewhere to hold her, like Lottie wanted. Somewhere nobody would look. Then he could find a deep hole to put her in. Because that's where she'd end up eventually, no matter what Lottie might be saying now.

He knew a building site where they were sinking pilings for a block of flats, and right next to a place where he could hold her, too. Easy stuff. He grinned, proud of himself, and walked out of the room and along the corridor past the bedrooms. He paused at Ray Grossman's door and looked in.

The nurse was in there giving the poor old bastard a wash-down. He could just see a bowl and a large tube of gel on the side of the bed. The sickly smell of roses filled the air. There was a grunting sound as the nurse struggled to move Grossman's body, and the slick noise of soap on skin. McManus swore silently to himself that he'd never go through that. What a scummy thing to endure, he thought. Like a baby. I'd sooner put a bullet through my skull.

He thought about making a call to the hotel where the Gavin woman was staying. Check she was in. Better than going out there and finding she'd already flown. As he passed Mitcheson's room on the way to the hall, he spotted a mobile phone lying on the bed. The idea of using Mitcheson's phone to track down the Gavin woman appealed to his sense of fairness.

He was about to dial when he noticed a message symbol flashing on the display. His in-built suspicions about the former soldier got the better of him. He punched the button and waited while the recorded voice went through its patter. There was a buzz of static and what sounded like a burst of distant laughter in the background, then a woman's voice spoke.

"John? It's Riley...I need to see you...it's urgent. Can we meet? Not in the same place as last time – it's too public."

McManus listened as Riley Gavin suggested somewhere called the Ascona along the coast road at midday tomorrow. She said goodbye and the recorded voice told him the message had been left at eight the previous evening.

He checked the address on the slip of paper Lottie had given him. It wasn't the Ascona, so they must have moved. Never mind – he'd find it. Couldn't be too hard, could it?

He was about to delete the message but decided against it. Better if he left it so Mitcheson could find it later. When he saw how close he might have been, it would kill him.

He grinned and switched off the phone, then went back into the living room and dumped it behind a cushion. There you are, soldier boy, he thought maliciously. By the time you get the message, she'll just be a memory...

34

Riley was edgy. So far Mitcheson hadn't responded to her message for a meeting. Palmer had gone off earlier to watch the Palacio, and although she had argued that she should cover it, he had pointed out that if Mitcheson did call, she should be ready to move quickly. The centre of Malaga wasn't the place to do that.

She finished her drink and went up to her room to go over her notes. After that she lay down on the bed to get some rest. If things were going to start moving, she'd need all the energy she could get. Within seconds she was fast asleep, head filled with tangled dreams of dogs, gun and Peter Willis and his wife, laughing as they queued for check-in at the airport.

As Riley gave in to a restless sleep, downstairs in reception a large man was pushing his way through a crowd of new arrivals clamouring for attention.

McManus used his bulk to get through and held up his car keys to the clerk. "Hire car for Miss Gavin," he announced. "She needs to sign. Can I use the house phone?"

The receptionist, relieved at not having another job to do, told McManus the room number and indicated an internal phone to one side. McManus smiled. This was going to be easy.

The moment the receptionist looked away he replaced the phone and slipped round the corner to check the layout of the exits and the room numbers. Then he went back to his car and parked it at the nearest side door to the emergency staircase. Re-entering the hotel, he went to the lift and punched the call button. In his pocket he fingered a length of nylon cord.

Mitcheson was feeling a growing sense of desperation. His phone had disappeared and he couldn't think where he'd left it. He had to warn Riley before McManus got to her. The man was like a bloodhound and wouldn't stop until he had her. He couldn't take a chance on using the phone in the hall because of the risk of being overheard, and he knew voices echoed in this place.

He checked through his clothes again, then scoured the house a second time, throwing chairs aside. Eventually he came across the cleaning lady tidying up in the living room.

"Have you seen a mobile phone?" he asked her, indicating his shirt pocket. "Cellphone? *Telefono*?" She stared mutely back at him, shaking her head, then turned to arrange the cushions on the chairs.

He continued searching, flicking open doors in the sideboard and checking the wastebasket, his nerves like a series of tiny needles under his skin. Give it two more minutes and he'd go crazy. He turned to watch the cleaner, finally running out of ideas and ready to take the chance with the phone in the hall. To hell with it; he couldn't stand by here and let McManus get his hands on Riley. Just then the cleaner lifted one of the cushions off the sofa and he saw the mobile nestling underneath.

She picked it up and turned to him, holding out the phone with her fingertips. She was frowning and making what he assumed was a Spanish tutting noise, plainly unhappy about something.

Mitcheson switched it on and saw the message symbol

flashing. He punched in the code and listened to Riley's message. As he did so, he felt a sticky substance on the back of the instrument and realised why the cleaner was unhappy, and was now scrubbing furiously with a damp cloth at the sofa. He turned the mobile over. *Red jam?*

His blood ran cold.

He dialled Riley's number.

Riley was shaken by a loud knocking at her bedroom door. Struggling to wake up, she levered herself off the bed, her mouth gummy and dry. She felt a stab of alarm, then told herself it was probably Palmer forgotten his keys. After all, who else knew they were here?

Another knock, this time more urgent, followed by a man's voice. "Police. Open, please."

Riley swore softly, and wondered how they had found her. After the police captain's warning, this meant instant deportation or worse. She stumbled across the room to the door, and had just lifted the safety catch out of its slot when her muddled brain triggered the realisation that the voice sounded wrong.

On the bedside table, her mobile phone began ringing.

She pushed furiously against the door and tried to slide the chain back into place, but the door slammed against her like a battering ram, propelling her backwards into the room. As she fell, she caught a glimpse of McManus's huge shape bearing down on her, a smile of triumph on his face.

Although winded, she broke her fall with the flat of her hands and desperately kicked out with her right foot, connecting with the side of McManus's left kneecap. He didn't even flinch but grasped her foot and twisted it painfully, flipping her on to her face. In his other hand he was holding a length of rope. With practised ease and two turns of the rope, he had Riley effectively neutralised on the floor.

He pressed a foot against the side of her neck and leered down at her. "Ain't no good strugglin'," he told her. "You'll only make things worse." He stepped over to the bedside cabinet where Riley's mobile phone was still ringing and stabbed the 'off' button.

"The good news is, your message got through to soldier boy. The bad news is, he couldn't make it so I've come instead." He flicked the curtain aside and peered out on to the car park. Satisfied the way was clear he came back and lifted her on to the bed. She could smell coffee on his breath and a strong aftershave that made her feel nauseous.

"Now listen, darlin'," he said, face close to hers. "I ain't messin', so don't piss me about. We're goin' walkies. Out of this room, down the back stairs and out to the car park. Simple and easy, okay?"

Riley stared up at him, her revulsion evident by the white-hot look in her eyes.

"Where are you taking me?"

"I said *okay*?" He prodded her stomach with a massive finger, doubling her forward.

She nodded. "Yes...all right."

"Good." He cupped a huge hand around her neck. "Do anything silly, I'll snap your neck like a twig. And believe me, darlin', I've snapped stronger than yours."

He untied the cord from her wrists and flung it to one side, then pushed her across to the door and opened it.

"Remember," he whispered. "One wrong move and you're dead." Then he pushed her out into the corridor.

Mitcheson switched off his phone, a sick feeling in his gut. The phone had started ringing, then been switched off.

Why should she do that?

He went out to the hallway and picked up a local business directory. According to the listing the Ascona was just along the coast road. He dialled the number. No reply. He swore, glancing at his watch. There was plenty of time before the afternoon meeting in Malaga. Lottie Grossman wouldn't like the idea of him going walkabout any more than McManus would, but that was too bad. They didn't own him lock, stock and barrel – not yet.

He found Doug standing by the front door, eyeing the surrounding scenery.

"I'll be back in a while," he told him. "Did McManus go out?"

Doug nodded. "Yeah. I'm still amazed the caveman can drive. He looked like he'd won the Lottery, too. What's going on?"

Mitcheson felt guilty not trusting a man he'd known for a number of years, but he couldn't take the chance. "I'll tell you later," he said. "Keep your eyes open."

The Land Cruiser was free, so he got in and wheeled it down the drive.

When Frank Palmer returned to the hotel for lunch, he walked along the corridor to Riley's room and was surprised to see the door open. Inside he found John Mitcheson standing at the window looking out. The bed was rumpled and Mitcheson was holding a length of nylon cord.

"I wouldn't have thought that was your scene," Palmer said softly.

Mitcheson snapped round, eyes seeking a way out. When he saw who it was, he relaxed slightly, but began to move towards the door. "Frank Palmer, isn't it?" His voice was calm and relaxed, as though meeting an old friend.

The investigator stepped aside and indicated the open doorway. He had no illusions about being able to take on the former soldier; the man was younger, fitter and had the advantage of desperation on his side. All Palmer would get in the process was a trampled body and bruised pride.

"You can go if you like," he said coolly. "I won't stop you. But I'd rather you told me what's happened to Riley first."

Mitcheson stopped and reassessed Palmer. "I don't know," he told him with obvious honesty. "I was supposed to meet her here at midday." He glanced at his watch; it was just gone eleven.

"Bit eager, aren't you?"

Mitcheson ignored the crack. "I think the message was intercepted by McManus. If it was, she's in real trouble."

Palmer indicated the cord in Mitcheson's hand. "Well, I doubt Riley's into bondage, so that could only have been left by your primeval mate. Where would he have taken her – the villa?"

"Not there, no. Lottie Grossman told him to deal with her. Where he takes her is up to him." He glanced at his watch again. "I have to be at a meeting soon. If I don't turn up Riley definitely won't survive."

Palmer nodded. "Well, that gives us a bit of time, doesn't it?" He glanced around the room, then went to the wardrobe where Riley's laptop sat on a shelf. Evidently McManus hadn't been interested in taking anything else. He left it where it was; Riley had already emailed her notes to Brask. He turned back to Mitcheson. "We'd better come up with something bloody quick. And while we're about it, you'd best figure out which side of the fence you're on."

35

Riley felt the skin tightening on the back of her neck and debated driving the Mercedes into the nearest brick wall. But she knew it wouldn't work. McManus was beside her with a handgun in one huge fist and the other hand resting on the seat-back behind her. The proximity of the gun repulsed her almost as much as the touch of his hand.

After leaving the hotel, he had walked her to his car with his arm clamped around her shoulder, then pushed her into the driving seat, handing her the keys.

"You're driving," he told her. "And forget about any silly shunts on the way. Make a wrong move and I'll top you where you sit." As he got in the passenger seat he produced a gun, which he held under his jacket with the muzzle pointing at Riley's stomach. "Yeah. Look at it, darlin'," he muttered. "Imagine what kind of bullet comes out of a barrel this big. Think of the damage it'd do to your body."

She followed his directions on to the coast road towards Malaga, then out to a suburb of narrow streets and shabby housing. Whining mopeds buzzed around the big German car, overtaking on blind corners and slipping through gaps which looked suicidally small. And everywhere delivery trucks of all shapes and sizes seemed to fill the streets, causing jams and minor altercations as motorists leaned out of the vehicles and shouted at each other. McManus's hand moved forward off the seat, resting heavily midway between Riley's shoulder and neck as a reminder not to try anything.

"Slow down." McManus leaned forward as they nosed

along a narrow street, then indicated a parking space ahead. "Pull in there."

Riley did as she was told and cut the engine, shivering as McManus's hand curled warningly over her shoulder. She saw why: a hundred yards ahead, a dark blue car was nosing out of the gates to a house next to a hoarding advertising a new block of flats. A uniformed policeman closed the gates, then stretched a length of plastic tape across the front before climbing into the car. Another policeman stepped out of the front door of the house and closed the door, pinning another length of tape in place, before joining his colleague. Seconds later the car was disappearing down the street.

McManus sniggered quietly. "That's handy. Everything stops for lunch in this country, did you know that?" He pointed forward. "Okay. Up to the gates."

Riley started the car and drove forward. She briefly considered ramming the ironwork in an attempt to escape, but she knew McManus would kill her before they even made contact.

"Keys," McManus ordered, his hand held out as soon as she stopped. She handed them over and he got out and untied the police tape, then opened the gates. Returning the keys, he told her to drive the car inside, then retied the tape before closing the gates behind them.

In one of the Hotel Palacio's small conference rooms, Lottie Grossman looked coldly at Andre Segassa. Alongside her sat John Mitcheson and Howie. They were watching Segassa's escort as he stood against the wall behind his boss.

Doug and Gary were in the corridor, watching the door-ways on each side and the fire exit at one end.

The Grossman party had arrived fifteen minutes early and, to Lottie's annoyance, was being made to wait. Segassa had come down to meet them, but had explained that his colleague was busy on the telephone. In the meantime he had arranged for coffee and sandwiches to be served.

There was a tap at the door and Gary appeared. Behind him stood a man with the wary expression of the professional bodyguard. His eyes flickered around the room and he nodded at the man behind Segassa.

"Man wants us to clear the corridor, boss," said Gary, clearly looking directly Lottie Grossman. "Says the big chief's on his way down."

Mitcheson kept his face blank, although Howie looked surprised. For a brief second nobody moved.

"Very well," said Lottie, and Gary disappeared, followed by the other man.

Lottie leaned closer to Mitcheson and hissed: "Has McManus called? He was supposed to let us know if he'd found the girl."

Mitcheson shook his head, feeling the slow burn of anger and despair. Even with Gary's casual display of transferred allegiance, he was asking himself the same question and trying hard not to freak out at the implications. Right now he was more concerned about Riley's safety than Gary's duplicity. "I haven't heard from him. He went out this morning like you told him."

"I'll have his balls," Lottie grated angrily, ignoring the pointed dig at her orders. "Who the hell does he think he is?"

Moments later an elderly man entered the room. With gold-rimmed glasses and a receding hairstyle, he looked more like an academic than a Moroccan narcotics dealer.

He nodded briefly at Lottie and sat down next to Segassa, produced a gold lighter and lit a cigarette.

"Can we get on with this?" Lottie Grossman said stiffly.

The man paused, cigarette midway to his mouth. He lowered it and stared at the woman with the beginnings of distaste. "You English are so impatient," he said softly. "And discourteous." He puffed on the cigarette, sending a cloud of strongly-scented smoke into the air. "Mr Bignell was also impatient, although always polite...in his own way."

"I'll try to remember that," said Lottie, a flinty look in her eye. "For now I'd like to get things moving. When can we have the first shipment, Mr..?"

"You can have the shipment tomorrow," the man replied, without giving his name. "Make the first payment now and the package will be landed in the afternoon."

Lottie seemed impressed in spite of herself. "That's quick work."

The man shrugged. "We already had the route set up, until you...took over from Mr Bignell. It works – why change it?"

"Isn't it risky, using the same methods?"

The man sighed and looked at the woman as if she was a child who had made a silly remark. Lottie's face coloured beneath her heavy make-up and her pudgy hands balled into fists on the table top.

Alongside her, Mitcheson was struggling to restrain himself. He wanted to grab the stupid old woman by the shoulders and tell her if she continued the way she was going, there wouldn't be any deal and they could all go home again. But at least he could continue his search for Riley.

"If you're using existing routes," Lottie pointed out doggedly, "your costs won't be as high, will they?"

Segassa spoke for the first time. "What are you suggesting – that we give you a special discount? Maybe…buy one, get one free?" The tone was mocking but his eyes were cold as a dead fish.

Lottie ignored the sarcasm. "Why not? We'll increase your volume by ten times what Bignell was shifting."

Segassa nodded. "You know how much Bignell was moving?"

"Peanuts compared with what we can take."

The elderly man stubbed his cigarette out in a glass ashtray and looked questioningly at Lottie. "Have you any idea what twenty kilos looks like? How difficult it is to… to manage?"

"I compare it to bags of sugar," Lottie replied simply. "And how I put it away is my business."

"No. Not quite." The man wagged a finger from side to side, the most animated he had been since entering the room. A faint pulse had started to beat in his throat. "If you make a mistake, Mrs Grossman, it could lead back to us. And that is very definitely *my* business."

In the silence that followed, a vacuum cleaner hummed in the distance. Outside the door a man cleared his throat.

"Now," the elderly man said, rising from his chair and placing his hands flat on the table, "at the risk of being discourteous also, I must go. Do you wish to deal, or not?"

Lottie glared at him, aware the Moroccan was in the stronger position. "All right."

The man nodded and glanced at Segassa. "You know what to do."

He stepped away from the table, then paused and looked back at Lottie. "Payment now, delivery tomorrow. No problems, we do more business."

"What about the other matter?" Lottie's voice was calm,

but with a hint of resentment.

The man nodded. "The travellers. Yes, there is a big demand. Maybe very big. Something we may have overlooked, perhaps." He smiled, self-mockingly. "First, let us see how this arrangement goes. Then we will talk again." He reached into his jacket and took out a white square of thick, glossy paper and flipped it on to the table. It skidded across the polished surface and came to rest against Lottie Grossman's hands.

"A small demonstration of how closely we control things around here, Mrs Grossman," he said pleasantly. "Please do not underestimate my reach."

He left the room and closed the door. Lottie turned over the square of paper and gave a sharp intake of breath. Mitcheson and Howie craned their necks to see what she was looking at.

It was a grainy photo of an elderly man lying on a bed, staring up at the camera. To one side lay a bowl and flannel, and a tube of soap gel.

36

Riley woke with the noise of machinery clattering nearby and a sour taste on her lips. In the distance a horn sounded. She struggled to sit upright and found she was lying on a double bed, her hands bound tightly behind her back with plastic-coated clothes-line. Underneath her was a mess of socks, cuff-links and old newspapers, several cheap plastic cigarette lighters and what looked like the contents of someone's rubbish drawer.

There was an unpleasant smell of stale sweat in the room, and the heat was unbearable. She peered over the edge of the bed and saw clothes scattered everywhere, mixed with crumpled cigarette packets, shoes and dented beer cans. A dresser against one wall looked as if it had been sprinkled with a fine coating of talcum powder, and the drawers had been left drunkenly open or upturned on the floor.

She tested her bindings and felt a rush of pain in her wrists. She swore silently and fluently, which did nothing to lessen the agony but made her feel slightly better about being in such a mess. She shifted over to the side of the bed and swung her feet on to the floor, kicking some of the rubbish aside. Among the papers on the carpet she saw a red passport. She kicked off one shoe and flipped the passport open.

The man looking up at her had been featured in the local paper a couple of days ago. Jerry Bignell. She was in the dead man's bedroom.

Palmer's first and only concrete location to look for Riley was the Villa Almedina. In spite of Mitcheson telling him Lottie had counselled against taking Riley there, he couldn't think of anywhere else to begin. At least the Villa's residents would all be at the Palacio meeting. That left just Ray Grossman alone in his room, with possibly the nurse somewhere near. Palmer decided he would look there first for McManus, and meet Mitcheson outside the Palacio if the gunman or Riley failed to turn up. He didn't like having to trust Mitcheson, but he believed the man's concern for Riley was genuine. Whether that concern would stand up if Palmer or Riley posed a threat to the group's plans, he didn't want to find out.

As soon as Mitcheson left for the Palacio, Palmer drove along the coast road and found a parking area within sight of the turning to the villa. He pulled in, turned off the engine and settled back to wait.

When he reasoned it was safe to assume the group had left, he drove up to the villa. His knock on the door received no answer, so he walked round to the back and tried the patio door. It slid open smoothly and Palmer sent up a prayer of thanks to the God of Carelessness and listened carefully. The only sound was some music playing softly in the depths of the house.

He stepped across to the hall door and listened. The music was louder and seemed to be coming from a corridor to his right. He crossed the tiled hallway and checked through a slit window overlooking the front steps and the drive. There were no cars in sight. Unless McManus had walked from the hotel with Riley slung over his shoulder, it didn't look like the thug was here. Unfortunately, that left several thousand other places to search.

Palmer followed the sound of music, sticking carefully

to the carpet down the centre of the hall. There was a smell of soap and medicines in the warm air, and he guessed there must be a bathroom along here somewhere.

He was just edging past an open doorway when he stopped dead, his breathing suspended. A man was lying on a bed inside the room, looking right at him.

Riley jumped as the bedroom door opened and McManus entered. In one hand he carried his gun, in the other a roll of electrician's tape. He approached the bed and looked down at her, his eyes dulled as if by sleep. "You haven't tried escaping yet, then? I'm disappointed." He reached forward with the gun barrel and lifted the hem of her skirt. When Riley wrenched her legs away he laughed with indifference. "Don't flatter yourself," he grunted, checking her bindings. "I ain't that desperate." As he breathed over her she recoiled at the smell of whisky. For sleep read drinking.

Riley stared up at him with a look of loathing. "Why are you doing this?"

He said nothing for a moment, but there was a taunting expression on his face.

"What's the matter? Pissed off 'cos soldier boy ain't turned up to rescue you?" He leaned over her again and said softly: "He's been feeding you, hasn't he? Letting you in on all our tiny little secrets." He reached down and rested the tip of the gun barrel against her cheekbone, then ran it achingly slowly around her face, first one way then back the other, scoring the metal into her skin in a way she found obscene and terrifying. He stopped for a moment, studying her without blinking, his breath hot and close. Then he pulled the gun barrel down her cheek and inserted the tip into her mouth, the cold steel clicking against her teeth. Riley gagged, the taste of gun oil heavy and musky, and tried to pull her head back, but there was nowhere for her to go. She closed her eyes tight and tried not to let out the scream that was building inside her.

"Well, no more," he said suddenly and stood up, leaving her shaking and nauseous with the ghost of the cold metal still vivid on her flesh. "No more." He began pacing round the room, tapping the barrel of the gun on various objects with a casual flick of his wrist. *Chink*. A small china dog shattered into fragments. *Chink*. A glass photo frame split and fell to the floor. *Chink*. A dirty cup broke in half. *Chink*. A plastic lighter frosted and issued a hiss of escaping gas.

Chink.

Chink.

Chink.

Riley opened her eyes and watched him, aware that the big man was behaving in an increasingly unstable manner, yet powerless to do anything to stop him. "I don't know what the hell you're talking about," she protested. "What do you want?" She had to keep him talking for as long as possible – to stop him from going after Mitcheson and to give her a chance to work out a way of escaping before he lost it completely.

"Nice try, that. Almost innocent." He approached the bed and glared down at her, breathing heavily. "*You think I'm stupid?*" he shouted. Then he stepped back again, looking confused. He stared at the wall, frowning and scrubbing furiously at his face with the back of his hand. "Something I was supposed to do," he muttered. "Call someone...let them know..." He spun round, eyes scouring the room and sweat springing out on his face. The heat was making him more agitated and Riley felt a sudden charge in the foetid atmosphere of the squalid room, as though a powerful force had intruded and was hanging in the air around them. Then McManus seemed to come to. He shook himself and peeled off a strip of the electrical tape from the roll he carried, ripping it with his teeth. Leaning forward, he put the gun barrel to the side of Riley's head and applied the tape across her mouth. Satisfied it was securely in place, he walked to the door. "Just so you don't try screaming for the neighbours. Not that they'd come running, exactly. Don't go away, will you?"

His footsteps shuffled away and she was left to the stifling heat of the bedroom and the nightmare certainty that if her nose became blocked, she would suffocate within minutes.

Frank Palmer didn't like upsetting people, but he was in a sour mood. He sat in a small café across the street from the Palacio, waiting for Mitcheson to emerge. He ignored the dagger looks from a large woman at the next table, who was grumbling loudly about passive smoking, and puffed at his cigarette. He was too busy going over the millions of places McManus could have taken Riley Gavin to worry about disapproving tourists.

He tensed when he saw Mitcheson come out of the Palacio's entrance and stand on the pavement. With him were the two men he recognised as Doug and Howie, and for a second his stomach lurched at the thought that Mitcheson had set him up. He was about to rise from his seat when Mitcheson nodded to the other two and they turned away and walked away down the street.

When they were out of sight, Mitcheson crossed the street and entered the cafe where Palmer was sitting. He grinned at the tense expression on Palmer's face. "Sorry if that gave you a scare. I couldn't just walk out –

they'd have been curious." He ordered lemon tea from the waitress, then looked at Palmer. "We need to give them time to get clear."

"Have you heard from McManus?"

"No. He hasn't reported in yet. Any luck yourself?"

Palmer told him about his visit to the villa. "I saw Ray Grossman."

"He's a sick man, but there's still some fire in his gut. Did he see you?"

"Only if he was looking up from the fires of Hell," Palmer commented coolly. "He was dead."

The large woman at the next table heard the comment and looked horrified.

Mitcheson gave her a nasty look and said: "Did you touch him?"

"You kidding? I stayed just long enough to see he'd definitely copped it and got out of there. It looked like a heart attack. Bad news for his wife, I suppose."

Mitcheson looked doubtful. "I wouldn't bet on it. I doubt she'll care. But I'm not so sure it's great news from my point of view." He explained what had been discussed at the Palacio, and the warning given to Lottie Grossman by the Moroccan. "She took it, but not well. I half expected her to tell me and the lads to kill him there and then."

"Good thing you didn't. So with no Ray Grossman to be used as leverage, she's got a clear field."

"Dead right. And it'll be my lads that cop the flack."

Palmer looked at him, expressionless. "You must have known that when you took this on."

Mitcheson nodded. "Kind of. But when we started out there was no mention of mixing it with a bunch of drug runners and illegal immigrants."

Palmer raised an eyebrow. "So why were you taken on?"

"Protection, mostly. Back then, Ray Grossman was in charge. He wanted some visible muscle to sort out a couple of problems. He heard of us through an ex-army buddy and hired us as a group. We were just to be there in the background for a few weeks. This was before he got really ill. When it happened it was quick and knocked him off his feet."

"Then his wife took over."

Mitcheson nodded. "I knew as soon as I met her that she was poison, but I never expected her to slip into the driving seat so easily." He shrugged. "Or maybe she was in it more than anyone realised. Anyway, she's got ideas above her station, unfortunately… like thinking she's the reincarnation of the Krays."

"Why didn't you quit?"

"We took a vote and decided not to. Big mistake."

"Where does McManus fit in?"

"He's not one of mine. He's been with Ray from way back. He didn't like me and the lads being brought in to help. He figured he could do it all by himself – which he has, so far."

"The killings?"

Mitcheson looked squarely at Palmer, the muscles working in his jaw. "Not all of them. A couple of my lads are down for one. The difference is, McManus enjoys it."

"Thanks for telling me," Palmer muttered. "What's his likely reaction when he finds out his boss is dead?"

The waitress brought Mitcheson's tea and he gulped it down. "Not good. He'll probably blame me." He looked up suddenly. "Christ – I've just had an idea where he might be. You ready?"

37

Riley listened intently for any sound of movement downstairs. She desperately needed to know where McManus was, but the constant noise of machinery from the building site next door drowned out all noise within the house.

She rolled over on the bed and edged her body round until she could feel the plastic lighters behind her. The pain from the bindings was intense, and she knew she had to do something before her hands lost all sense of feeling.

She grasped one of the lighters and twisted it until she could put her thumb against the flint-wheel. The first two tries were useless – her fingers were practically numb and her thumb kept slipping off the wheel. She gripped harder and tried again. This time she felt the heat as the flame caught, but instantly burned her fingers and dropped the lighter.

She picked it up and tried again, but the bindings were so tight there was no room to direct the flame against the plastic for long enough to burn through. She dropped it to the bed and lay back, sweating furiously, her breathing coming in short gasps.

She rolled over on her side and wiped her face against the pillow, and felt the corner of the tape catch on the fabric. With renewed energy, she rubbed harder, gradually feeling the tape coming unstuck.

Then the machinery was switched off.

The silence was stunning. It was as if she had been struck stone deaf, every sound in the world cut off by the throw of a switch.

She waited, not daring to move in case McManus came up to check on her.

When there was no sound from downstairs, she rolled over. Every instinct told her she hadn't long left. McManus sober was bad enough; drunk and resentful he was unpredictable and lethal. She had to do something *now*. She used her knee to move some of the paper rubbish on the bed to see what lay beneath.

It was more rubbish; some socks, two or three different kinds of cheap cufflinks, packets of condoms, several ball-point pens, batteries and other assorted junk. Even a set of gaudily-coloured nail clippers bearing a motif of Malaga.

Nail clippers. She twisted round and scrabbled for them, opening the lever-arm first time. She wiggled the cutting jaws on to a strand of the plastic line and forced the lever down; there was no time for finesse, but the last thing she could afford to do was drop the clippers off the bed.

She felt the jaws cut through the line. Thank God for quality crap, she thought gratefully. I'll buy a dozen pairs if I get out of here…

She twisted her hands, hoping the binding would part, but there was no movement. She moved the jaws again, clamping them over another strand. Hand shut and—damn… slipped… She tried again and this time heard a snick as the jaws closed and felt the plastic part. She gripped the clippers tightly and twisted and pulled with desperate strength in an attempt to force the bindings to slide loose. This time there was the slightest give, and she began to rub her hands back and forth, trying to spread the sweat over her wrists and make them as slick as possible.

There was a faint crunch outside the bedroom door, and Riley had just enough time to lie back and cover the clippers before the door was flung open and McManus entered, red-eyed, his handgun by his side. He looked angry and lost, and it was obvious he had continued drinking. In his other hand he carried a telephone receiver, the broken wire trailing along the floor.

He swayed slightly as he approached the bed, a wave of alcohol surrounding him. He bent down and forced her off the bed to her feet. "Come on," he grunted. "It's *siesta* time and you're going sleepies." He turned towards the door and dragged Riley behind him, losing one of her shoes in the process.

"Where are you taking me?" she mouthed, the sounds distorted behind the gag. As they reached the top of the stairs she tried to hook her foot round a metal banister upright, but McManus tugged her after him like a rag doll.

She bumped down the stairs on her knees and was slammed against the wall at the bottom. McManus pushed the barrel of his gun against the side of her face and leaned on her, his face less than two inches from hers.

"It's not your lucky day, is it?" he breathed, his eyes wild and staring. "Not your lucky day at all." He let go of her and threw the broken telephone receiver to one side. "Won't need that no more."

"What's happened?" Riley asked, trying to delay him. This time her words came out more clearly, although McManus didn't seem to notice.

He tugged her towards the back door. "Happened? Shit's happened, that's what. I've just heard the boss has gone and died on me...and now I've got nowhere to go. Bloody rich, isn't it? After all these fucking years, too, the bitch!" He slammed his gun against a mirror on the wall, shattering the glass. Blood dripped from his hand where he'd been cut, but he seemed oblivious to it.

He dragged her out into the sunlight, the sudden brightness painful to the eyes, the heat intense.

Facing them across the courtyard was a makeshift plasterboard wall. Beyond it Riley saw a towering crane and the skeletal structure of the new building where, until a few minutes ago, men had been working. Now there wasn't a sound.

McManus dragged her over to the wall and slammed her against it, jarring her teeth. Dust fell around her, stinging her eyes and gritty on her tongue. Her mouth was now so dry she couldn't have called out even if she'd wanted to.

McManus reached up and tugged at the top of one of the boards with his free hand, grunting with the effort until it sagged and fell to one side with a dry, rasping sound.

He pushed Riley through the gap and stood looking around for a moment, his great head swaying from side to side. Then he grunted and propelled her towards a small square of posts and planks at one corner of the development. Above the posts hung a large metal shute with a cut-away mouth, shiny and battered with use. A cement lorry stood close by.

As they neared the planks, Riley could see they guarded a deep shaft lined with boards and sprouting rusty metal rods thick as a man's thumb. It was the foundations of one of the main support pillars for the building.

McManus peered over the edge and grinned drunkenly. "Long way down, I reckon," he taunted her. "You any good at diving?"

He began to pull the nearest planks aside and Riley struggled furiously as she realised what he was about to do. McManus seemed unaware, intent only on clearing any obstacles. She waited until he bent over to clear the lip, then twisted her body until she was side on to him. With every ounce of her strength, she stabbed her leg out and downwards, the side of her shoe connecting with the outside of his knee.

Even on a man of McManus's build it was a weak point. There was a crunch as his knee gave way, and he roared with pain and anger and fell sideways, his flailing hand grabbing hold of her clothing and dragging her down with him. He grunted and swore, launching himself on to his knees over her, his eyes blazing with a fierce light and spittle spraying from his mouth.

"Bitch!" he shouted, and grasped her shoulders ready to flip her over the lip of the shaft. As his hands fastened on her, Riley remembered her father telling her that one thing no man ever expected a woman to do when defending herself was to use her head.

"In your dreams, you pig!" she screamed and, as McManus pulled her towards him, she launched herself forward, using his own strength against him.

As her head slammed into his face she felt his breath against her skin and heard a crunch as his nose took the full power of the blow. His hands released their grip and he fell back with a roar of pain, blood spraying down his front.

Riley scrambled away from him, looking for a way out from the building site. Somewhere nearby a car stopped in the street and doors slammed. *Police?*

McManus staggered upright and lifted his gun, spittle and blood dripping from his face, a look of shock and outrage twisting his features. She kicked again, this time at a pile of cement powder at her feet, trying to scoop it up into his eyes.

"*McManus!*" A man's voice shouted from behind her.

There was a blur of movement as somebody ran past her, and she heard a loud slap of something hard against flesh. Then she was grabbed around the waist and dragged away through the gap in the wall, away from what was happening at the lip of the shaft.

The last image she had was of two figures; McManus teetering on the edge of the hole, his arms scrabbling for a hold on thin air; and another man, standing before him. Then McManus seemed to dance backwards before plunging silently out of sight. The other figure began turning away, his face set and hard.

John Mitcheson.

Riley sagged against the man holding her and looked up to see Frank Palmer smiling down at her. "Palmer, you idle bastard," she muttered, fighting the urge to throw up. "I thought you were supposed to be protecting me."

"Yeah, right," Palmer retorted calmly. "Tell that to McManus, why don't you?"

38

Riley opened her eyes and stared out at the passing scenery. She was in the back of Mitcheson's car and they were driving past a row of shops and estate agents, with the tall shape of a holiday hotel in the background. The sky was deep blue without a cloud in sight, and the pavements were crowded with tanned bodies in shorts, T-shirts and sunglasses. She vaguely recognised the outskirts of Malaga on the way to their hotel and slumped back on to the seat, stunned with relief.

"Welcome back," said Palmer, handing her a bottle of water. "You went out for a few minutes there."

She took it gratefully and swallowed half the contents. It was warm and slightly metallic. "What happened?" she asked. Her throat was sore and her voice sounded as though she'd been smoking cigars all her life. She was surprised to find she had both shoes on. "You got my other shoe." Her clothing was another matter; she felt grubby and soiled and covered in a gritty substance. Cement powder. Then she remembered.

"We cleaned up," said Mitcheson, before she could ask. "No clues."

"Except for McManus," she said. She also remembered the cigarette lighter but decided the chance of the police latching on to it was too remote. "Will they notice him?"

Mitcheson shook his head. "I doubt it. That shaft looked deep. Unless he survived the fall and begins to shout, they won't even look. We left the Mercedes where it was."

Riley shivered, imagining the process when the men

returned from their siesta and began pouring cement into the shaft. The gruesome thought was countered by remembering that it could so easily have been herself down there if things had gone differently. "He knew Ray Grossman was dead."

They both looked at her. "He told you?" said Palmer. He looked at Mitcheson. "He must have rung the villa. That's not good."

Mitcheson said nothing.

"He was really upset," Riley continued. "He was drinking heavily and saying he was being cheated."

"I wonder if he told them where he was," Palmer pondered, lighting a cigarette.

"If he did it won't do them much good," Mitcheson responded coldly. "Anyway, as far as they know, he's taking care of Riley...and probably having some fun in the process." He glanced in the rear-view mirror. "Sorry."

Riley preferred not to think about it. If she dwelled on what might have happened, she knew she'd be useless from here on. Right now she had to blot it out of her mind and concentrate on the next moves.

"Won't they look for him?" she asked.

"I doubt it. Lottie'll go berserk but that won't last long. He was always more Ray's man than hers. She'll just convince herself he's had enough being bossed around by a woman and scarpered. The worst he's done is taken the Mercedes. She might put the police on to him for that, knowing her. She's a vindictive woman."

Riley tapped Mitcheson on the shoulder. "What about you?" she asked. "You're not going back to the villa, are you?"

He shrugged and pulled out to overtake a gaggle of cyclists. "I have to," he said quietly. It sounded like the end of the matter, and Palmer glanced across at him, smoke dribbling from his lips. He glanced at Riley and raised an eyebrow.

Riley sat forward on her seat. "Mitcheson, are you mad?" she asked bluntly. "They're about to start running drugs and people into the UK and you think you can carry on working with them? Anyway, why do you *have* to? You talk as though you've signed a blood oath with them."

They had reached the Ascona. Mitcheson pulled into the car park and cut the engine. He looked at them in turn.

"It was me who got the lads into this," he explained. "I was offered the job through a contact providing I brought some men in with me. I knew they were having a hard time after leaving the army, so I recruited them."

"And you feel responsible? But they're big boys now."

Mitcheson nodded. "They served under me in Bosnia." He glanced at Palmer. "Ask him – he knows what I mean."

Palmer shrugged, then got out of the car, followed by Riley. She leaned back in and stared at Mitcheson with a cool expression. "I'm grateful for what you did back there, John," she said quietly, "but I'm not giving up on this one. That woman's got to be stopped. The only way I know is to gather all the information I can and let the police have it. I've already sent a report back to England. Brask will probably run it past the *Review* editor to keep him sweet until I get back. But if he wants to break the story immediately, that's his privilege."

He returned her stare. "Thanks for the warning. I'll bear it in mind." He smiled briefly. "I'm glad he didn't hurt you."

"Get out of it, John," she insisted. "You've got a couple of days at most." Then she turned and walked into the hotel.

Palmer watched her go. He knew she was suffering and

would need some care after what she had been through. On the way to the car he'd asked her if McManus had done anything and she'd said no. He believed her but it still couldn't have been pleasant. He leaned on the car roof and pulled a sheet of paper from an inside pocket. He unfolded it and scanned it quickly.

"Got a fax from a friend of mine in London this morning," he said casually. "He works in military records in Whitehall." Mitcheson looked up but said nothing. "Says here you got in a jam after a couple of tours in Bosnia. Some of your blokes were caught adding a few items to their baggage, apparently, when it was shipped to the UK. Pistols, mostly, some ammo, the odd bit of high-tech battlefield equipment – even an Uzi. War souvenirs, your boys claimed. Surprised they thought it was worth it, the way things are with terrorist scares."

"Is this leading somewhere?" Mitcheson asked coolly. "Only I ought to be going before they miss me."

"Sorry," Palmer remarked dryly. "I forgot you were so conscientious. Where it's leading is, those items of hardware being shipped out of Bosnia by your mates weren't war souvenirs, were they? And neither were they the only items in the bags going back."

Mitcheson frowned. "What do you mean?"

"Is that really what your lads told you at the time? That they were souvenirs? A little something to show the grand-kids? What grandad did in the war in Bosnia?" Palmer shook his head. "It's about time you got wise, Mitcheson."

Mitcheson reached out and grabbed Palmer's wrist. "What are you driving at, Palmer? What else do you know – and why the sudden interest?"

Palmer looked down at the hand gripping his, then with no more than a casual flick, he had Mitcheson's hand bent painfully backwards.

"That," he said conversationally, "was one of the first tricks I learned in training. Useful for when drunken squaddies object to being arrested and try to grip you by the throat. I did my training at a small depot near Chichester, in case you're interested. It's also how I got the information about you and the others." He released Mitcheson and stepped back.

Mitcheson gave him a sour look, then smiled faintly, massaging his wrist. "Redcap, huh? I should have guessed." He seemed to assess Palmer for a moment. "That bit about the bags from Bosnia. What did you mean?"

"Drugs," Palmer informed him. "They were shipping drugs and using the weapons as a diversionary tactic. It worked well for a time, too. Stash a gun where it'll be found and all hell breaks loose…enough to make everyone look in the other direction. That way they also concentrate on anywhere guns can be hidden. And that leaves lots of places where they can't be but where drugs can. Which is where the real money is. As a bonus they even got to sell any weapons that did get through. Until they got careless, anyway."

"How come I never heard about this?"

"The army covered it up. They didn't want it known that any of our UN chaps were shipping in drugs bought on the Serb black market. Bad publicity, you see. Especially involving men with good records. Unfortunately, you went in to bat for them, didn't you, without thinking about it? As an officer that was enough to ruin your career." His eyes bored into Mitcheson with growing amazement. "You really didn't know, did you?"

Mitcheson shook his head. "No. I did wonder, but they denied it. Just souvenirs, they said. Seemed best to let it go after that, the way things turned out. As you say, it was enough to kill my career prospects." He looked through the windscreen, his eyes suddenly cold. "I had no idea."

"You were used, Mitcheson," Palmer said brutally. "Just like you're being used now. Pity your lads don't set as much store by loyalty as you do."

He stepped back and watched Mitcheson drive away.

39

Mitcheson sensed the atmosphere the moment he arrived at the villa. Gary nodded without meeting his eyes, and he could see Doug scouting the trees to one side. Howie was standing by the pool as backup.

Lottie Grossman was in the living room, smoking and staring out at the water. Painted and powdered as usual, she seemed amazingly calm considering her husband had died and one of her men had disappeared with a valuable car.

"Glad you could make it," she muttered, echoing her late husband's words. "Ray's dead." She began clicking her nails together in irritation, and Mitcheson readied himself for the inevitable blast. He wondered what was annoying her more – her husband's death or McManus's disappearance.

"I thought I'd follow Segassa and his boss," he said. "Just in case we need to know where their base is. Sorry to hear about Ray."

Lottie looked surprised. "You followed them? Where to?"

"A hotel the other side of Malaga. It's probably a temporary base. They must have come in specially for the meeting but I doubt they'll hang around long." He wondered if it sounded as plausible to her as it had to himself as he walked into the house. Nothing like living on the wing to get the blood going.

"Good thinking," she said, eyes sweeping over him. After a moment her face seemed to click shut on the subject but he could see she was still burning over something. Her next words confirmed it. "I still don't like it. McManus called earlier. Unfortunately, one of your men answered the phone and told him Ray was dead and he rang off without saying where he was. We don't know if he got the Gavin woman or not – and we still haven't seen this Palmer who's working with her. If McManus hasn't got the girl she could still make trouble."

"Maybe he's dealt with Palmer as well."

She shrugged and took a deep breath, then said with studied calmness: "I'm flying my husband's body home tomorrow or the next day, after the local coroner has signed a release. And after we've completed the deal."

"Okay." Mitcheson gently let his breath out, relieved she seemed to have been temporarily diverted from focusing her paranoia on him. "What about the payment?"

"Tomorrow. At the same time as the delivery."

Mitcheson raised his eyebrows, remembering how adamant the Moroccan had been. Payment today, delivery tomorrow.

"I arranged it with Segassa by phone," Lottie informed him smugly. "After all, how could I know they wouldn't just skip with our money?"

No wonder she looked so pleased with herself, he thought. It made sense, but it put more pressure on him and his men. Taking delivery of illegal goods was problem enough; having to exchange them simultaneously for large amounts of money was compounding the risk.

Her next statement was like a cold shower. "There won't, of course, be any money."

"Come again?"

"We take the drugs and keep the money. Simple."

He stared at her. "You can't be serious. Those people can't be messed with, for God's sake. They're killers – we've already seen that."

Lottie seemed unconcerned. "The others don't agree.

It's manageable."

So she'd already run it by the others. Well, now he finally knew where he stood. It looked like Palmer was right: his hold over the men had been severed. Or maybe it had never really been there in the first place.

"But what you're doing will kill off the whole supply-line. What about the illegals? How the hell do you think Segassa's boss will deal with you for people when you've screwed him over drugs? We'll be lucky to leave Spain in one piece." He stared at her, trying to figure out whether she had gone completely insane or if she knew something he didn't. Then it hit him. "You've come to a separate deal with Segassa."

"I can't afford to lose another man, Mr Mitcheson," Lottie admitted, not bothering to deny it. "If McManus comes back, all well and good. Somehow I doubt it. And while the men are good at what they do, I need you to organise them." She stubbed out the cigarette. "Andre Segassa has been waiting to establish his own operation and will deal with his own contacts on the other side. I need to cover things here. I'll double your contracted amount and pay another seventy-five thousand on completion."

As she was speaking, Gary entered the room and stood by the door. At the same time Howie drifted across the patio to stand directly outside the glass doors. Doug was nowhere to be seen, but Mitcheson knew he wouldn't be far away. It was a clear and chilling indication of what would unfold if he told Grossman he didn't want any part of her plan.

"All right," he nodded and, because it was probably expected, added, "but make it a hundred thousand... There's more risk involved."

Lottie Grossman smiled, her painted lips a small, obscene rosebud of victory. He was speaking a language she understood. "Agreed. Let's have dinner and go over the plans, shall we?"

While Palmer sat smoking by the window, Riley finished her next batch of notes and dialled up to email them to Brask. The fat man had been effusive when Riley phoned him earlier, saying the first batch she sent had already aroused a lot of interest. The *Review* editor was pushing for more.

Encouraged by Palmer to focus on work, Riley had sunk herself in the detailed task of collating the facts and adding her own comments. It had prevented her being overtaken by thoughts about the near miss with McManus at the building site.

As the machine beeped obediently, Riley looked at Palmer. "You think Mitcheson will come through?"

"I reckon." He'd shown Riley the details Charlie had faxed from London concerning the extent of Mitcheson's involvement in the Bosnia business. Her relief had been obvious. "But time will tell."

When he'd gone, Riley closed the laptop and lay down on her bed, staring at the ceiling. The image of Mitcheson's face became that of McManus's, leering down at her with blood streaming from his smashed nose, eyes glinting with hate and frustration. She shivered and wrapped her arms across her chest, and wondered if Mitcheson would have nightmares about the gunman's death down the shaft.

The following morning Riley's mobile signalled a message from Mitcheson. His voice was low and unemotional, and she guessed he must have been calling from the garden of the villa. She listened intently, then rang Palmer and arranged to meet him downstairs for breakfast.

By the time he joined her she was demolishing a plate of bacon and eggs.

He sat down and poured a cup of coffee before lighting his first cigarette of the day.

"For Christ's sake, Palmer," Riley protested, waving the smoke away, "at least let me get some food down before you smoke us both to death. God, you're so unhealthy. Did the package go off?"

He nodded and doused the cigarette. "Done and dusted, boss. So what's the news from our man on the inside?"

"According to John, Lottie Grossman's got it into her head she can cheat the Moroccans and take the drugs and the money. She's sweet-talked the one called Segassa into dealing direct with her instead of through his boss, and got Mitcheson's men seeing things her way. He thinks he'd have joined McManus by now if he'd showed signs of backing out."

Palmer whistled silently. "So much for army buddies. And Lottie must be off her trolley. Segassa will bide his time then skin her alive."

"Should we warn Mitcheson about Segassa?"

Palmer shook his head. "It won't change anything. When and where's the deal going through?"

"There's a stretch of coast just before Motril where the government's doing some underwater survey work. Boats coming and going all the time, and another one won't be noticed. The Moroccans have tested it out twice recently and reckon it's safe. They're going for an exchange at midday today."

"Did he say how?"

"The Moroccans are using a flotation device to drop the drugs off from a small fishing boat. The device keeps the package just below the surface. The Grossman boat dumps a small buoy over the side with the money, and each boat picks up its package as it goes by."

"Neat," Palmer commented. "With two ex-Royal Marines in Howie and Doug, it'll be a doddle."

"Right. And the boats go their separate ways with nobody the wiser."

"Until the Moroccans find they've been cheated. If Segassa doesn't do his part it could be messy."

Riley looked sourly at him. "You're probably right. John doesn't like it, either."

"So what's he going to do?"

Riley frowned. "He didn't say."

40

Had anyone stopped the *Soukia* as it ploughed a course off the island of Alboran they would have found an ordinary fishing boat that had been making the same run for years. A cursory inspection would have uncovered nothing more interesting than nets, ice-boxes and wet-weather gear, with a crew of three tanned, grizzled men in their fifties.

The only unusual piece of equipment would have been a set of scuba gear with some minor modifications which one of the men was sitting on while he mended a stretch of damaged netting. Attached to the equipment by strong plastic strapping was a large rubber-cased box that no fishing vessel normally carries, and which the man was ready to dump over the side should any naval or coast-guard vessels come too close.

In the tiny wheelhouse the skipper cocked his head to one side and answered his mobile phone. He listened for a while, then glanced at a map and gave their position before switching off the phone.

Midday off the coast near Motril, and they could begin their journey home.

Riley pulled the car off the road near a short stretch of beach and glanced at her watch. It was 11.30. She looked across at two small hotels nestled against a backdrop of sandy rock and coarse, scrubby trees. The Hotel Palma was neat and brightly painted in white and sea-blue, while its rival, the Flores, was a modern aluminium and glass creation. The road here followed a sharp curve in the coastline, clinging to a steep drop down to the sea, and other than the small line of sand which had largely been man-made to bolster the two hotels, there wasn't much to attract tourists.

Offshore a cluster of small vessels was moored in haphazard fashion, with bright marker-buoys bobbing gently on the waves among them. Other vessels moved back and forth, heading east and west towards Almeria and Malaga. Most were gleaming white with flashes of shiny chrome attachments, and crewed by people for whom this was a highway to pleasure and relaxation.

Palmer raised his head from the back seat and picked up a pair of binoculars he had purchased that morning in Malaga. They wouldn't have impressed a genuine naval officer, but they were quite sufficient for his needs.

"I hope you don't intend claiming for those on expenses," Riley said dryly.

"Of course not. I put them on yours." He focused on the moored craft. There was little activity except for a small semi-rigid boat with two men on board. They were holding station near the marker-buoys and as he watched, a black-suited figure popped up from the water and passed up what looked like a large, yellow underwater camera. One of the two men on board took it from him, while the other helped him clamber over the rounded gunwale.

"Might be part of the survey crew," he said. "Looks like they're getting ready to go to lunch."

Riley was looking towards the hotels, where a few vehicles were parked and a coach was unloading tourists. A Land Cruiser was just pulling in from the Malaga direction, its gleaming windows masking the occupants.

She had been toying with the idea of seeing if they could

rent a sea-facing room for the afternoon, but dismissed it. It would have been a good observation point but would probably lead to gossip about their arrival. And she doubted the Grossman group was the only one interested in current comings and goings at this particular point today. .

She pulled a floppy hat from the back seat and grabbed a beach bag. "Come on," she said, donning her sunglasses. "Time to hit the beach. I think the enemy's arrived."

Palmer followed her glance towards the Land Cruiser in front of the Palma hotel. "Right. But which enemy are you talking about?"

He clamped on a baseball cap and got out of the car, dropping the binoculars into a plastic bag. His pale legs stuck out from a pair of tan shorts, and his loose cotton shirt flapped in the breeze.

Riley looked at him and raised her eyebrows. "Palmer – you're a sight."

"Don't knock it," he answered cheerfully. "I've had my moments."

"Yeah…but when?"

They walked down on to the beach and sat just below road level. From here they had a good view of the sea, the beach and, if they peered over the top, of the hotels and car park as well as the road from both directions. There were few people on the sand, and they guessed many had gone in for lunch. Out at the survey site, the boats were silent and deserted.

They settled back to wait. Occasionally Palmer raised his binoculars to scan the horizon, while Riley applied sun-cream to her arms and legs.

After a few minutes Riley heard a car door slam, and risked a peek back at the Land Cruiser. She was just in time to see a man walking away from the vehicle and entering the Palma. It was too brief a look to see whether it was John Mitcheson or one of his men.

A crunch of tyres on gravel drew her attention to the other end of the car park, as a nondescript white Toyota stopped near the Flores and parked away from the other vehicles. When no one got out, Riley nudged Palmer.

"Fancy some lunch, Frank?" she asked. "My treat."

He rubbed his eyes. "Lead the way, boss. As long as there's a gallon of iced water involved, I'm game."

They picked up their bags and walked across to the Flores, away from the Land Cruiser. As they neared the Toyota, Riley risked a glance from behind her sunglasses. She could just make out the shape of a driver through the glass, but no detail.

Inside, the Flores was cool and airy. A lounge area ran along the front of the building, with a canopy over the glass to provide shaded viewing of the sea and beach. Riley ordered sandwiches and drinks, and they sat down and waited to see what happened.

Six miles out from the coast the *Soukia* was nearing the end of its run before landing its catch at a small harbour near Almeria. The skipper scanned the horizon, eyes alert for a boat approaching or the sudden arrival of the Spanish coastguard. He also checked the sky for the telltale dot of a helicopter; the drugs patrols were using newer and more modern methods to track down boats like the *Soukia* and the risk was increasing daily.

Yet they had been lucky for a long time. Easy runs with no problems other than having to deal with Bignell, the drunken Englishman. Now, though, things had changed; the Englishman had gone and a woman had taken his place. He hawked and spat over the side. She wouldn't last, the fat woman. She didn't sound as though she knew what she was doing. Still, there would always be someone else to take her place, eager to trade for the powdered gold or anything else with a commercial value.

A shout from one of his men made him look ahead. A speck was curving round on an intercept course towards them. He throttled back and shouted for his men to get the package ready.

The speck became a fast, white launch favoured by the pleasure-seekers on the beaches of Spain. A would-be rich man's toy that would not stand the first big wave that hit it. Ideal for this kind of job, though.

With another glance skywards to check for aircraft, he waved a hand and his men jettisoned the rubber package and scuba-gear over the side, where it sank just below the surface, its position marked by a small coloured buoy.

He saw a similar marker-buoy fall away from the approaching launch, and increased his own speed towards it. The launch growled past a hundred metres away, its twin screws lifting its nose clear of the waves. There were two men on board, both in their middle thirties, looking tanned and fit. The skipper noticed they stood in the launch with a relaxed stance, like men accustomed to the sea. With a faint hint of anxiety he realised these men weren't amateurs.

As the launch fell back and curved round to pick up the package, the skipper picked up his mobile phone and watched. It was as he thought; the boat had not even stopped and was now powering back towards the mainland. Very smooth.

He slowed the *Soukia* alongside the marker-buoy and watched his men lean out with a hook to snag the rope.

After the other boat's display of expertise, he hoped they caught it first time and didn't expect him to come round for a second try. He was about to press the send button on the mobile to confirm all was okay, when he saw that, instead of a rope and package, there was nothing attached to the buoy but lead weights which kept it upright in the water.

He turned to shout at the launch. To his horror, instead of disappearing towards land, it had slowed and crept up alongside and was now reducing speed to match his own. One of the men was standing against the gunwale. He was holding a gleaming black machine pistol.

The skipper desperately slammed the throttle open and felt the engine rumble beneath his feet. With his free hand he stabbed the send button on the mobile, but it was too late. The gun chattered briefly, and he looked back to see both his men knocked overboard as they tried to run.

As he screamed out what was happening into the phone, hoping someone was listening, the launch surged forward until it was alongside the wheelhouse. The man with the gun grinned mirthlessly, his face absurdly young, and changed magazines. Then, as casually as if he was spraying flowers, he pressed the trigger and spewed the contents of the new magazine through the open wheelhouse door.

41

The white Toyota was halfway across the car park before it registered on either Riley or Palmer that something had happened. With tyres screaming it skidded on the gravel and out on to the road heading towards Malaga, nearly hitting a local bus coming the other way. In the Flores lounge, tourists craned their necks, muttered disapproval, then returned to their meals.

"Someone forgot an appointment, you reckon?" Riley asked.

"Either that or someone closer to home," Palmer replied enigmatically.

"Segassa's men?"

But Palmer was already rising, and Riley grabbed her bag. "You pay – I'll get the car," she said, and hurried through the sliding doors out to the car park.

Palmer called the waiter over and settled the bill. As he was about to follow Riley, a figure stepped up alongside him. He turned and found himself looking at the smiling face of Doug.

"Well, as I live and breathe," Doug smiled, "if it isn't Frank Palmer, ace investigator." He prodded Palmer in the ribs with something hard. It was a large automatic pistol with the safety catch off.

"I haven't got my computer with me today," Palmer said dryly, "if that's what you're after." He risked a quick glance across the road to where Riley was digging in her bag for her car keys. He guessed the ex-Marine hadn't spotted her and turned to keep the man's attention on himself.

Very carefully, he put his cigarette lighter down on the table beside his binoculars.

"Good one, Frank," Doug smiled. "Very funny, considering your position. Come on – we're going for a ride, you and me." He picked up the binoculars and motioned for him to lead the way out of the door. They walked across to the Land Cruiser, where Doug opened the door and shuffled Palmer into the driver's seat. Then he hopped into the rear door, the gun never shifting away from Palmer for an instant, and threw the binoculars into the back. "Okay, Frank. Let's head for Malaga."

Palmer pulled out of the car park and followed Doug's directions. He'd never driven one of the big cars before, and found the size uncomfortable after the small hire car he'd been using. The gun at his back didn't help. As he passed Riley, she was leaning on the roof of the car, staring out to sea, unaware of what had happened behind her. He sighed with relief and pressed his foot down.

"Have you been following me?" he asked Doug. He could feel the man's gun resting on the seat against his back and detected the familiar smell of gun oil.

"You kidding? I thought it was the other way round. That's what you snoopers do, isn't it – follow people?"

Palmer said nothing, aware that if he let too much slip it could endanger Mitcheson's position. It wouldn't take the gang long to work out that Mitcheson's earlier absence could have been for entirely different reasons than searching for McManus. And as one of the handful who knew the arrangements for bringing in the drugs at this point along the coast, the finger of suspicion would soon be pointing Mitcheson's way.

"Where's the girlfriend, by the way?" Doug asked.

"In Malaga. Shopping," said Palmer.

The gun tapped on his shoulder. "Speed, Frank. Keep it down, there's a good fella. We don't want to get hauled over, do we?" He chuckled at the thought, then leaned closer to Palmer. "Now, while we're all comfortable and that, what were you doing out here? Sunbathing all by yourself? You don't look very tanned – and where did you get those shorts?"

Palmer racked his brains for a reason that would sound halfway plausible without dragging Mitcheson into it. If they suspected the ex-officer was looking for a way out, they would have no choice but to deal with him the same way as Bignell.

"The white Toyota in the car park back there," he said finally. "Did you see it go like a bat out of hell?"

"Yeah – I saw that. Thought he was going to bend himself round that bus for a moment. Spanish drivers, eh? What about it?"

"He was supposed to be one of Bignell's men. He said he had information about the set-up."

"Set-up?"

"The drugs route Bignell had been using. He said if I came to this beach, he'd show me where the stuff used to be landed. They used the survey boats as cover, he reckoned." Palmer added a touch of accusation to his voice. "He must have spotted you and decided to take off."

The seat back shifted as Doug leaned back to consider the details. Evidently it sounded likely enough to the ex-Marine. He shrugged and pointed through the front window. "See that sign for new apartments?" They were travelling along a short, deserted stretch of road with arid grass and rock on either side. Up to the right on the hillside, two or three ramshackle farm buildings were the only signs of local habitation. A giant hoarding advertising

234

a building development was coming up on the left. "There's a small turning just after it. Swing left there."

"Where are we going?"

Palmer sensed the grin on Doug's face. "We're going shopping, Frank. Like your girlfriend."

Riley swore silently as she waited for Palmer to appear, and drummed impatiently on the roof of the car. Whatever had got into the Toyota driver she felt sure it was connected with the Grossman business. And if that was the case, she hoped it wasn't going to be bad news for John Mitcheson.

Out on the horizon a boat was cutting a white path through the waves, its prow high in the air. It looked as though it was heading down the coast towards Malaga and the vast boat-parking lot they called a marina. Where the hell was Palmer?

When she looked round towards the hotel to see where he'd got to, she felt a sudden jolt in her stomach. The Land Cruiser was gone.

Palmer followed Doug's directions and swung round the hoarding on to a narrow track heading towards the sea. The surface was rough and overgrown with grass but the Land Cruiser flowed over the bumps and through the potholes with barely a sign. They passed derelict huts and some rusting machinery before emerging between two small hills on to a tiny plateau above the sea. The water was a deep, brochure blue, and melted into the sky along the horizon. As they neared the edge a white arrow cut across the blue surface of the water and moved inshore, the boat bouncing from wave to wave.

Doug told him to park the vehicle facing back the way

they had come, then climbed out, motioning Palmer to follow. "Come on, Frank. I've got some work for you. I hope you're feeling strong."

They followed a narrow path down the side of the slope to a flat, rocky platform just above the waterline. Palmer felt suddenly vulnerable here; he wasn't the world's best swimmer, and either side of the platform the water looked dark and threatening. It was a geological oddity, and he guessed the lack of room and the swirling currents made it unattractive to tourists. Ideal, however, for drug-runners.

A powerful-looking white launch was nosing in towards the platform and Palmer recognised the muscular form of Howie standing at the wheel. A younger, smaller man sat on the prow clutching a rope with a small grappling anchor attached. In his other hand he held an automatic, a quizzical look on his face.

"Easy, Frank," Doug warned him. "The little fella's a bit touchy on the trigger."

Howie was evidently expert at handling boats, and nosed the launch against the rock with the barest kiss, while the younger man tossed the anchor across. Palmer let it bounce on the rock before bending to settle it into a crack where it would hold fast.

"How'd it go?" Doug called across as the engine died.

Howie nodded and jumped ashore. "It went. What's he doing here?" His gaze was not unfriendly – merely curious.

Doug grinned and looked at Palmer. "You remember Frank, don't you? Of course you do. Frank's volunteered to help us carry the goods." His eyes turned cold and he hefted the pistol. "The alternative being we shoot him right now and drop him in the water."

42

Riley crossed the road back to the Flores and checked everywhere. The feeling of unease in her stomach increased dramatically when she saw Frank's cigarette lighter still lying on the table. Palmer wouldn't have gone without it. She asked one of the waiters to check the washrooms. He came back shaking his head.

She ran outside and across to the car, a clear image in her head of the Land Cruiser. If only she had kept an eye on it.

She floored the accelerator, pulled the small car round in a tight circle and set off towards Malaga. If Palmer was anywhere, she was betting it had to be in the Land Cruiser, and she could only be a few minutes behind it.

Traffic was light and consisted mainly of slow-moving hire cars and the odd delivery van. Riley was able to leap-frog them quite easily. She shut her mind off from why Palmer had been taken and what his captors might have in mind. If they intended to kill him, they could have done so in the car park and no one would have been able to stop them.

The questions still remaining were: who had been in the vehicle, and why were they there? Top of the list was to watch over the exchange, but it didn't rule out the possibility that somehow the Grossman group had got wind of her and Palmer's presence and had decided to take whichever one they could get.

But if so, how had they found out? Had Mitcheson talked? Unlikely. And why not take her, too? Maybe they didn't need both of them.

A horsebox had pulled in to a side turning near a large advertising hoarding, and the driver was scrubbing the windscreen. Riley swerved round the protruding back end of the vehicle and put her foot down. If all else failed, there was one place left to go. But as double insurance, she pulled out her mobile phone and dialled Donald Brask's number in London.

When the Land Cruiser emerged from the side turning a few moments after Riley had passed, Palmer was in the back seat, hands tied in front of him with a length of rope.

In the front, Doug was driving while Gary lounged in the passenger seat, eyes flicking back and forth to watch Palmer. Howie had been left to take the boat back along the coast to the marina in Malaga.

All talking had stopped as the two men kept their eyes open for police or customs. Palmer guessed the easy part for the men had been out at sea. Here inland was another ball game, and even a simple traffic accident greatly enhanced their chances of being subjected to closer scrutiny than they wanted.

After Palmer had been forced to carry a large rubber package up the path to the Land Cruiser, the men had tied him up and left him in the back while they reported in by mobile phone – presumably to Mitcheson and Lottie Grossman. He hadn't been able to catch any of their conversation, but the description by Howie and Gary of their sea trip had been animated and triumphant. When Gary had produced a machine pistol from the launch and what looked like two empty magazines, he could see why.

They arrived back at the villa and Palmer was bundled out and made to lie down in a utility room at the back.

Lottie Grossman appeared shortly afterwards and stood gazing down at him as though he was an insect that had wandered in from the garden. She held a pruning knife with a curved blade. He found it amazing she could be gardening while people were being killed and kidnapped. It was the first time Palmer had seen the woman close-to, and he was surprised at her age. At a time when most people were thinking of taking things easy, this painted harridan seemed intent on breaking the mould by starting up a whole new criminal enterprise. Oddly, while her clothes looked expensive, the thickness of her make-up gave her the appearance of a cheap, gaudy doll.

He spotted Mitcheson in the background, his face blank. The other men hovered close by, evidently waiting to see what their leader was going to do. Palmer began to understand what it was like to be a bug in a laboratory, awaiting vivisection.

The tension in the small room was palpable, and Palmer felt a sudden need to belittle the woman and show he wasn't intimidated by her efforts to be the ruthless gangster. It was childish and potentially dangerous, but he smiled and said: "Sorry to hear about the old man, Lottie. Must have come as a big relief to have that old bastard out of your hair."

She turned away without a flicker of reaction. When she came back she was holding a black automatic pistol gripped in both hands. She pointed it at Palmer's head.

The expression on Mitcheson's face would have had Palmer laughing in other circumstances, and even Doug stood with his mouth open in shock.

"No!"

As the woman's finger tightened on the trigger, Mitcheson leapt forward and pushed her arm upwards.

He stared down into Lottie Grossman's face, reaching for the gun with his other hand and extracting it gently but firmly from her grasp.

The others stood rock still, the pool pump the only noise.

"We need him," Mitcheson continued, passing the gun behind the woman's back to Gary, who checked the safety catch. "We can use him as insurance. Until we know for sure that the Gavin woman's out of the picture, we need some leverage."

Lottie Grossman blinked and looked down at Palmer, her breathing heavy. Then she turned to the other men. "Do you agree?"

They exchanged looks, clearly baffled by her decision to include them on the investigator's fate. Doug was first to react. Flicking a brief glance towards Mitcheson, he nodded. "Makes good sense," he admitted.

The other two nodded and Lottie Grossman turned back to Mitcheson. "Very well. Keep him here until we leave." She looked at her watch. "My husband's body will be released at three. We leave for the airport as soon as it's on its way. I've had clearance to use the plane instead of a commercial flight. Gary, make sure the pilot's ready with his flight plan? Good. The rest of you know what to do."

As they left the room, Palmer let his breath out in a trickle. Jesus, he thought. Me and my big mouth. That was close.

He thought about what the woman had said. Leaving this afternoon? He sneaked a look at his watch. It was nearly one-thirty. Where the hell had the time gone? And what were they going to do with the drugs they'd picked up?

He settled back to work on loosening the rope around his wrists. The knots were efficient and the rope slightly damp, which didn't help, but he couldn't simply sit there and wait. While he flexed his hands to work up a sweat, he listened to the sounds of movement throughout the villa. Doors and drawers were being closed and what sounded like cases being dropped on to the tiled floor at the front of the house. It was obvious they were preparing for more than a simple departure until next time. They were evacuating the place. Voices were muffled and low, but he thought he recognised Mitcheson and the two baseball fans. The young one, Gary, seemed to have least to say, but he put his head round the door from time to time to check on Palmer.

"Any chance of a drink?" Palmer asked. He was feeling dehydrated, but more than anything he wanted to test the man's reaction. If Gary refused him, it meant Palmer's future was going to be very limited, no matter what the general vote on his usefulness had been.

Gary went away without a word and returned several minutes later with a glass of orange juice. He stood over Palmer while he drank, then took the glass off him as soon as he had finished. Palmer had the feeling Gary was disappointed Mitcheson had stopped Lottie blowing his head off all over the utility room wall. On the other hand, giving him a drink must mean they had a use for him.

He handed back the empty glass and settled back to listen and continue working on his bonds. It was surprisingly tiring work and the flexing of his arms and wrists made his whole upper body feel unbearably heavy. He shook his head and stared up at the ceiling, a gritty feeling around his eyes. Must be the heat, he thought. And the shock of being picked up and nearly shot. Or maybe I'm getting old. He stopped what he was doing for a moment and felt his head dropping like an enormously heavy weight, his thoughts becoming scrambled. He tried to lift it again, sucking in air, but it was no good. Way too tired...

Riley slid over the low stone wall and pushed through the trees surrounding the villa to watch the preparations to leave. The patio furniture was tidied away and through the windows she could see dust covers being placed on the chairs and tables inside. From the front of the house she could hear the slamming of doors as vehicles were loaded with luggage.

There was no sign of Palmer. She'd have to get a look inside the house to see if he was here. She glanced at her watch and wondered how Brask was getting on. She'd relayed to him what had happened to Palmer, and that it was time to bring in official help, preferably on both sides of the Med. He'd been doubtful the police would pay any attention without some official corroboration from the Spanish side, but promised to try. He would also try to get Customs & Excise excited about the Cessna, since that, at least, might be carrying some of the guns used by the ex-soldiers. Even if they came up with traces of ammunition or gun oil, it would show that focusing some attention on Lottie Grossman's activities would be worthwhile.

A car started at the front of the house and faded away down the drive. Riley chewed her lip. It looked like they were off. There might not be a better time to do it.

She pushed through the branches until she was clear of the overhang. Seconds later she was running across the lawn, body hunched and expecting any second to hear a warning shout. She hit the back of the villa and ducked down, her breathing harsh and loud. That's it, she promised herself; when this is all over, I'm joining a gym. All this work and no play's turning me into a soft pudding.

She pressed her ear against the brickwork and listened. Apart from the hum of an electric motor there was nothing. She crept along the rear wall, peered round the corner…and ducked back as voices sounded nearby.

Something scraped behind her. She began to rise but found a powerful hand pressing down on her shoulder. Another hand clamped over her mouth.

"Easy," Mitcheson hissed in her ear. He held on to her until she subsided, then let her go.

"Where's Palmer?" Riley whispered, spinning round. Her heart was thumping in her chest and a wave of nausea threatened to rise in her stomach. "Is he okay?"

He placed a finger against her lips. "No time. We're off to the airport. Lottie's taking a private plane back to England. Ray's body's inside. Gary's going too, with Palmer as insurance…He's been sedated. The rest of us are following by scheduled flight to Heathrow this evening."

"And the drugs?" Riley's face was centimetres away from his, and she could smell his aftershave, see her reflection in his eyes. Something told her this man couldn't lie this close up to her.

He hesitated for a moment, then said: "They're strapped to Palmer's body."

"What? They're going to take him through customs?"

"No. They've filed a flight plan to Luton for customs purposes, but she's paid the pilot for a last minute diversion to Rickmansworth, claiming engine trouble. Less likely they'll be searched there, especially with a coffin on board. In any case, they're counting on enough time to get Palmer away before anyone arrives."

Someone called Mitcheson's name from the front of the building. He clamped his hand back on Riley's mouth but she angrily pushed his fingers away. "Where are they

243

taking Palmer?"

"Horton Road commercial estate, West Drayton. Unit twenty-four. Once they're in the UK they'll have no further use for him. I'll try to stop it but I can't promise anything."

As he stood, Riley put a warning hand on his arm. He frowned. "What is it?"

"I've arranged for the police in the UK to be called in. They haven't got your name, but they'll be waiting for the plane…at Rickmansworth. It's where I guessed they'd land."

Mitcheson frowned. "Christ. That's all we need. Okay. I'll see if I can get them to go in somewhere else, although if Palmer's caught it'll be pretty obvious he's not doing it voluntarily. Anything else?"

"There was another car along the coast where Palmer got picked up. It's either the Moroccans or the Spanish police. They could be on their way here already."

He nodded. "We haven't got long, then. Thanks for the warning."

"What are you going to do?"

"Whatever I can for Palmer, I promise. You keep your head down. Take care." With a brief touch on her arm, he was gone.

43

Riley shivered as a vicious wind cut across the top level of Terminal One car park at Heathrow, bringing a faint sting of rain on her cheeks. Dark clouds had brought the evening in earlier than usual, a stark contrast after the heat and light of Spain.

She'd been hoping to go out to Rickmansworth to try to intercept Lottie Grossman's plane, but in the end knew there was too high a risk of missing them. They would have already arrived and Palmer would be long gone by now, spirited away before he was spotted. On the off chance, she'd called the airfield and asked if the Grossman Cessna had returned, but the woman on the other end had been guarded about flight movements.

In the end, with daylight making it too risky to hang around a trading estate too long, she decided to wait at Heathrow for the Malaga flight to arrive and follow Mitcheson and the others to their destination. She was praying nothing would happen to Palmer until the group was together.

She checked her watch. Nearly time to go. She hurried down to the ground floor and found a quiet spot away from the noise. Brask answered on the first ring. As soon as Riley left the villa at Moharras, she'd called and told him what was happening. He had promised to get whatever official interest he could. Now he sounded less than hopeful.

"I've bent every ear I can, sweetie," he said, "but there seems to be a marked reluctance to do anything. The only thing in our favour is there aren't customs facilities at

Rickmansworth to clear the body, so Grossman must be planning to just drop in and take a punt on getting it through without being spotted. However, that may be the official view – I don't know what the uniformed pinheads may be planning on the quiet, of course. For all I know they may be getting together the massed ranks of the Metropolitan Police Band and Customs & Excise and descending on Heathrow and Rickmansworth even as we speak."

"If they are, they're being bloody quiet about it," Riley replied. "The trouble is, I'm only guessing Mitcheson's flight number, and all Rickmansworth would say was they weren't expecting Grossman's plane, anyway."

Brask breathed sympathetically down the phone. "Well, there's nothing more I can do. Sorry. The best I can offer is some muscle at the commercial place your friend Mitcheson mentioned. It'll probably take Palmer and the others some time to get through formalities, so I doubt they'll be out of the airport for a while yet."

Riley shook her head. "Forget it. These men won't think twice about cutting their losses; if they spot a bunch of security guard-types armed with nothing more than fists and rubber torches, there'll be a bloodbath."

Brask said nothing and the line hummed with static. Riley hung up, feeling suddenly helpless and cut adrift, and wondering where Palmer was.

Frank Palmer was feeling sick. He was lying on a seat in the rear of a transit van that smelled of paint, and the constant bumping and swaying didn't help. For some reason he couldn't work out, his body felt on fire and perspiration was streaming down his face into his collar.

Unable to lift his head, all Palmer could see was the floor

of the van a few inches away and the wooden legs of the bench seat he was lying on. The floor was scuffed and bare and showed signs of rough use. Movement showed a man's leg and foot, but there was no conversation to show how many people were in the vehicle with him.

He tried to crane his head round to see more, but his muscles wouldn't respond. His body wanted to lie down and go back to sleep, yet his instincts were screaming at him to get a grip and start running around before it was too late.

A hand grasped his chin and forced him upright, and he found himself staring through the front window of the vehicle at a busy motorway. It looked familiar and was obviously England, but his brain couldn't yet make the right connections to tell him where he might be.

He was sitting behind the passenger seat and the driver was reaching back to examine him. Gary? Doug? Howie? It was Gary…he remembered the boyish face handing him a glass of orange to drink in the house. That was when he'd felt tired and fallen asleep. Bastard.

The van turned several times, and Palmer opened his eyes. He was lying down once more, dribbling on to the seat. He must have fallen asleep again. He got a vague impression of houses and shops, and he reasoned sluggishly that they were no longer on the motorway. Then the vehicle slowed and went over a bump, and he felt a strong hand tighten on his arm to stop him toppling off the seat. It seemed to release a surge of clarity into his brain, and his thoughts swam and became momentarily more lucid. He'd been drugged. Like a lemon in some cheap Portsmouth boozer. He shook his head, trying to brush away the fog and find clear air on the other side. Riley was going to be so pissed off at him for getting

247

caught like this.

Then he remembered she'd been caught too, once. Only he and – what was that bloke's name? – Mitcheson, had galloped to her rescue like knights in rusty armour-for-hire. But she hadn't really needed rescuing, had she? She'd kicked seven kinds of piss out of that McManus bloke and would've chucked him down the hole if Mitcheson hadn't got there and done it first. Or had he? Shite, he thought, I feel sick...

He held his breath and concentrated, remembering an airport – somewhere hot this time. He'd been lolling about on legs like spaghetti, feeling unbearably heavy and unable to control his movements. Somewhere along the way he recalled being sick down his front. No one had bothered cleaning him up, and when he'd tried wiping the mess off his chest, his hands had been slapped away. After a while he'd almost got used to the smell.

Along the way, under strong overhead lights, someone had asked if he was fit to travel. No, he'd wanted to shout out... I'm not fit. I'm sick and carrying more narcotics than a Boots delivery truck, for Christ's sake!

But nobody had been listening. He'd been manhandled up a set of narrow steps and strapped into a seat. Alongside him was a long metal box fixed by brackets and straps to the floor. He wondered who'd got the cheap seat. Then someone fed him some liquid through a straw and he was sick again. Soiled and uncomfortable, and with a vague sense of shame settling on him, he'd gone back to sleep, feeling the floor lifting beneath him and the pressure building in his ears.

He thrust his hands into his trouser pockets and huddled in on himself, eyes tight shut. That was better; the nausea was receding. Still bloody hot, though. Couldn't figure out why. He was surprised to find he was no longer trussed up like a Norfolk turkey. That was better... He sighed and flexed his fingers in his pockets, remembering some distant lesson in a tin hut somewhere about examining extremities to gain awareness in times of – what was it – disorientation? Jesus, he was so fucking disorientated, he couldn't even recall what his extremities were. But the movement made him remember something more recent. It tugged at his consciousness and slipped away, a ghostly thought, then came back stronger. That other bloke, Mitcheson, had been helping load him into the Land Cruiser at the villa, and had pressed something into his pocket, like he didn't want anyone to know. A going-away present.

Palmer extended his fingers, feeling the cloth inside his pockets. He felt something hard and the memory came flooding back. It reminded him of the games he'd played with his sister a lifetime ago on cold, wet days when there was nothing else to do. They would take turns at putting their hands into a box and saying what was in there. Dead easy. Half the time he got it wrong – especially when she put in stupid girlish things like walnuts and hair-clips and pens. But not when it was his turn. Like tennis balls, a matchbox or the plastic frogmen he'd saved up and bought to play with in the bath.

Or the pruning knife his dad had given him on his twelfth birthday. The one with the wooden handle and curved blade.

His fingers slid along the familiar shape, and for a moment he wondered if his childhood memories were playing tricks. How could he have his old pruning knife in his pocket after all these years? He'd lost it years ago. Then the image burst through in another bubble of clarity, and he remembered. Good old Mitcheson. So you came through in the end? Only thing is, what the hell can I do with a pruning knife if I can't stand up?

44

Mitcheson swayed against the rolling of the taxi as it passed under the M4, watching Doug and Howie on the back seat. He guessed they were probably dreaming about how they were going to spend all the money Lottie Grossman had promised them. Whatever they were thinking, they seemed uneasy in his presence, like kids meeting up with a former teacher and not quite knowing whether to call him Sir or not.

He glanced through the side window and saw they were passing the Holiday Inn, the road curving north through landscaped banks and artificially created gardens.

They were nearly there.

He felt a thudding in his chest and came as close to praying as he had done in years. It wouldn't have been a traditional prayer, but it would have amounted to the same thing. Save Palmer, save himself. Make it all right.

Not that Doug and Howie would give a toss about saving anyone. To them, wasting Palmer was just another job. He guessed Gary would do it. He didn't turn a hair – never had done. Killing was what he did. No problems.

He wondered if Palmer had discovered the knife yet.

He glanced at his watch. By now Lottie Grossman would be on her way to Jordans, her husband's body trundling somewhere else in the back of a funeral van. Unless everything had gone pear-shaped.

He wondered if the drugs had got through. Unless the police were waiting it would take a brave official to question the arrival of a coffin and insist on a search.

Lottie Grossman had detailed Gary to do that job and told Mitcheson and the others to get on with cleaning up the villa and making sure the Moroccans weren't around. He stopped thinking about it when the taxi turned into a commercial estate. The place was nearly deserted at this time of day, with just a few cars parked in front of some units, lights burning against the falling gloom.

They swung into a small cul-de-sac and Doug told the driver to stop in front of a row of three small workshops with oval glass panels set into metal doors. Two of the units had name-plates. The third, in the middle, was blank. Nearby stood a skip full of twisted car body parts and scrap metal.

The workshops were dark. They waited for the taxi to turn the corner before unlocking the small personnel door in the middle unit.

Riley hurried across to the taxi rank, scanning the area in case Mitcheson or the others should appear. She gave the driver the address of the unit Mitcheson had mentioned and sat back, heart pounding, willing the traffic to keep moving.

As they emerged from the tunnel and split into the feeder lanes to the A4 and M4 link roads, Riley dialled Brask's number again. "Any news?" she asked.

"Psychic child," he breathed down the line at her. "I've just had a call from a detective sergeant in the drugs squad. He was asked to have a look at the Cessna out at Rickmansworth, but it was too late. Everyone bar the pilot has gone."

"What?" Riley exploded, causing the taxi driver to look anxiously in his mirror. "Of course they've left…how could they be so incompetent?"

"It happens," he said calmly. "I hope you're not going to do anything silly, sweetie. I've got other jobs lined up for you already. Leave the rest to the police."

"I can't," she retorted. "Anyway, I wouldn't miss this for anything. I owe Palmer for getting him into this in the first place. You'd better tell the *Review* what's happening. This is going to hit the papers tomorrow morning and I don't want the editor thinking he's been scooped out of a story. The details behind this aren't going to be known by anyone else, so I don't want him going into a panic."

"Will do, sweetie. Take care."

As she switched off the mobile, the cab pulled into the commercial estate and coasted past the rows of near-empty buildings. The driver slid the glass back.

"I think number twenty-four's down a side road somewhere. You sure you want dropping here? There's not many people about."

Riley handed him a note with a fat tip. "Don't worry," she said, grateful for his concern. "There'll be someone else along shortly."

When he'd gone, she walked along the road until she reached a turning into a small cul-de-sac. On her left a high brick wall bordered a van-hire depot. To her right stood an unkempt shrubbery, before the road opened out in front of three small workshop units with metal doors. There were no cars in sight but she could see a light in the middle unit. She slipped into the bushes, pushing through dense laurel until she arrived at the wall of the nearest workshop.

The brickwork was cold and damp from a recent down-pour. There was no sound from within. She slid along the wall to check for a back entrance, but found it blocked off by a high fence.

Riley headed towards the front and poked her head round the corner. Whoever was in the middle building was being very quiet, and she doubted there was any work going on inside.

Just across from the units was a rubbish skip. It was a perfect observation point but getting in there unseen might be a problem. She took a deep breath, ready to sprint across the road.

The air inside the workshop was musty. A pile of junk mail lay scattered by the door. The floor was empty except for some tea-chests and a heavy bench set against one wall. On the top lay a jumble of hand-tools, a kettle and jars of coffee and sugar.

Howie plugged in the kettle and spooned coffee and sugar into polystyrene cups. The drone of the water heating sounded loud in the empty space.

Mitcheson idly inspected the tools on the bench. Home-handyman stuff, screwdrivers, pliers, hand-drill, with a selection of screws and nails in plastic boxes.

He upended a tea chest and sat down, watching Howie drum a spoon on the coffee jar while Doug stood by the metal door keeping watch through the viewing panel.

Howie handed out the coffee and they stood sipping, glad of something to do. Now would have been the time to talk about future plans and hopes...what any group of men did when about to split up and pass on. But it wasn't going to happen. Their positions had shifted over the last few days, and Mitcheson was aware that he'd been kidding himself about any kind of bond between them. Maybe there had been when the bullets were flying and they were screaming down a narrow, militia-infested road near Bihac; or out by the airport at Sarajevo in a white APC, hoping there were no landmines or Serbs with rocket-launchers trained on them. But not any longer. The promise of easy money had seen to that. And maybe a growing desperation to make something, anything, of their lives rather than face life as a security guard in a shopping centre, growing soft and fat and being the object of scorn from kids with nothing better to do.

Twin lights blazed across the garden area as a van turned into the cul-de-sac and stopped outside the middle unit. The driver got out and looked around, then went to the passenger door and opened it. Riley heard him grunting as he helped someone out. As they stepped into the pool of light spilling from the observation panels, she recognised Frank Palmer. He looked pale and drawn. The man holding him was Gary.

A single access door opened alongside the metal door, and a face showed briefly before retreating inside. As soon as the door slammed shut, Riley was on her feet and running over to the rubbish skip, where she took cover behind its comforting bulk, her nose twitching at the strong smell of paint, burned metal and petrol.

She breathed deeply, recalling Mitcheson's comment about how once they had no need for Palmer they would do away with him. She had to do something…but what? She had no weapons, and if she waited for the police to come, Palmer would be beyond caring.

She rubbed her nose as the sharp smell of petrol aggravated her nostrils.

"Jesus!" Doug snorted, and stepped back at the sight of Palmer's vomit-stained clothing as Gary pushed him inside. The investigator sank to the floor, his face slack and pale under the lights.

"Think yourselves lucky," Gary snarled. "I had to put up with that stink all the way from Malaga." He glared at Palmer as if he had been ill deliberately, and dragged him to his feet again, grunting with the weight. Then he slapped him twice across the face: hard, solid blows which echoed in the empty space above their heads.

Mitcheson recognised what Gary was doing. He wasn't merely being brutal; he was psyching himself up to carry out the next task. Pump up enough hatred or disgust for the victim and it made the killing so much easier.

Mitcheson slipped his hand in his pocket and felt for the screwdriver he'd taken off the bench. As a weapon it was about par with the plan he hadn't got to get out of here with Palmer's life intact. But it would have to do.

With Palmer upright against the wall, Gary produced a knife and flicked it open one-handed. He turned to Doug with a cold smile. "I need a hand with this."

45

Riley pulled a bottle from the skip. It felt half full of liquid and she sniffed at the top, instantly pulling back and gagging on the eye-watering smell of paint-thinner. She placed it carefully on the ground and looked for something else. Her fingers settled on a half-inch thick metal rod. That would be heavy enough.

She bent down and peered carefully at the bottle. From a repeat-arson case she had researched the year before, she had learned some interesting facts. One was that some kids really did hate their schooldays and would get out of them almost any way they could. Another was that making a Molotov cocktail was surprisingly simple. It was also dangerous.

She reached into the skip and searched around until she felt some cloth. Pulling it free she tore off enough to stuff into the neck of the bottle, then shook the contents around until the cloth was saturated with the paint-thinner.

There was no one at the window. She picked up the metal rod and ran across to the unit and squatted against the wall. From inside she could hear the rumble of voices.

She stood upright until she could see through the nearest window, keeping her face back from the glass in case one of the men looked her way. The one known as Howie was standing by a workbench, a cup in his hand. Behind him a kettle steamed in the cold atmosphere.

Mitcheson was in the centre of the room facing the door, his expression blank and unemotional. She wondered what was going through his mind right now.

Moving further she caught a glimpse of Gary and, behind him, a partial sight of Palmer. Doug was moving to join them and Palmer seemed to be leaning away as if he was drunk.

In the distance she heard the faint *wup-wup-wooo* of a police siren beginning to build. Great timing, boys, she thought. Pity it's a bit too late.

Holding the rod between her knees, she pulled Palmer's lighter from her pocket and held the bottle with the rag trailing down. It was now or never…

Palmer felt himself being dragged upright. The nausea had gone but while he could hear and understand most of what was happening around him, he still lacked full control of his limbs.

He felt somebody pulling at his jacket, and glimpsed John Mitcheson a few feet away, hands in his pockets. Doug was coming towards him with Howie close behind. Palmer shook his head and tried to piece together Gary's request for help and the other man moving in to assist him. Assist him with what?

He caught a flash of light on shiny metal at the periphery of his vision and knew instinctively what it meant. He tensed himself for the blow he knew was coming, for the cold shock of steel cutting into his body. In the background he heard Mitcheson shout: "Wait!"

Instead of the pain of the blade, however, he felt something move, and a great weight seemed to slip from his shoulders. Was this what it was like to be stabbed?

Something was sliding down his legs. He looked down, vaguely expecting to see a part of his anatomy lying at his feet. Instead there on the floor was his soiled jacket, and on top was a pale yellow jerkin made of webbing. It reminded

258

him of the hunting jackets worn by Olympic marksmen, with pockets and loops for all their equipment.

This jerkin, however, contained hard, tightly-packed bundles sewn into the webbing, giving it the appearance of a bulky flak-jacket. One of the packages had sprung a leak and a trail of white powder had spilled on the concrete floor of the workshop.

No wonder I was so bloody hot, he thought stupidly. I would have been the one to cop it if I'd been searched. All they had to say was I'd begged for a flight back rather than take a commercial one.

The thought helped drive out the fogginess, replacing it with a surge of anger.

Gary pushed him away until he bounced off the wall, and smiled with contempt. "Christ, to think I had to sit with you all that way," he muttered coldly. He held out his knife hand and stepped forward in a fluid motion.

Palmer sagged instinctively to one side and sucked in his stomach. His back scraped against the rough brickwork as he took his hand from his trouser pocket and slashed with the pruning knife across Gary's wrist. The sharp blade cut deep, severing tendons, muscle and flesh all the way to the bone.

As Gary screamed, the metal door behind him pulsed with light, then exploded in a ball of red and yellow flame. Heat poured through the cold air and tongues of flame came licking through the gaps, reaching out for the men inside. A fire alarm went off with deafening intensity.

Mitcheson propelled himself forward and intercepted Howie as the ex-Marine threw his cup aside and ran towards Palmer. He hit him with a shoulder-charge, stopping him short, then chopped him across the throat, dropping him to the floor.

Doug reached down to grab the jerkin and lurched towards the door. As he did so, Gary reached behind his back with his good hand and brought out an automatic pistol. His eyes were crazed, flecks of spit gathered around his mouth as the shock of pain began to hit him. He backed towards the door, making beckoning motions at Doug.

"Doug, c'mon," he muttered shakily, holding his bloodied hand under his other arm. "Throw it here."

Outside, the police sirens grew louder. Mitcheson edged towards the door, hoping Gary would be distracted by the noise. In his hand he held the screwdriver.

"What are you doing, Gary?" Doug yelled. "What about Howie, man?"

"Howie's down," Gary replied, his face in spasm. "It's every man for himself. Throw me the jacket!" He swung the pistol round and pointed it at Doug's face, his stance rock-solid in spite if his obvious pain. "You know me. I'll use it."

Mitcheson ran forward, knowing he could never make it in time. At the same moment, the door behind Gary opened inwards and a figure ducked inside. There was a swish of movement through the air, and a sickening sound of metal hitting flesh. Gary's head flew back, eyes open wide with shock. Then he pitched forward. As he did so, his finger tightened on the trigger.

Doug took the bullet in the chest and was kicked back under the impact, the jerkin falling at his feet.

Riley looked across at Mitcheson and threw the metal rod aside. "John," she said. "We're quits."

Mitcheson nodded and walked over to help Palmer to his feet. Frank nodded at Howie on the floor and spluttered: "Thanks for that. What kept you?"

For a moment they all stood looking at each other in the dying light. Then Palmer waved his hand, taking deep breaths to clear his head. "Wassamatter, Mitcheson?" he slurred drunkenly. "You want an invitation? Piss off, for Christ's sake. Me 'n' Riley will finish off here…"

Mitcheson looked at Riley for confirmation. She nodded, and he smiled and stepped past her into the night.

46

Riley parked her Golf and walked into the main foyer of the Sheraton Heathrow. She took the lift to the first floor and found the room number she wanted. She stood for a moment, indecision threatening to win over curiosity, then she took a deep breath and knocked.

The door swung open under her hand. Inside, she saw an open suitcase on the trestle, clothes packed neatly inside. The air was touched with a familiar aftershave.

A polished circular table near the window held a bottle in an ice bucket, the ceiling light glinting off two glasses. John Mitcheson was standing by the window. As she closed the door behind her, he turned to greet her, smiling hesitantly.

"I'm glad you could come," he said with evident relief, and reached out to touch her shoulder.

Riley smiled back and indicated the bottle. "If I hadn't, you'd have had to drink all that by yourself."

"Yeah, well, to be honest, I ordered it but now I don't feel thirsty."

"That's okay – I'll drink, you watch."

Mitcheson busied himself opening the champagne and filled two glasses. He handed her one and raised his own.

"I'm not sure what I should be toasting," he said awkwardly. "It can hardly be to us, can it?"

Riley shook her head. She lifted her glass and sipped the cold wine, the bubbles fizzing on her tongue. "Where are you going?"

"The States, for a while. Seems best after all that's happened."

She nodded. After the violence at West Drayton, she'd only tried his mobile once, to let him know she'd managed to keep his name out of the story.

"Lottie Grossman's disappeared," she said, stirring her drink with her finger. "Did you know that?"

"I heard. I get nervous every time I see a blue rinse or a pair of gardening gloves."

"It's not funny," Riley cautioned. "She's probably got money stashed away...and that woman's got a long memory."

"I promise to watch my back. You should do the same."

Howie and Gary had been arrested and were refusing to talk, but how long that would last was anyone's guess. In the meantime they were being encouraged to consider helping with drug squad enquiries in England and Spain. The length of their sentence, it was rumoured, would depend on how much help they gave.

"Will they implicate you?"

"Gary might," Mitcheson said. "Howie I'm not sure about. That's why I'm leaving for a while. I'll see how things pan out."

"Good idea. Frank told me what they'd done in Bosnia. Not nice people."

"How is Frank?"

"Smoking too much. He's off to Germany on a job. He said to say thanks for the pruning knife. What did he mean?"

Mitcheson shrugged. "It's a guy thing. Anyway," he added lightly, "if I remember, it was you fire-bombing the place and beating Gary to a pulp that saved us. Otherwise we might have been in real trouble."

Riley rolled her eyes. "Yeah, right." She handed him a slip of paper. "Frank says this man needs a security consultant. It's in San Francisco, if you're interested."

Mitcheson nodded and tucked the paper in his wallet. "Tell him I appreciate it."

"He knows."

They smiled, both aware that they were circling each other, awkward and tense and suddenly with little to say.

"You never did get that holiday," Mitcheson began, looking into his glass. "I suppose you'll be making up for it now this is over?"

Riley took off her earrings and dropped them on the side table. "I might be," she replied. "The trouble is, since the Grossman business, I've got work coming from all directions." She kicked her shoes off and sipped her wine. "But you know what they say… All work and no play."

"I feel responsible for ruining the last one," Mitcheson said, his voice uncertain.

Riley undid the top button of her dress, then sipped more wine, her eyes on his. "Don't worry – I'm sure you'll make up for it sometime."

She undid more buttons, revealing a froth of pale blue lace, and swung her foot to and fro. Mitcheson stood very still, mesmerised.

Two more buttons popped and the dress whispered apart. She flicked the material aside, allowing Mitcheson to see her all the way down.

"Maybe… " Mitcheson's voice was strained. "…maybe you could make it to San Francisco."

"Maybe." Riley shrugged her shoulders and the dress fell to the floor. She stepped towards him and placed her glass on the table. She did the same with his, then took his fingers and held them against her.

"I may be an independent sort of girl," Riley breathed softly, releasing his hand. "But the last bit really is up to you… "

In the glove box of her Golf, Riley's mobile was ringing. After six rings the answering service took over and recorded a message. It was from Donald Brask.

"Riley, sweetie," he chided heavily. "Get off the nest, there's a good girl. I've got a job for you…"

More action-packed crime novels from Crème de la Crime

Working Girls
Maureen Carter

Dumped in a park ... throat slashed.... schoolgirl prostitute Michelle Lucas died in agony and terror.

The sight breaks the heart of Detective Sergeant Bev Morriss of West Midlands Police. She thought she was hardened, inured, but gazing at Michelle's pale, broken body she is consumed by a cold fury.

She knows this case is different – this is the one that will push her to the edge.

Plunging herself into the seedy heart of Birmingham's vice-land she struggles to infiltrate the deadly jungle of hookers, evil pimps and violent johns. But no one will co-operate, no one will break the wall of silence...

When a second victim dies, Bev knows time is running out. If she is to win the trust of the working girls – she has to take the biggest, most dangerous, gamble of her life – *out on the streets...*

A Kind of Puritan
Penny Deacon

Dead and dumped. Jon was nobody ... no money ... no influence. So who dropped him in the river?

Bodies are bad for business so when one is dredged up the Midway Port developers want it buried. Deep. But Humility found the body and she's not going to let it go. Not until she knows who killed the guy everyone said was harmless.

She's a low-tech woman in a hi-tech world and no one wants to give her any answers. But with her best friend's job on the line, a series of 'accidents' at the Port, and the battered barge she lives on threatened with seizure, she's not going to give up.

The mystery leads her to the cruellest parts of the city where people kill for the cost of a meal and it's dangerous to get involved. When she has to seek help from the local crime boss she knows his price is likely to be high.

It's a world where she's not sure anyone is who they claim to be, and where one death leads to another... and the next one could be hers!